NADA AWAR JARRAR

A Good Land

D1090200

HarperCollins*Publishers*

HarperCollins*Publishers*
77–85 Fulham Palace Road,
Hammersmith, London W6 8JB

www.harpercollins.co.uk

Published by HarperCollins*Publishers* 2009
1

A catalogue record for this book
is available from the British Library

ISBN: 978 000 7221974

This novel is entirely a work of fiction.
The names, characters and incidents portrayed in it are the work of the
author's imagination. Any resemblance to actual persons, living or dead,
events or localities is entirely coincidental.

Set in Sabon by Palimpsest Book Production Ltd
Grangemouth, Stirlingshire

Printed and bound in Great Britain by
Clays Ltd, St Ives plc

Mixed Sources
Product group from well-managed
forests and other controlled sources
www.fsc.org Cert no. SW-COC-1806
© 1996 Forest Stewardship Council

FSC is a non-profit international organisation established
to promote the responsible management of the world's forests.
Products carrying the FSC label are independently certified
to assure consumers that they come from forests that are managed
to meet the social, economic and ecological needs
of present and future generations.

Find out more about HarperCollins and the environment at
www.harpercollins.co.uk/green

For my mother,
with all my love

And for Marianne,
I will always miss you

'For the meaning of life differs from man to man, from day to day and from hour to hour. What matters therefore, is not the meaning of life in general but rather the specific meaning of a person's life at a given moment.'

Viktor Frankl

PART ONE

Layla

Beirut is the city of dreams, at once magnificent and fragile, filled with instances of grace, ephemeral pockets of loveliness that can overwhelm even courageous hearts. There is colour here and brilliance, the hum of movement and its attending sounds; there are buried sorrows and there is transcending joy; and everywhere, flowing through the intricate, complex layers that are people and places, breathes unrestrained life.

Yet the city no longer possesses an obvious beauty. Very little of the lush greenness I knew when I was growing up and which once defined our many neighbourhoods remains. Beirut is invariably overcrowded with people and construction that is haphazard and garish, and areas that once hummed with life lack character and a real sense of community. What is it then that makes us love it so?

I live between the east and west of the city in a yellowed building tucked away at the end of an alleyway that begins on a bustling main road. The building has no elevator. Instead, the tenants have to struggle up a long stairway that wraps itself round the exterior walls of some of the floors and plunges into the building's interior on others.

My second-floor apartment shares a wall with the

outside stairwell which is often noisy, in the early mornings when other tenants are rushing off to work or school and late at night when some of them venture home again. And although it is part of a more recent addition to the building, the flat has uneven floors in places so that, walking through it, I can feel myself leaning towards uncertainty, teetering on the brink.

There is enough room in the kitchen for a table where I have most of my meals, sitting on one of the two chairs. Afterwards, standing at the sink, I look through the window out onto the alley as I do the washing up, a plate and utensils, a glass and a pot or pan, day-dreaming into the future. And at night, lying in the windowless, small bedroom at the back of the apartment, I fall asleep sheltered by layers of comfort, my bed and the sheets and blankets that touch my skin, and the walls around me that enclose a deep, undisturbed darkness.

The neighbourhood is heavily populated, older buildings crowded in by newer and higher construction and pavements that are either narrow or totally non-existent. Small shops that sell all kinds of wares line the streets and the constant flow of traffic on the main road adds to the noise level and the impression of overcrowding. Stepping out into the street every morning, I am quickly enveloped by the energy that surrounds me and filled with hope, with the sense that wherever I turn, something is certain to happen.

I walk past a shop that sells tyres and spare parts for cars, a butcher's, and a dry-cleaners that also doubles up as a telephone and fax centre. I turn onto the main road where cars jostle their way up the one-way street, almost nudging each other as they move in fits and spurts, their horns blaring. On one corner, inches away from oncoming traffic, a man sells fruits and vegetables from a large wooden cart, and beyond that there is a flower shop with fresh as well as artificial flowers in plastic vases placed outside its front window.

At a tiny corner café minutes from home, I order my usual cup of coffee and stand at a counter overlooking the street, sipping it slowly. Most days, I am the only woman there and the men on either side of me move away as soon as I arrive, their gazes averted. It is their way of giving me room and making me more comfortable, I know, but it is a kindness I cannot acknowledge since it might be considered too forward of me to thank them outright. Instead, I remain silent and look out onto the street, gathering my thoughts about me and observing the many passers-by.

In returning to Lebanon after long years away, I envisioned exactly this life for myself: moments quietly accumulating with me in the midst of a sea of people and activity, separate in some ways but linked nonetheless to the steady, relentless movement that fills the day.

I am on the stairwell when I hear the thud, feel it move from my belly down into my feet, the tips of my toes tingling with fear. I have heard this sound before and it is not, I know, the echo of a slamming door somewhere in the building, nor the din of heavy machinery from the construction site down the road.

Within seconds, neighbours come out onto the outside landing to investigate.

'What was that?' someone asks.

'I'm not sure,' I reply, my heart beating fast.

'Sounded like a car bomb to me,' another neighbour says. 'God knows we heard enough of them during the war to know.'

'Look, there's smoke rising over there!'

We turn in the direction of the sea to see a black cloud forming.

'It's coming from the Corniche,' I murmur with dismay.

A neighbour from the flat next door puts her hand on my arm.

'Were you on your way to work, Layla?' she asks.

I nod.

'Maybe it's best you don't go out today. Until we find out what's going on, that is.'

She is still in dressing gown and slippers and looks pale without her usual make-up.

'Reminds me of the American embassy bombing in 1982,' she continues, shaking her head. 'That's exactly where the smoke came from then.'

'It's Hariri,' someone shouts up the stairwell moments later. 'I just heard it on the news.'

We look at each other. 'Hariri?'

Hariri is the billionaire businessman who served as prime minister for two terms after the end of the civil war. A larger than life character, he is credited with being the driving force behind Beirut's reconstruction efforts and, most recently, has been pushing hard for changes in the country's electoral laws.

'Why would they want to kill him?'

'Layla!'

I look up to see Margo gesturing from above, her mass of white hair more unruly than usual.

'Come up, sweetheart.'

I run up the stairs and wrap my arms around my old friend. I seem unable to stop myself from shaking.

'Something terrible has happened, Margo, I'm sure of it,' I say, hearing the shrill of ambulance sirens in the distance.

We step inside and Margo turns on the radio in the kitchen.

'Try one of the local stations,' she tells me with her grainy voice. 'You can translate the Arabic for me.'

It takes me a few moments to adjust the dial on the radio. I sit down to listen. The announcer's voice falters as he speaks. I eventually turn to Margo.

'Oh, my god. It is Hariri. They're saying a huge car bomb has targeted his motorcade. They think he's among those who have been killed.'

Margo frowns.

'It sounded like a massive explosion. And at this time of day there would have been lots of people about on the Corniche.'

She pulls open a kitchen drawer, takes out a packet of cigarettes and a lighter and sits down on one of the stools by the sink.

'I suppose any one of his political rivals might have done it,' I say, shaking my head. 'Or even an outside power. They've all been known to try to settle their differences with violence.'

'Poor man,' Margo says.

'How could anyone do such a terrible thing?'

She reaches up and attempts to smooth back her hair.

'I don't know, sweetheart. But it's hardly the first time something like this happens in this country, is it?'

'But we thought all that was long over, Margo. We've had peace for a while now. Surely it should have lasted longer than this?'

'It's no use trying to understand,' she says, removing a cigarette from the packet. 'Violence isn't supposed to make sense.'

You should know, Margo, I begin to say but stop myself in time.

'I dread to think what might happen next,' I murmur instead.

Margo lights up

'No one can know that, Layla.'

It is not the reassuring answer I had been looking for.

'You're right, Margo,' I say, feeling a little foolish.

'It's alright, sweetheart,' she says gently. 'It's normal to want to be reassured at a time like this.'

By the end of the day, the death of Hariri is confirmed, along with the deaths of fifteen others, some from his entourage as well as some innocent bystanders. I watch the terrible images on the television. The huge crater in the road, the damage to surrounding buildings, and what look like charred human remains amongst the shattered glass and rubble. There is a great deal of speculation on the news about who might have carried out the assassination and grim predictions about the likely consequences.

For the first time since my return to Lebanon, I ask myself if I did the right thing in coming back. I could have continued to enjoy a quiet life in Australia where my parents and I had fled years earlier because of the civil war here. Mixed in with the anxiety and fear, I'm also feeling angry about what has just happened. How dare they do this after all that this country has already been through?

I sit on the sofa in my small living room with a blanket wrapped around me and eventually fall into an uneasy sleep.

I grew up in a neighbourhood not far from the waterfront where spring rains sometimes flooded the streets and, in summer, whiffs of sea air provided relief from the dank, persistent heat. My father and his brothers owned a petrol station on the Corniche of Ras Beirut, and my mother, a beautiful woman with a calm demeanour, taught at the school that I attended.

I remember childhood as a breezy existence that was only interrupted when civil war broke out, the grown-ups around me taking on a sudden heaviness in their manner, an anxious air, their brows often furrowed. Throughout the turmoil that ensued, my parents continued to love me quietly, not without intensity, but modestly and with deliberation, a love that did not demand reciprocation but rather offered me a good measure of freedom. Encouraging my progress in whatever I attempted to do, they did not push me to prove myself, and whenever I went to them for answers that no one else seemed able to provide, they would consider my question seriously before giving a reply, building in me a sense of self-worth that would stand me in good stead in later life.

Of those childhood years, I also remember the fragile feel of my body, long, thin limbs and my heart beating through my chest. I would run with a host of other children in the neighbourhood through the streets and across the busy thoroughfare. Then, sensing the growing strength that was mine, climbing over the blue railing at the edge of the promenade and onto the boulders at the other side, I would breathe in the sea air and watch the fishing boats bob up and down in the water.

After enduring several years of Lebanon's sectarian and bloody civil war, my parents packed up all our belongings and moved to Australia to start anew. Arriving in Adelaide, we were warmly welcomed by relatives who helped my mother and father find work and eventually a home of our own. I was an adolescent then, awkward and unforgiving and unwilling to join in the grown ups' apparent enthusiasm for this new adventure. Still, as soon as life began to take on a predictable pattern, I was sent to the local school and eventually settled into the reality of being so far from the only home I had ever known.

We lived in a bungalow in the suburbs that had lemon and orange trees in its small garden and a front lawn that I liked to walk on barefoot, the newly mown grass rubbing against the soles of my feet and making them tingle. On Saturday mornings, my mother would take me into the city for hot chocolate and dessert at one of the cafés in the central shopping district. We would talk and browse through the shops and return home to find my father in the living room watching television or, when it was warm, in a straw hat and sunglasses relaxing on a deck chair in the garden.

Now my parents seemed like different people, took on separate selves that had not been apparent before they left Beirut. There were moments also when my own life seemed illusory and undeserved, until I felt I might one day have to rouse myself from it and face reality, though I did not know when nor how that would happen.

I made friends, children like myself from a rapidly growing Lebanese diaspora, as well as young Australians to whom I felt attracted because they were boisterous and happy and unburdened by complicated pasts.

With time, I began to see those intervening years between leaving Lebanon and longing to return to it as a reprieve, an opportunity to garner the strength I would eventually need once I went back. I got through high school as if in a dream and once at university felt as though I was discovering another dimension to myself, one that was adept at maintaining this dual existence with composure. Then, after gaining my doctorate, I worked for a few years, making plans to go back home despite my parents' inevitable objections. I cannot, I told them once it came time to leave, fully embrace this life when the one we left behind us still clings to me even as I attempt to escape it.

I came back to take a job as a lecturer in English literature at the American University, feeling safe in the knowledge that I once again belonged somewhere that mattered. Yet now that I have been here for some time , living the uncertainties that we all have to face , I am sometimes less sure of my intentions than I had been as a young girl, as though my initial resolve had dissipated over time, leaving me with a yearning that I can no longer clearly understand.

There are times when, unable to sleep, I put on my slippers, wrap a shawl around myself and tiptoe up the stairs to the upper landing where the lights of the city flicker through the dark. I lean over the concrete banister and sniff at the air and imagine I hear the sounds of Beirut calling to me, soft whispers that rise from the sea and then gently float up into the waiting sky, memories of a past I cannot leave behind.

The morning after the assassination, I sense a stir in the building and go out onto the landing to find out what is happening.

'They're taking the remains for burial in downtown Beirut,' a neighbour tells me as he's going down the stairs.

'Where from?' I ask him.

'From his villa up the road,' he shouts up the stairwell.

I go back into the apartment, grab my handbag and rush outside again. Once on the street, I am surprised by the number of people who are walking singly or in groups in the direction of Hariri's home. Despite the crowds, everything seems eerily quiet. I eventually find myself being pushed along by the swarm behind a coffin hoisted onto the shoulders of a group of young men and draped with a large Lebanese flag. I recognize two of the bearers as Hariri's sons. An ambulance inches its way ahead of us and I wonder when the men will tire and have to relinquish their burden to it.

As we move slowly forward into the neighbourhoods that lead into Beirut's downtown, people continue to join us. Soon, I can no longer see the coffin. I look up at the buildings on either side of the road. The balconies are crowded with onlookers, some of whom are waving at the throng. Again, I am struck by the despondent mood

11

that surrounds me. Passions usually run high at funerals in this country but everyone here seems subdued with grief. The silence only serves to heighten the ominous nature of the occasion.

I lose my footing and stumble before managing to pick myself up again. For a moment, as I look down to regain my balance, I notice some of the shoes worn by those walking next to me. Elegant feet in precariously high-heeled boots next to a pair of well-worn, fake leather lace-ups in an ugly shade of mustard; white trainers with their instantly recognizable logo alongside two very grubby feet in plastic slippers that make a slapping noise as they move. I lift my head and blink with astonishment. Although popular among much of Lebanon's upper classes, Hariri has never struck me as a man of the people. Yet here we apparently are, rich, poor and everything in between, marching at his funeral.

On the outskirts of Martyrs' Square where the politician and others killed in the explosion will be buried, hundreds of thousands of people are already gathered. The atmosphere here seems different, less restrained. I feel myself being forced forward by the crowd and in my rising panic, grab onto a street lamp to steady myself. I climb up onto the low ledge at the base of the lamp and take a look around for a way out.

A short distance to the left of me, Druze sheikhs in their long, navy blue robes and white and red headdresses walk past. Right behind them are Christian Maronite priests, their heads bowed and large brass crosses swinging round their necks. They have come from the mountain villages east of Beirut where the two communities have lived together for hundreds of years. Where are the Muslim clerics, I wonder? As if on cue, a group of Muslim sheikhs approach from the distance. They are in long robes too and move in unison, like a rolling wave, many with their arms crossed in front of their chests. From their headdresses, I can tell that there are both Sunnis and Shiites among them.

I hear shouts from the crowd up ahead and try to make out what is being said. The chanting catches on and soon everyone around me seems to be shouting for a free and independent Lebanon. I am not surprised. Until recently, the Israeli army had occupied the whole of southern Lebanon for nearly thirty years, and the thousands of Syrian troops who came here in the early stages of the civil war have still not left. This has not been a truly sovereign nation for decades. I realize that my own anger and frustration at the undue influence neighbouring countries have over Lebanon are being echoed here. And while I cannot bring myself to join in the political slogans, I begin to see that this sad occasion is providing an opportunity for all of us to express how we feel about the continued presence of foreign troops in our country.

I step down and take a deep breath. The dread at being so tightly surrounded by people has suddenly left me. We are united, I think quietly to myself, before allowing myself to be swept away once again by the crowd.

The university is built on a hillside overlooking the Mediterranean and boasts all the trees and plants that disappeared long ago from other parts of Beirut. Pines, palms and chestnut trees, sweet-smelling frangipanis, azalea bushes, delicate camellias, rhododendrons that produce huge pink and blue blossoms in spring and bougainvillea that turns a brilliant purple, a feast for the eyes. All this and swathes of greenery too, lawns and evergreen shrubs, rubber plants and gorse bushes; and then the eternal backdrop of the azure sea that stretches horizons so far one senses release at the end of it.

My office is in one of a number of two-storey stone

buildings with red rooftops that dot the campus. It is small with laden bookshelves lining its walls, and is almost overwhelmed by a heavy, battered desk that has served many other lecturers before me. By the window, only a few inches from the door, is an old armchair that I sit in when I am reading or merely want to think, looking out now and then at the greenery or at students stopping to chat or walking to and from their classes. At times, I lean back in the armchair and close my eyes for a moment and, breathing in the silence around me, try to picture the me that came before this, the promise that brought me back to this city of light and shadows.

When I was a child, my mother told me stories that she made up as I sat in bed waiting to fall asleep. They were not fantastical tales, but described the adventures of a little girl who, like me, lived with her parents in Ras Beirut in an apartment not far from the sea. Eventually, I took on the role of story teller too, adding details to *mama*'s accounts of the girl's life, changing an ending whenever I felt it needed it and seeing myself the heroine of an unyielding imagination. My father, on the other hand, bought me books, sat me in his lap and, opening them carefully, read out the title and the writer's name before moving on to the story itself, anticipation in his lilting voice. I would look at the illustrations as he read and run a finger along the lines of words in wonder, and feel them swirl around in my head like clouds in the wind.

There are times when I think the two notions of story telling and books have forever become muddled up in my mind. Even as I grew and eventually learned to read, I still thought of books not as words on paper that needed to be deciphered, but as something alive and malleable, stories which I had in one way or another inspired, at least in part, and which could change depending on how I chose to understand them. Now, when I read, I cannot shake off the feeling that I am somehow part of the process, an element of a wheel that turns and in constantly turning creates movement where there might otherwise be stillness, dreams up the stories of my own uneven existence.

I speak to my parents on the telephone and long to be engulfed once again by the green and peppery scents of Australia, by its white, expansive shores and a sky above so vast that it is easy to lose oneself in it.

'No, I am not lonely, *habibti*,' I tell my mother. 'It's impossible to feel loneliness here, life is much too immediate.'

'But the situation . . .'

'The Syrian troops have finally withdrawn *mama*, and things are quiet again. People have to get on with their lives regardless of the political mayhem around them. Please don't worry about me. I'll be fine.'

'All these assassinations are very worrying,' my father says once he gets on the phone. 'Things may get worse, Layla. Syria might retaliate and Israel certainly won't sit idly by if the situation explodes. It's all too reminiscent of the events that preceded the civil war. I think you should come back here where it's safe.'

I understand my father's concern. The car bomb that killed the former prime minister shook the country and has since been followed by killings of other politicians and journalists brave enough to speak their minds. I'm beginning to see that political stability is not something we can ever take for granted here. Still, I have felt a growing stubbornness in me not so much to ignore what is going on but to keep going in spite of it.

'*Baba*, the Lebanese aren't going to start killing each other again,' I try to reassure him. 'The civil war is over for good and things will eventually settle down, I'm certain of that.'

Although in leaving Lebanon all those years ago my

15

parents believed they were securing a better future for me, I find the fact that they now choose to remain in Australia without me more poignant than ironic, especially since they seem genuinely afraid for my safety, more affected by Lebanon's ups and downs than those of us who live here could ever allow ourselves to be. I suspect also that there is a measure of guilt at play here, the sense so many Lebanese living abroad have that they have abandoned their country just when it needs them most.

I hear my father sigh.

'I'll never understand the hold Lebanon has over you,' he says.

'But you already do understand, *baba*,' I protest. 'In many ways, it was you and *mama* who passed it on to me.'

I do not think of myself as particularly defiant or brave. I have at times had to admit that in staying here I am only resigning myself to the inevitable, acknowledging a pull that I know I am unable to resist. And whenever I am challenged to provide an explanation for my actions, either by my parents or by my own misdirected musings, I hesitate. I am weak, I want to say to anyone willing to listen. This enthusiasm you think you see in me is only my heart wavering this way and that.

I see Margo for the first time a few months after my arrival in Beirut. She is on the stairwell of the building making her way slowly but deliberately up to the third floor. She stops and looks straight at me.

'Hello,' she says with a smile.

I nod, feeling ashamed that I have been caught staring.

'My name is Margo,' she continues. 'We're neighbours, you know. You must come and visit me soon. I live in the flat just above yours.'

I look closely at her, the way her head shakes a little

as she speaks, her skin, pale and lightly powdered, pulling gently downwards at her chin. She is not Lebanese, I can tell, but I am not certain where she might come from.

'Yes, I would like that,' I say after clearing my throat. 'I'm Layla, by the way.'

Arriving a few days later at the open landing of the third-floor flat with a bouquet of flowers in my hand, I stop to look up at the sky before knocking at the door and hearing Margo's greeting.

Moments later, I am sitting in a deep blue armchair with my new friend on the floor opposite, her back against the sofa, her short legs stretched out on the carpet, pink felt slippers on her feet, and her ankles, covered in mottled skin, showing beneath the hem of beige corduroy trousers. Even at this first meeting, I see how important this friendship will be in my life, an anchor in a recurring storm.

Margo tells me she married an air force pilot who was killed over Germany during the war. A handsome young man of French aristocratic line, he chose her on a whim, she says, and later made her abort two pregnancies because he believed it was no time to bring children into the world.

I listen to her slow, accented English and watch closely as her grey eyes, small and surprisingly clear for her age, sparkle in the telling, her hair short and white and so thick it curls into clumps behind her rather large ears. The tremor in her voice means I have to listen very carefully to follow and as the lined skin of her face moves with her words she appears ageless, a kind of female Peter Pan, magical and only real when I want her to be.

Pronouncing the name of her husband in the French way, with a long vowel sound in the middle and a silent 'n', Margo says John had been the love of her life. That is why she never remarried after he was killed.

'It was not so much that the men I met later in life were no match for him, you see. In fact, in many ways, one or two of them were better than my John, much kinder to me than he was.'

She pauses.

'It was just that I could never bring myself to feel as much as I did with him, to go through that kind of intensity again with another human being.'

'It must have been very difficult for you when you lost him,' I say gently.

Margo nods.

'But I managed, as most people did during those terrible times.'

She lifts her cigarette to her mouth and draws deeply on it, her lips pressed closely together over it in the manner of a committed smoker. When she finally lets out a cloud of smoke like a long sigh, I feel myself breathe again.

'Surely after the war finally ended life was easier, Margo.'

'I suppose we all felt relief that the end had come, yes, but things were difficult for a long while afterwards.'

She looks up at me with her heavy-lidded eyes.

'I don't mean just the physical deprivations, the food rationing and belt-tightening we had to do,' Margo continues. 'It was more that everyone was exhausted with the effort of surviving the war and people still had to cope with all of its consequences.'

I try to imagine what it must have been like, to have lost so much and been broken, to have to struggle to put yourself together again when all you really wanted to do was to curl up into yourself and wish existence away. I shake my head.

Margo gives me a questioning look.

'Don't look so worried, sweetheart,' she says, laughing softly. 'It's all over now and things did work out in the end. Let's have some more coffee.'

In spring, during the almost sub-tropical rains that fall over Beirut, I step into Margo's apartment, shut the front door behind me and feel as though I can finally stop and gather the scattered parts of myself together again. In this sitting room and in this solid armchair, rain descending outside the partially opened window and chaos far behind me, I know I am accepted just as I am, lost and sometimes lonely and looking for answers that elude me.

Margo listens attentively, cigarette constantly in hand, her head shaking slightly or held to one side, her eyes blinking every now and then and her mouth making an 'O' of astonishment just at the right moment. And as time passes and the light in the room continues to tilt away from us, our faces falling into half-shadow, she manages to make me feel, imperceptibly and with the help of an occasional murmur, less needy somehow and worthy of her favour.

It will be some time before I will learn to interpret the nuances in her conversation or catch the subtle hints behind her deliberately pronounced words. But I know that the exchanges which will follow, suspended as they are with silences that let in intermittent sounds from the street below, will always be rich with layers of meaning, fragile things that I can only guess at and which I might later hope to understand.

Alone at night, I dream Margo's stories, a long drawn-out dream with a multitude of characters and Margo, her white hair luminous, her body youthful and strong. For a moment, we are interchangeable. I am Margo sixty years ago, a resistance fighter in the Second World War in a field in France in the dead of night, the smells and sounds around me as sharp-edged as briars, my breathing heavy and filled with what feels like smoke, and in the distance a flickering light from a lone farmhouse, my heart hopeful and in my head the myriad thoughts that accompany nervous excitement.

She has told me of once parachuting face down in daylight onto a bush of thorns and lifting her head to watch a fine stream of blood trickle from her eyelid and onto the grass where each blade was magnified a thousand times until she could see a tiny forest of green and hear an immutable silence. That is when I finally understood, she said, how life is preciously small, its details, so often invisible, a kind of greatness, unremarkable acts of kindness ever present, even at the very worst of times.

She regrets being too headstrong in her youth, of failing to see her father's point of view while he was still alive, and of being too crotchety in her old age; and once, standing outside the mesh fencing that surrounded a group of German prisoners of war, a young soldier, unkempt and with fear in his eyes, approaching, her asking for a cigarette: she took one out of its packet, lit it and then, the soldier watching, threw it on the ground and stepped on it for good measure.

What could have possessed me to do something so cruel, Margo muttered quietly to herself? Since the only god she believes in is the power of one's own conscience, I know this is one transgression among many that she can never forgive herself for. I know also, because of my love for her, that she is so much more than her past or her present, more than her misdeeds and regrets; that within the immeasurable spaces of Margo's heart lies the freedom to be without judgment, beyond fear. And at a time when my own anxiety over the situation here seems to be growing beyond my control, her strength is formidable to me.

This is what I also see in my dreams: Margo holding her front door open, the sun from the living room window lighting the air behind her so that she appears to glow through the outlines of her body. She is looking out with wonder, with the certainty of infinite compassion, and on the other side, trembling a little, is me.

*   *   *

When I first knew Margo, she volunteered at a centre for disabled children not far from where we live. She was stronger then than she is now and looked forward to the two afternoons a week she spent supervising a play group. She spoke to me often of the children, explaining that many of their disabilities were due to the poverty they lived in, lack of immunization, perhaps, or unsupervised home births. Yet despite the challenges they faced, Margo always insisted, the children made every effort to enjoy their afternoons in the playground.

'They love the new climbing frame that we had put in recently,' she tells me one day. 'Now we're trying to collect enough money for a sandbox. That should be great fun for them.'

'Children like that sort of thing, don't they?'

Margo's eyes narrow.

'You haven't had much exposure to children have you, sweetheart?'

'I just don't think I'd be any good with them, that's all.'

'Well, you won't know unless you try,' says Margo. 'Why don't you come with me next Saturday? We could do with some more help.'

The playground is small but very colourful, with several swings, a large slide and the climbing frame that Margo has told me about. We walk into a small structure at one end of the playground and Margo introduces me to some of the other volunteers she works with.

'The children will be arriving soon,' she says, turning to me. 'Let's go meet them.'

There are over a dozen girls and boys between the ages of four and ten, some in wheelchairs being pushed by their adult helpers, others on crutches or with walking frames, and still others approaching on their own, walking carefully and as if on the tips of their toes. I watch in silence as Margo greets each of the children,

21

asking them how they are and encouraging them to have a good time.

I nervously walk up to a young boy as he tries to climb up to the top of the slide. He has a metal brace on one of his legs.

'Would you like me to help you?' I ask quietly.

He looks at me and nods.

I try to push him up the steps from behind and when that doesn't work put my hands under his arms and half-lift him to the top. Once there, the little boy sits down, places his good leg on the slide and then picks up the other with both hands and swings it over while I hold onto him. Then he stretches both arms out like wings and plunges down the slide, landing with a loud thump onto his bottom. I run to him, thinking that I will find him in tears and will have to comfort him. Instead, he is smiling widely.

'Can we do that again?' he asks me.

'Yes,' I say, suddenly feeling sad. 'Of course we can.'

I spend half an hour or so wandering around the play-ground with the other volunteers, watching the children and sometimes approaching to help them. I am not quite sure how to play with them as the other adults are doing and soon begin to feel inadequate. When Margo calls me to go back inside with her I sense that she has noticed my predicament.

'They'll be coming in for a snack soon,' she says. 'I'll need you to help me with that, sweetheart.'

We roll *labneh* sandwiches and place them on individual paper plates, then we pour orange juice into plastic cups and set them all on a large table in the middle of the room.

'There are some packets of biscuits on the top of the fridge, Layla. Could you bring them down for me? We'll have to open them up and place them on those platters over there.'

I give Margo the biscuits and begin to collect plastic chairs from around the room and place them around the table.

'Don't do that yet, sweetheart,' Margo stops me. 'Some of the children will be sitting at the table with their wheelchairs so it's best to wait until they come in to sort it out.'

I am unable to move.

'Layla? Are you alright?'

I shake my head and sit down.

'You're crying,' Margo lays a hand on my shoulder. 'What's the matter, sweetheart?'

'It's heartbreaking, Margo,' I sniff. 'They're so small and it's so difficult for them. How do they cope?'

Margo reaches into her sleeve for a tissue and hands it to me.

'Come on,' she says gently. 'Let's go back outside. I need a cigarette.'

We sit on a bench in a corner of the garden. I wait for Margo to say something but she is too busy lighting her cigarette. I take a deep breath and look out at the children. The sun has gone behind a cloud and the playground is now in half-shadow. It suddenly seems as though the children are moving in slow motion, swinging forwards and backwards on the swings, moving up and down through the climbing frame or just sitting in their wheelchairs, waving their arms above their heads. When, moments later, the sun comes out again and casts its rays over us, I realize that rather than awkwardness, it is grace that I have just witnessed.

'I lived in London near a park that had a pond and a wooden bridge that floated above it in a gentle arch,' Margo interrupts my reverie. 'I used to go there now and then with a bagful of stale bread and throw it down to the ducks and geese that swam beneath the bridge. It was beautiful there, so green and quiet.'

23

She looks at me and grins.

'And although it's very different here,' Margo continues, 'it's beautiful too, don't you think?'

I laugh.

'How is it Margo that you always manage to read my mind?'

'Look at them, Layla. They're totally absorbed in their playing and are oblivious to anything but the moment they're living right now.'

'Yes,' I sigh. 'They can't help but be beautiful, can they?'

She draws on her cigarette and blows a thin cloud of smoke in my direction.

If I had ideas when I first knew Margo that there was anything romantic or exciting about the war she fought in, she soon changed my mind.

'There was urgency, yes, and immediacy, but not pleasure,' she tells me as we sit on the landing in front of her apartment one evening.

'But you met the love of your life in the resistance,' I protest. 'You and John were so brave.'

'The war only made it more difficult for us, Layla, not easier.'

'Surely, you only started to feel that way much later on, Margo. I can tell from the stories you've told me that you knew at the time what you were doing was important.'

'Stories, yes,' Margo sighs. 'But it wasn't long before we stopped thinking of ourselves as heroes, although I didn't understand why until later.'

I wait for her to continue.

'I remember once being in Paris while expecting John back from a mission. It was early summer and many people had left the city because of the occupation. The streets, homes and shops seemed completely deserted to me and it was sad too. The truth was, of course, that there were still many Parisians there just getting on with their lives and trying to avoid attention.

'I walked into a café for something to eat and there was a middle-aged woman serving. I noticed after a while that she was the only one working there, so I asked her why that was. She just put a plate of food in front of me and walked away without replying.

'I didn't stop there, of course. I finished my meal and went up to the counter where she was rinsing out some glasses and asked her why she was running the place on her own.'

Margo clears her throat and looks out into the distance.

'The woman was clearly very irritated with me but she finally gave me an answer. She said that her husband had been taken away by the Germans and that although her son and his young family had fled, she had refused to go with them.

'But why would you want to stay, I asked her. "I'm waiting it out," she said. I didn't understand what she meant. "I'm waiting it out," she told me again, "because I know it won't last, war never does, and someone has to be here to put the pieces back together again when it's all over".'

Margo wraps her arms around herself.

'I felt so small. There I was feeling important when I suddenly realized that our fight would be won by people just like her who stubbornly held on to their daily existence and resisted just by insisting on living their lives as they always had.'

I lean over to take her hand and we continue to gaze up together at the darkened sky.

'I love you, Margo,' I say.

I walk through the open front door of Margo's apartment and find a man in the sitting room. He is grey-haired and pleasant looking and stands up as soon as I arrive.

'Oh, hello,' I say, reaching out to shake his hand. 'I'm Layla. A friend of Margo's.'

'How do you do?' he says, with a smile. 'And I'm Fouad.'

'Layla, sweetheart,' Margo says, coming in from the kitchen. 'How nice of you to drop in.'

I turn to her and smile.

'I won't keep you, Margo,' I say. 'I just thought I'd come by to say hello.'

'Oh, sweetheart, please sit down. I've been wanting you to meet Fouad for a while now. He's a dear friend from years and years ago.'

Margo has mentioned Fouad to me before. I nod and smile.

'Why don't I go make some more coffee?' Margo says as I sit down. 'I'll be right back.'

Fouad and I look closely at one another. I am very curious about anyone from Margo's past.

'So how long have you known Margo?' I ask, a little surprised at my own boldness.

'Hm. Would you believe over fifty years?'

He chuckles at my astonishment and his eyes disappear into his face with his smile.

'We met when I was a student in London right after the war,' he continues. 'It doesn't actually feel like that long ago, but I suppose it is. What about you? How do you know Margo?'

'Oh, we're neighbours. I live on the floor below. I met her when I moved in here a few years ago.'

I want to ask him what Margo was like when she was young but I am afraid of appearing too forward.

'You want to know more about Margo and her past, don't you?'

I'm startled by his question.

'Am I that transparent?'

'I don't blame you,' he says, leaning forward in his seat.

26

'I would be curious too. She's a remarkable woman and she's been through a great deal.'

'She's a very special friend,' I say.

'What is he telling you?' Margo appears in the doorway with a tray.

I help her carry it to the table and pour the coffee.

'Just how wonderful you are, my dear,' Fouad says. 'But Layla already knows that, I think.'

Margo sits down, lights a cigarette and looks at me through a cloud of smoke, her eyes half-closed, her head tilted to one side.

'Fouad helped me through a very difficult period in my life,' she says. 'I owe him a great deal.'

We talk mostly about Beirut and the unfolding of our lives here. With Margo looking on, I tell him about my work at the university and am then delighted to hear that he graduated from there, too many years ago to admit to, he laughs. Like me, Fouad is Beirut born and bred, though since the death of his wife two years ago he has been living in their house in the hills above the city because it is easier to be alone there, he explains, with a garden for solace and a mountain of memories to sort through.

'You must come up with Margo next time she visits, Layla,' Fouad says. 'Get away from the strain and stress of living in Beirut. We don't hear about the antics of our politicians up there. It's like being in a different country.'

'I would love to, thank you,' I reply and look at Margo for a reaction.

'Yes, of course you must,' she says with a smile. 'It would do you lots of good.'

At home later, I replay the visit in my mind. Margo has always been guarded about her friends, especially those like Fouad from the distant past, and although I am certain he knows much more about her than I do, I don't think she would want him to talk to me about it. It is not the first time I experience bewilderment in her presence. It is as if there are aspects to her life that I will never understand, the darker side of an otherwise resplendent moon.

I think of love as a state of being that I might one day find myself in without previous intention. This is how I feel about Beirut, after all, an attachment that I am not conscious of ever acquiring, my love for it having no beginning nor a likely end, a bond that is impossible to abandon because it has become so much a part of me.

Soon after my return to Beirut, a colleague in my department who had been born in America to Lebanese parents asks me to come out to see a film with him. The film, based on a novel about immigrants in a Western city, is very moving, and afterwards, over a light dinner at a quiet restaurant not far from the theatre, we discuss it at length, examine the motivation behind the characters' actions and the strengths and weaknesses of the plot.

'I imagine the reverse is also true, that it has been difficult for you to adjust to being here again, after all the years away,' David says as we eventually make our way home.

'This country has changed so much since I was a child,' I sigh.

'And you are very different as well, aren't you?'

I laugh nervously and stop to look up at him for a moment.

'Yes, that too, I suppose.'

With time, I discover in David an underlying kindness that puts me at my ease. It is not just being with him that makes me contented but also the anticipation of our encounters, the certainty that they will continue to be a part of today and of the days to come. We speak of work and of our pasts, the small town in Virginia where David's parents had settled and his childhood there, my experience of the civil war and the years that followed my family's departure. We also indulge our mutual love of literature by discussing favourite authors and books, the successes or otherwise of our endeavours as teachers and our ambitions for the future. David taught in the United States for many years and could have expected to get far in the academic world there, yet still chose to come to Beirut.

'Why come here now, David, when things are in such a mess?' I ask him as we sit in my office one day.

'Life in the West is not always what it might seem,' he replies. 'I just wanted to get away, to experience something new and different.'

He is in the armchair by the open window and for a moment a passing breeze ruffles his fair, smooth hair.

'And is it different enough for you?'

David shifts in his seat and looks at me.

'So you were only looking for something exotic and you plan to leave eventually, is that it?' I continue, surprised at the sharpness in my voice. 'Once you've had enough of new and different, I mean.'

'Have I said something to upset you?'

I suddenly feel ashamed of myself.

'I'm sorry.'

'Layla, are you alright?'

He stands up and walks towards me.

'I'm fine,' I reply. 'Just fine. Why don't we go get something to eat?'

Soon after this conversation, David left Lebanon to return to America, just as I had suspected he would. I am here to stay, I say out loud alone in my bed at night, and nothing will happen to change that.

On days when Margo seems particularly frail, her small body shaking more than usual, her speech more deliberate, she is more inclined to talk about herself if I ask her a question about her life and wait for her to begin at some undefined point in her past, to unravel stories like tangled twine.

We go for a walk through the university campus and sit on a wooden bench surrounded by the trees and plants Margo so loves.

'My mother adored flowers and our house was always full of them,' she begins. 'It's no wonder really that I grew up dreaming of being a gardener, although father was horrified at the thought.'

When she turned sixteen and her parents discovered that Margo had fallen in love with the gardener, they hurriedly shipped her off to finishing school in Switzerland. And although the young man was soon forgotten, she never quite lost her love for growing things. Now, in place of a garden of her own, Margo tends the pots and plants in pots at her doorstep.

'What happened after they sent you away?' I ask.

'My parents were hopeful I would change and there was a part of me that wanted to please them but I still managed to disgrace myself at finishing school doing things that were bound to infuriate everyone, like smoking and drinking and getting up to all sorts of mischief with the boys.'

She sighs, takes a cigarette and lighter out of her pocket and lights up.

'I was eventually sent back home, of course. I think that's when I realized that I was never going to get my parents' approval so I might as well stop trying. Still, when the war began and the time finally came for me to go, it was difficult to leave them.'

There is a sudden kind of croak in her voice now, age and years and years of smoking, I suppose, that makes me jump every time I hear it. I don't know if she uses it for dramatic effect or if she really does not know how startling it can be.

'Ah!' Margo opens her mouth wide.

Then she shakes her head and smiles.

'I told them I wanted to go to London to study English and they agreed even though I don't think they believed that was what I really intended to do. I suppose they didn't object because they didn't know what else to do with me. I packed my bags and made my farewells and when I looked back to wave goodbye, they seemed already to be fading from sight. Mama, papa and Emily standing on the balcony of our flat in Prague, looking silently down at me as I got into the taxi that took me to the train station.'

'Don't you mean Paris?' I ask, puzzled.

But Margo does not reply.

'I never saw my parents again,' she says after a long pause.

I clear my throat.

'What happened?'

'The war went on and on until some of us thought it would never end and when I returned they were no longer there.'

I remember in Adelaide once talking to the grandfather of a friend of mine who kept referring to 'the war' during our conversation. It was a while before I realized that he was not talking about the civil conflict in Lebanon that had so affected my own life but to the Second World War which, for his generation, had defined the 'before' and 'after' of their existence, the single event that had changed them and their world forever.

'Everything changed once the Americans came in, of course,' Margo continues. 'It would have gone on a lot longer if they hadn't.'

She watches two students walking past. They are absorbed in their conversation and do not notice us.

'I went with them later on into the camps in Poland and Germany later on.'

'The American troops?'

She nods.

'I served as a translator during the liberation.'

'You went into the concentration camps?' I ask, my fascination with Margo's tale turning into horror.

She looks at me with concern.

'It's OK, Margo,' I say, recovering my composure. 'Please go on.'

Perhaps it is something she needs to talk about, I think to myself. But Margo only shakes her head.

'After the war, I returned to France to find my sister Emily,' she eventually continues. 'My parents were already lost by then and she and her husband were living in Paris.'

'She must have been very relieved to see you.'

Margo gives me a sidelong glance and a wry smile that lasts only seconds.

'She wanted nothing to do with me, accused me of running away during the war just when the family needed me most and said I had been selfish and ungrateful. I couldn't really argue with that. Still, I was shocked that she should feel that way about me. We were very different, she and I, but I always thought of us as close.'

'Didn't she know you had been working with the resistance?' I ask, feeling indignant for Margo's sake. 'She should have been proud of what you had done.'

She shrugs and blows smoke through her nostrils.

'That wasn't the way things worked out. Afterwards, I realized I would have to make my home somewhere else.'

'Where did you go?'

'I moved to London and eventually settled down. It was easier that way.'

She pauses.

'I thought so much about going home after the war had ended that it took a bit of getting used to at first , being alone and in England . In the end I managed to find a way of life that worked for me and I was happy there for a while.'

'But how did you end up coming to Beirut?'

'Some time later, Fouad and his wife came to London for a visit and they invited me to return here with them for a holiday. I liked it so much that I didn't really need them to persuade me to stay.'

I feel emboldened to talk about something I had been puzzling over since we first met.

'It seems a strange place for you to end up in, though,' I say quietly. 'I mean, given your background and all the things that had happened to you. It's not as though you had any connection to Lebanon.'

'I had nothing to keep me here, no one to keep me here, that's true. But that's why I wanted to stay, I think. Besides, where else would I have gone after leaving London?'

There is a note of cynicism in her voice that surprises me. I sit back in my seat and look up at the leaves of a tree whose branches arch gently above the bench we are sitting on. They are a dark, polished green in places and have a soft silvery sheen about them in others. I am suddenly struck by the symmetry of their irregular shapes and the beauty in their contrasting colours.

I begin to wonder if Margo might now regret her decision to remain in Lebanon, especially given the political instability we are now experiencing.

'So where do you feel you belong, Margo?' I finally ask.

She drops her cigarette to the ground, puts it out with her shoe and pulls herself up with her stick.

'Wherever I happen to be, sweetheart, whoever I happen to be with,' she says. 'With you here, now, and some-where else later on. It's all the same, after all, don't you think?'

I laugh loudly.

'You know that's not how I feel, Margo,' I protest, gesturing at the view before us. 'This country is everything to me, this city. It's where I grew up, where I became who I am.'

'Mmm. But perhaps one day that feeling too will change in you.'

My uncle and his wife still live in the old neighbourhood by the American University, though they moved some years ago into a larger apartment that has a partial view of the Corniche and the sea beyond it. Every once in a while I visit and when the weather is fine, we relax on the balcony in the shade of a large beach umbrella and chat while the hum of traffic and people goes on below.

My cousins left home years ago, but my uncle and aunt remain a surprisingly forward-looking couple, unwilling to hark back to the miseries of the civil war and enjoying the here and now of Beirut days.

This city, my uncle insists every time I see him, is still the best place to be. It has everything and everyone I could ever need in it and more, he says.

Several years ago, he and his wife came to visit us in Australia and seemed to enjoy their holiday, but when the time came for them to leave and my father suggested they set up home there, my uncle adamantly refused. The civil war had just come to a shaky end and they were both anxious, he said, to get back and play a part in rebuilding Lebanon.

I did not know it then, but my uncle's determination played a part in my own longing to return, and confirmed my conviction that what I had always seen as my roots on this earth were worth preserving, that in abandoning them I might also be losing the very qualities that defined me. How does one live, I began to ask myself, without a clear sense of self in a world where individuality is constantly being eroded?

'You know, *amou*,' I tell my uncle during one of our conversations on the terrace. The air is warm but not uncomfortably so. 'In many ways you're very different from my father.'

'Oh?'

'I mean you both grew up here, set up business and eventually married and had families. Yet he was prepared to give it all up and move away, without looking back once.'

I shake my head to emphasize my disapproval.

'There's no right or wrong in what we each chose to do, Layla,' he says.

'He left home and dragged his family away with him, without allowing anyone else a say in it.'

'You were too young to make choices then, *habibti*, and your mother was very happy to leave the war behind. They did it for you, after all.'

'You have children too,' I protest. 'Why did you decide to stay?'

He sits up and looks at me.

'I suppose I couldn't imagine myself and my family being happy anywhere else.'

'Is it really as simple as that?'

He shrugs his shoulders and leans back in his chair.

'Why don't we just try to enjoy the afternoon and stop worrying about things we can do nothing about?' he says not unkindly.

Would it take only a change of perspective to make me comfortable with myself wherever I happen to be, I wonder later. Could Margo be right, am I simply misleading myself in thinking that there is only one place, one way for me to be?

Margo is not old in my eyes. Her hair is white, her skin is furrowed and lined and the colour in her eyes seems to have faded to translucent, but her spirit is unblemished by age, as though in living so long and so much she has merely reverted to innocence and fooled the inevitable movement of time. It is strange but often, when we are together, I feel wiser and less vulnerable than she, the protector rather than the one in need of protection.

'Margo, are you on your way somewhere?'

She is standing at the end of the alleyway leaning heavily on her stick and looking around her with some bewilderment.

'Layla, sweetheart,' she says, her voice anxious. 'Fouad just dropped me off. He couldn't find anywhere to park his car so I told him to go on home.'

'Why don't I walk with you up the stairs?'

I reach out to take her arm but she shakes her head.

'I . . . I'm feeling suddenly tired, sweetheart. I think I need to rest for a moment.'

She is looking pale and I am concerned she might fall down. I knock on the door of one of the ground floor flats and ask them for a chair.

'I'm sorry for being so much trouble, sweetheart,' she says, sitting down.

I hand her the glass of water that the neighbour has given me and she sips at it slowly.

'Perhaps we should take you to see a doctor?'

'Margo, are you alright?' Fouad asks, walking into the alley.

He leans over to wrap an arm around Margo's shoulders.

'I found a parking spot further up the road,' he says. 'I didn't want to leave you to walk up the stairs on your own.'

'Please don't fret you two,' Margo says, patting Fouad's arm. 'I'm feeling better now.'

'I'm glad you were here for her, Layla,' Fouad says.

'You are beginning to look better, Margo,' I say. 'The colour's coming back into your cheeks.'

'I was a bit worried there for a moment,' Fouad says looking at me. 'We were on our way down from the mountains and Margo said she wasn't feeling too well. But she wouldn't let me stop at a doctor's to have her checked.'

'I'm a useless old thing sometimes, I know,' Margo interrupts him. 'But I'm perfectly alright now, and I'm ready to make my way up to the flat.'

'I'll come with you,' Fouad insists, helping her up from the chair.

Margo looks at him and shakes her head.

'Actually, I was on my way back upstairs,' I say. 'I just realized I've forgotten something. Why don't I go with you Margo?'

'If you're going to be with her, Layla, that'll be fine. She's always had a hard time accepting help anyway.'

He bends down and gives Margo a hug, then pulls away again, looking at her with a depth of tenderness that makes a deep impression on me.

Once upstairs, I ask Margo if she would like me to help her into the bedroom.

'You know I've always thought of myself as self-sufficient,' she says, shaking her head. 'I suppose it's easy to do when you're young and strong, but old age changes all that.'

She laughs and I reach out to touch her hand.

'I'm always here for you, Margo.'

'Yes, I know, sweetheart. It's just that sometimes I can't help wishing . . .'

She looks down and brushes the front of her sweater with her hand.

'You know, I never thought this would happen to me,' she continues. 'I always believed I would remain strong enough not to have to rely on anyone.'

She pauses and looks up at me again.

'It's ridiculous, isn't it?'

On the outside landing, by Margo's front door, is a plant pot perched on a stand. Inside it is a small nest and four baby birds, their disproportionately large and bare heads quivering on thin necks, their beaks wide open.

'This is amazing,' I exclaim, peering into the pot.

'They hatched only a few days ago. The mother comes and goes all the time, feeding them and keeping them warm.'

'She doesn't mind you being around?'

Margo shakes her head.

'Not so far, anyway. But I do try to be discreet.'

She motions for me to go inside.

'She must have sensed she and the babies would be safe here,' I begin as we take our seats in the living room.

Margo gives me a quizzical look.

'Not many birds escape being shot here, Margo, despite the laws against it. The mother bird obviously realized that you would not harm them.'

I hesitate.

'I'm not surprised, though,' I continue. 'It's exactly how I feel whenever I come here, safe from harm. You are the most tolerant person I know, Margo.'

'I'm glad you feel that way, sweetheart,' she says with a smile. 'Sometimes, though, I feel you think too well of me for my own good. I have done some very foolish things in my life, you know, things that I'm not proud of.'

'I can't imagine you doing anything bad, Margo. Mistakes are different. We all make those.'

'Some mistakes can be deliberate.' There is a hint of impatience in her voice. 'When I think now of how I treated my parents while they were alive, of all those I've hurt in the past . . . I'm not trying to shock you but to encourage you to see people as they really are, my dear, even if you do love them. Particularly if you love them as you do.'

I begin to protest but Margo interrupts me.

'At one point in my life, just after the war, I thought drinking was the best way of dealing with my problems. I drank so much that some days I'd wake up not knowing what I had done the night before or who the man or woman beside me was and I came very close once to killing myself.'

I shake my head.

'You were lost and confused, at the time, Margo. So much had been lost despite the fact that you had all fought so hard for things to change for the better.'

Margo reaches for her cigarettes.

'People are not always motivated by the right reasons,' she says quietly. 'Sometimes we do what seem like brave things only because we are too afraid to stop and look more closely within ourselves.'

I frown and watch as she attempts to light her cigarette with shaking hands. I should have known you when you were young and needed direction and the world did not seem big enough to contain the despair that threatened to overwhelm you.

I remember telling Margo one morning that I was planning to take students from my writing seminar out for a drink. I explained that I occasionally met with students outside the classroom in the hope that we will get to know one another better . Often, in this less formal environment, I am struck by a promise in them that I had not been aware of before.I was pleasantly surprised when she showed interest in meeting them.

'I would love for them to meet you,' I say. 'Would you like to come with us?'

'Why don't you bring them here instead? We can serve food and drinks in the living room and those who want to can spill out onto the landing for more space.'

'There are only seven of them so I suppose it would work,' I say. 'But wouldn't it be too much trouble for you?'

She shakes her head.

'I think I would enjoy having young people around the place. Even if it's just for one evening.'

'Alright, but I'll prepare every thing we need, Margo. I don't want you to go to any trouble.'

The weather is mild the evening of the party. When I arrive, Margo's front door is held open with a large pot that contains a young jasmine tree only just beginning to flower.

'Is that new?' I ask, gesturing towards the plant. 'It smells wonderful.'

I place two large plastic bags filled with foods and treats on the kitchen floor.

Margo smiles and nods.

'I've put out some bowls and platters on the dining room table for you to put the food in, sweetheart,' she says.

'Thank you, Margo. I'll need to make some room in the fridge as well. They'll be delivering the drinks soon.'

It usually takes time for us to relax and shake off the air of classroom formality, but not long after the students arrive the evening's conversations begin in earnest. When I introduce them, I can see that my students are impressed by Margo, one or two of them not knowing quite how to react to this diminutive, elderly woman whose eyes look straight into theirs, unflinching and knowing. I also begin to see that Margo relies on that moment of hesitation her demeanour imposes on those who meet her for the first time to study them closely, while their guard is down.

Still, there is kindness also in her assessment, I think, an acceptance of whatever it is she sees because she harbours no compulsion to captivate or even change it.

Half-way through the evening, I find one of my male students sitting next to Margo in her usual spot on the floor. They seem deep in conversation and I am curious to know what they might be talking about so I ease myself into the armchair opposite and wait to be invited to join them.

'Here you are, sweetheart,' Margo says, looking up at me.

Youssef is the one student I feel I have not quite managed to get through to. He is almost excessively serious and visibly withdraws into himself every time I try to get him to talk. Yet his writing reveals a remarkably profound inner life for one so young, even if it does tend to lack focus, and often leads him to go off on tangents that are more confused than creative. I have met with him several times in my office to give him the direction he needs to achieve his true potential, but with no success.

'This young man is telling me how much he enjoys your classes, Layla,' Margo says. 'He says he finds them inspiring.'

I try not to look too surprised.

'Youssef is a good student,' I say with a half-smile. 'I'd just like him to be more willing to participate in the classroom and listen to my advice once in a while.'

Youssef turns to me and frowns.

'I think he finds it difficult to feel completely comfortable around others, don't you?' Margo says, reaching out to pat him gently on the arm before turning to me.

'Some things cannot be forced, Layla,' she continues with a firm voice.

There is such sympathy in her eyes and such relief in his that I am momentarily taken aback and am aware of having missed something crucial in this intimate exchange.

41

I stand up and walk away, feeling as if I have been summarily dismissed by them.

Later, as I finish off the last of the washing up, Margo comes into the kitchen and stands by me at the sink.

'Please sit down, Margo. It's been a long evening and you must be very tired.'

'I had a good time, Layla. Thank you for bringing them here.'

I reach out for a dish towel and change my mind.

'Perhaps I'll leave the washing up to dry itself on the rack,' I say. 'I'll come back tomorrow morning to clear it all up. Is that OK?'

'Of course it is, sweetheart. We're both tired and should just head off to bed, I suppose.'

'Thanks again for letting me have the party here, Margo,' I say, heading to the front door. 'It went even better than I thought it would.'

'Layla,' she calls after me.

'Yes?'

'It eventually gets easier, you know, as long as you don't try so hard to make everything better.'

I am uncertain of what she is trying to tell me at first.

'Does it really?' I ask.

She smiles and shakes her head.

'Perhaps a time will come, my darling girl, when you will feel the release in simply accepting some things as they are without trying to change them.'

'And rely only on happenstance?'

'But isn't that what it ultimately means to be trusting, Layla?'

I have noticed, once or twice, a man in our building who seems familiar, yet I cannot remember ever having met or spoken to him. He is of medium height and wears glasses and has a small beard that is flecked with grey and I am

drawn by an air of resignation about him that I sometimes think might instead be an indication of humility.

Perhaps it is this impression of reticence that I recognize
in him, I think one morning when we meet on the stairs.
We nod at one another and I smile. The encounter, however
brief, makes me determined to try to strike up a conversation with him next time we see one another, though I
don't really understand why that should be so, nor why
this man should seem so appealing to me.

Margo and I often speak about lovers in our very
different pasts, my experiences seeming more awkward
than authentic, poor substitutes for what I imagine would
be the real thing, the passion and the romance. Whenever
she talks about her husband John, a picture emerges in
my mind of the intensity of a love that, had circumstances
been different, might not have lasted. Relationships that
endure, I tell Margo, like those of my parents or my uncle
and his wife, seem to have an element of the mundane
about them that I know I would find unacceptable.

There is a professor of music at the university, a man
with a mane of dark, thick hair and a voice so resonant
that he seems sometimes to sing as he speaks, who intrigued
me when we met. But the first time I went into his office
and noticed the dust-free shelves lined with books in
descending size, the neat desk and empty in and out trays
placed at precise angles on its surface, and the general
impression of tidiness taken to a disconcerting extreme, I
longed to get out again.

Margo and I laughed about it afterwards. She said she
was surprised I had not yet realized that men tended to
be creatures of habit, surrounding themselves with a sense
of security that is based on objects and rituals rather than
emotions. Was your John like that? I asked her then. She
fell silent for a moment. He probably would have been,
if he had lived, she eventually answered. Would you have

43

loved him still, I persisted. Perhaps even more, she said quietly, and I failed to understand what she meant at the time.

When she speaks about herself, Margo tells me it's like peeling away the many layers of an onion to arrive at its essence. There is so much hidden away from view, she says, that even when I think I have finally arrived at some kind of truth, there is another lurking beneath it.

I watch her as she cups her hands, holds them together and opens them up again, and imagine the process as endless, hidden levels of meaning that once arrived at become instantly out of reach.

'It never stops this self-searching then?' I ask.

Margo smiles wryly.

'Even for someone as old as I am, sweetheart.'

I long ago sensed Margo's ability for detachment, not only because there are some things about her life that I will never know and am not in any case prepared to probe, but also because she manages to maintain a distance from the events and people she encounters that comes from being older and so far removed from immediate concerns.

Still, she is also marvellously adept at living in the moment, at making of everything and everyone around her a discovery.

'We have lost the ability,' Margo repeats again and again, 'to simply stop and stare.'

I feel that with Margo I am encountering truths that would otherwise have eluded me, depths of being which I might not have been able to reach on my own. In accepting the people and circumstances that surround her, she shows me the way of compassion, and in being so steadfast, she gives me courage. Whenever I attempt to voice these feelings to her, I eventually find myself giving up because I know they would lose too much in the telling.

Once, standing together in the hallway of Margo's flat,

I tell her that she has remained innocent in her dealings with others, despite her age and all that had happened to her.

'At times, you seem almost like a child to me, Margo,' I say. 'It's almost as if at some point in your life, you simply gave up being certain about anything at all.'

I hesitate, suddenly unsure.

'But perhaps I have been unable to fully understand you,' I continue.

Margo leans against the wall and makes her way slowly towards the front door. When she eventually turns around to look at me, there are tears in her eyes. I reach out and touch her cheek with one hand.

'Oh. Oh, my dear friend,' I say, shaking my head.

I notice him at the butcher's one morning, both of us waiting to be served. I catch his eye and smile but when I attempt to approach him, he is already on his way out of the shop. I cannot shake off the feeling that I know him from somewhere.

A few days later, I go to a bookshop not far from the university and my suspicions are confirmed. He is a well known writer who is greatly admired in this part of the world and I have read three of his most celebrated books.

I choose a novel by him that was recently translated into English. On the back, there are quotes from critics who describe it as 'moving' and 'one of this excellent writer's best books yet', as well as a headshot of him in his younger days when he did not have a moustache or a beard.

When I arrive at his doorstep, there are no plants outside the front door, nor any other sign of welcome. I ring the bell and hear a faint shuffling inside before he opens the door.

'Hello,' I say with a smile. 'I'm Layla, your neighbour from upstairs.'

I put out my hand and shake his. He appears too surprised to say anything, his eyebrows are raised slightly and his lips are held tightly together.

'I hope I'm not disturbing you,' I continue, beginning to feel nervous.

He remains silent.

'I'm sorry. I expect you must be working and I interrupted you.'

He begins to say something when he looks down at the book in my hand.

'I wondered if you would sign this for me.' I lift it up for him to see.

He nods but does not smile.

'Yes, of course,' he says finally. 'Please come in.'

He leads me into the small entrance hall and turns to go into the living room.

'I have one if you like,' I say, handing him a pen.

A smell of burnt bread permeates the air.

'I'm sorry,' he says, opening the book and laying it on the hall table. 'What did you say your name was?'

'Layla,' I say softly.

He bends down to write.

'I hope you enjoy it,' he hands the book back to me. 'Although I have written two others since, you know.'

'Yes, I know. I haven't read this one yet, though.'

He nods and gives me back the pen.

'There was something else I wanted to ask you.'

He looks taken aback.

'I teach at the American University. I wondered if you would be willing to come and give a talk to my students. It's a literature course. I know a number of your books have been translated into English and I'd like my students to become familiar with your work.'

He takes off his glasses and rubs his eyes.

'It's something to think about,' he says, putting his

46

glasses back on again. 'Although I'm not particularly good at giving talks, you know.'

Then he accompanies me to the front door, opens it and finally smiles as I step out onto the landing.

I turn to shake his hand and repeat my thanks but he has already shut the door behind me. On my way back upstairs, I feel disappointed, as though I have been let down, not so much by the writer but by my own awkwardness.

Once inside my apartment, I open the book. His writing is small, the letters even and clean. From Kamal, it says, To Layla and future friendship.

I arrive at Margo's and find her rummaging through the bottom drawer of the big dresser in the living room. I clear my throat and she looks up at me.

'The front door was open, Margo. I knocked but you didn't hear me.'

'Come in, sweetheart. I'm just looking for something.'

'Shall I put the coffee on or would you like some help?'

She sits back on the floor.

'I thought I had a photograph of John here somewhere. I wanted to show it to you.'

'Oh?'

'We were in a café with a group of friends and someone took a picture of us. I was sure it was here.'

I sit down beside her. The contents of the drawer are tangled up together, piles of papers and photographs and notebooks and other bits and pieces.

'Why don't I try to sort out through all of this for you?'

I look at her and see hesitation in her eyes.

'But these might be private things,' I say hurriedly. 'I'm sorry, Margo.'

'No, no, it's alright. I just . . . It's all such a mess.'

'We can do it together. What do you think?'

We begin by taking everything out and making separate piles. Things that look like official documents which I try not to read despite my curiosity, and others such as receipts for electricity and telephone bills which I place in a manila envelope and tell Margo to keep. There are also a number of books which Margo agrees should go on the shelves in her bedroom, and in the far corner of the drawer, a thick wad of money kept together with a rubber band.

'There are a lot of dollars here, Margo. Are you sure it's safe to keep them in this drawer?'

She shrugs.

'It's for emergencies. Someone might need it one day.'

'Oh, Margo. You've been giving your money away again, haven't you?'

'I've got plenty of it, sweetheart.'

'You need to hang onto it for yourself. You may need it one day.'

She gives me one of her sidelong glances.

'You mean if I want to suddenly up and leave here or become incapacitated and have to go into a home?'

'No, of course not. I would never let that happen to you.'

'The only way I'm leaving this place is in a box, Layla. This is the last home I'll ever have.'

I sit back and shake my head.

'I hope that won't be for some time yet, Margo. I need you.'

'Yes, I know you do, but you won't be alone always, darling.'

We do not find the photograph of John among those we go through. There are pictures of Margo as a child with her mother and sister and others of her when she was a young woman, either portraits or group shots with friends. She points to a few of the faces and tells me who they are but otherwise says very little and I do not try to push her.

*   *   *

I remember a fisherman when I was a child who spent hours every morning untangling his net after a night's fishing just off shore. His small boat bobbing up and down in the tiny marina at the end of the Corniche near my home, he sat on a wooden stool puffing on a cigarette that was lodged between his lips as he worked, occasionally taking it out to sip on a cup of coffee placed on the ground by his feet.

He fascinated me, not only because of his tanned, leathery skin, his wild grey hair and the way his small eyes shone like pebbles whenever he looked up from his net, but also because he seemed so nonchalant, so detached from everything around him.

I mustered the courage one morning to go right up to him and when he did not object, sat down on a rock and watched him at work. He looked at me and grunted but said nothing, turning his attention back to his net, his coffee and cigarette. I allowed myself to look closely at him then, the huge chafed knuckles of his hands and his gnarled feet in plastic slippers, toenails thick and yellow and unevenly cut.

'Do they hurt?' I suddenly blurted out.

The fisherman looked up, his eyebrows raised.

'What?' he asked with a gruff voice.

I froze with fear.

'What did you say?' he repeated.

'I just wondered if your feet hurt. They . . . they look funny.'

He frowned hard, looked down at his feet and wiggled his toes.

'A bit stiff but they're fine,' he said.

The butt of his cigarette fell to the ground as he spoke and I hurriedly stepped on it to put it out.

'You could have started a fire,' I muttered, shaking my head.

The old man burst out laughing then and I found myself giggling in return.

'Cheeky thing,' he said, reaching out to pat me on the head.

We became fast friends after that, though he only ever muttered a greeting when I arrived at the marina to meet him on Saturday mornings, and when we did make conversation it was always brief and to the point. I asked him about his nightly fishing trips on the dark, rolling sea and about what it felt like to be out there on his own and whether he would take me out with him on his excursions. The water at night is as thick and as smooth as blood and anyone who fell into it would be swallowed up in no time, he replied with a mischievous grin. I shuddered at the thought but still did not give up the notion that anything was possible, even for me, if only I were brave enough to attempt it.

It is late afternoon and the Corniche is bathed in soft light.

'I grew up one street away from here,' I say, pointing away from the main road. 'I used to come to the Corniche with my friends to play. There was an old fisherman I made friends with, at that small marina just under the bridge there. I wonder what's happened to him.'

Margo stops to look in the direction I am pointing, then she makes her way to one of the concrete benches that line the pavement and sits down.

I motion to a vendor on a bicycle to stop and I buy two pieces of *kaak* from him.

I sit down next to Margo, make a hole in each of the layered pieces of bread and fill them with the thyme and sesame seed mixture that comes with them.

'Here you go, Margo,' I say, handing her the *kaak*.

By dusk parents with strollers are walking leisurely up and down the pavement. Looking around me, I am once again struck by the mix of people, elderly men in fold-out chairs, veiled women alongside others in body-hugging jeans and tight t-shirts, young children on their bicycles, joggers with their i-pods blotting out the world, and out on the rocks, fishermen with their rods and tackle. There are vendors also, either carrying their wares on their backs or standing next to large wooden carts from which they sell green almonds dipped in salt, boiled corn on the cob, pumpkin seeds and peanuts in the shell and Beirut's version of brioche and other pastries.

'This is the one place everyone can enjoy,' Margo says as if reading my mind. 'That's one of the reasons I chose to live in this part of the city when I decided to settle here.

'At first, I stayed with friends who have an old house up in the mountains with a beautiful garden. I've told you about them, haven't I? Fouad and his wife May. I loved it up there and stayed for several months before eventually coming down to Beirut.'

I nod. I have heard this story before, although Margot seems to have forgotten that I have met her friend Fouad before.

'That first walk on the Corniche was something,' Margo smiles. 'Like being in the south of France again, although it's a lot less polished here, of course.'

We look to the right, to the hills and mountains in the distance. It is a clear spring day and except for a small area of white on the highest summit, most of the winter snow is gone.

'This is beautiful but I love the mountains too,' I sigh. 'I dream of having a small house there one day, somewhere I can go to breathe fresh air and quiet.'

'Do you imagine a solitary life for yourself then, sweet-heart?'

I turn to her.

'What choice do I have? I've never been successful at

relationships, you know that, Margo. Besides, as I get older it seems even less likely that I'll meet a man I can really be with.'

Margo looks down and brushes some crumbs off her lap.

'I don't like to think of you always being on your own,' she says quietly.

'What kind of life do you wish for me then?' I smile.

'You will have a man to love you and children of your own too. It will all come when the time is right, I'm sure of that.'

Two young boys run past the bench, one of them tripping and falling down. Before I can stand up to help, he quickly picks himself up again and walks away with a slight limp. When I turn to Margo again, I realize that she looks very fragile today and feel my heart skip a beat.

'What about you, Margo? Is this the kind of life that you wished for yourself?'

'What makes you ask me that now, sweetheart?'

I hesitate and reach out to touch her arm.

'Have you really been happy here, after all? Sometimes I think that maybe it's not about place but just you, Margo. So many people come to you to be comforted, but do you have anyone to listen to you when you need solace?'

The myriad sounds of the Corniche continue around us, the sea a deep, even blue with almost no sign of waves in it.

Margo sighs.

'You're right, Layla, it's not about place,' she says, her voice trembling a little. 'It never is about where you are or even the people you happen to be with. But somehow I don't think I've really managed to help you understand that.'

'I know wherever I choose to live will have advantages and disadvantages, Margo,' I say a little impatiently. 'I'm not that unperceptive, you know.'

'No, of course you're not.'

I clear my throat, hoping I have not offended Margo with my retort, and pick up the piece of *kaak* in my lap. I take a large bite from it, the sharp scent of the thyme inside it filling my nostrils. I am surprised to feel tears in my eyes and blink them back hurriedly so that she will not see them.

'So what is it then, Margo?' I try to smile as I ask the question. 'What is it that I need to know to be really happy?'

She opens her hands out in front of her as if she were preparing to say a prayer.

'More and more these days,' she begins slowly, 'when I look back on all the things I have done with my time, I understand that regret is, after all, futile.'

She places her hands in her lap once again.

'What matters, sweetheart, is not what you do but how you do it, whether or not you give life the passion and seriousness it deserves and whether you have the courage and honesty to do this, not just every now and then, but every moment, right until the very end.'

She pauses.

'It's as hard as that?' I finally ask.

Margo laughs.

'Or as simple as taking pleasure in all of this,' she says, gesturing at the scene around us. 'As easy as finally letting go.'

PART TWO
Fouad

His parents had named him Fouad, another Arabic word, among many, for the heart. This was a sign that his passions would always lead him.

The family lived in the heart of Ras Beirut, on the ground floor of a two-storey house near the American University, his mother and father, grandparents and an aging housekeeper, his brother and two sisters and himself, with fruit and flowering trees in its spacious garden and a low wall around its borders where cats often sat bathing in the sun and passers-by stopped to sniff the heady scent of jasmine in spring.

Fouad shared a bedroom with his older brother Marwan that had a window overlooking a busy street corner. On weekday mornings, being a light sleeper, he would wake up to the call of tradesmen announcing their wares or the whistle of boys running past, down towards Bliss Street and the many neighbourhoods that bordered the university compound.

Getting up to shake Marwan out of his slumber, Fouad would open the shutters to let the sunlight in and pause for a moment to sniff at the air, the thought of the day ahead already filling him with anticipation. Then, washed and dressed, his dark hair smoothed back off his brow, he would run into the kitchen to see his mother making *labneh* and cucumber sandwiches for the children's school lunches and the housekeeper stirring the beginnings of that day's stew at the stove. His grandmother, seated at the kitchen table with a bowl of French beans from the garden in her lap, would look up briefly to greet him before bending down again to her task, knobby fingers breaking the pods in two then stringing them on either side in one fluid movement.

The apartment was large with high ceilings and elegant arches for doorways, its floors tiled in repeating patterns of brilliant green and a burnt orange that recalled the colour of the dirt on the street outside, its walls solid and reassuring. The entrance way led into two big reception rooms and a dining area behind which was the kitchen and bathroom and beyond that the back door to the garden. The five doors on either side of a long hallway opened onto the bedrooms as well as a small box room where trunks and other objects were kept out of sight. Outside the front door was an elegant landing with a wide stone stairwell leading up to the apartment above where an American professor at the university and his wife had lived for as long as anyone could remember.

Going outside into the garden, Fouad would find his grandfather, his grey head disappearing behind the greenery and then coming out again, his clothes already brown with dirt, a small trowel in one hand and in the other a handkerchief that he used to wipe his brow. These hours that he spent tending the plants and flowers, the fruits and vegetables that would eventually be served at the family table, were, grandfather always said, the most important of the day.

'Jiddo,' Fouad called out, waving a hand.

'Over here.'

Grandfather was bent over a bed of parsley, the still tiny shoots fragile beneath his fingers, a delicate green that would eventually turn darker, sharp and savoury to the taste.

'Good morning, *habibi*,' *Jiddo* looked up and smiled. 'Not too long before we'll be having *tabbouleh* with our dinner. The mint will be coming up soon as well.'

Fouad nodded.

'Are you off to school then?'

Fouad watched his grandfather slowly straighten himself up.

'I haven't had breakfast yet,' he said, waiting for *jiddo* to remember his promise from the night before.

A light breeze appeared and it seemed to both of them as if the garden were suddenly unfolding, the trees stretching further up towards the sky and the flowers shaking themselves awake, the plants glistening with intention. He heard his grandfather's resonant laugh.

'I haven't forgotten,' *jiddo* said. 'Here you are, *habibi*.'

He handed Fouad a coin.

'There's enough there for something for Marwan as well.'

'Thanks.' Fouad took the money and turned back into the house.

'Let's go,' he called out to his brother.

Father came out of his bedroom and placed a hand on Fouad's shoulder. He smelled fresh and bright, like lemons do when you first cut into them, and looked very handsome in a dark suit and his red *tarboosh* perched on his head.

'Good morning, son. Rushing off as usual?'

'Hello, *baba*,' Fouad replied, fingering the coin in his pocket.

Marwan appeared from the bedroom, his eyelids drooping with unfinished sleep. Fouad shook his head and motioned for him to follow.

'Where are your sisters?' Father asked.

'Waiting for us by the gate,' said Fouad, grabbing his brother by the arm. 'We're going.'

The two boys walked their sisters, Samia and Afaf, to the evangelical school for girls in the Hamra district moments away from home, and then doubled back towards Bliss Street and the international college they had both attended since they were very young. On the way, they went through fields filled with flowering cactus and, in season, sour sops and daisies, kicking the dirt and pebbles with their shoes and grinning at the rising dust.

Once on Bliss Street, Fouad took the coin his grand-father had given him out of his pocket and showed it to Marwan.

'For *kaak*,' he said.

A tram came roaring past. Fouad looked up, catching a glimpse of a carriage and passengers crowded inside. He felt Marwan grab the money from his hand and run towards the *kaak* vendor on the other side of the street.

'I don't want *zaatar* in mine,' he called after his brother.

Then Fouad smiled because the day had begun exactly as he had imagined it would.

They went to the movies on Saturdays after school, to the Roxy and the Empire cinemas in the Bourj in downtown Beirut, getting on the tram during morning break to buy the much sought after tickets, then back again to wait impatiently for classes to end and the weekend to begin.

The films featured Fouad's favourite stars, Stewart Granger and Clark Gable, Ginger Rogers and Betty Grable with her famously beautiful legs, gutsy westerns and spy thrillers in black and white or lively musicals that attracted girls from the French Protestant College to the cinema who sat where the boys could watch them too.

Fouad would stare resolutely at the screen as Marwan

and his friends tried to attract the girls' attention, sometimes even striking up a whispered conversation until a litany of shushing echoed through the theatre, and still he watched, focused and fascinated, the heroes himself in different guises, his head filled with fast-moving pictures.

Then on the way home in the clattering tram, squeezed between an old man in a straw hat and a woman with a small child in her lap, perhaps catching the eye of a young girl as she sat quietly in her seat across from him, her brown hair falling softly to cover one side of her face, her hands wringing nervously in her lap, and finally the faint glimmer of a smile before she quickly turned away again. His heart fluttering briefly in his chest before settling down, his feet involuntarily shuffling back and forth on the floor of the carriage and the clang clang of the overhead bell in his ears, he jumped up to the exit and leaned out of it, both hands clinging to the railing, the wind in his face, blowing away his embarrassment and reminding him that he was destined for greater things.

1939 and just turned nine years old, Fouad heard of war breaking out in Europe. Tiptoeing into the living room late one night, he crawled under the dining room table and watched his father and grandfather as they listened to the news on the radio and discussed the situation, their voices hushed and solemn. Lebanon's position as a French mandate, *baba* said, means it is bound to be adversely affected by events in Europe. *Jiddo* sighed loudly. The French will never give us our independence now, he said. They'll use this as an opportunity to stay on, you mark my words.

The next day *mama* began stocking up on food, huge bags of *burghul*, rice and flour, of lentils, split peas and broad beans arriving at their doorstep, Fatima the housekeeper picking them up one by one and placing them in a row beneath the pantry shelves, her back bent low and the hem of her long, cotton work dress lifting to reveal old, tired legs. She shooed Fouad away, off you go young man, not answering him at first when he asked her what all the food was for, then turning to him to say: We're not going to go hungry this time, not if I can help it.

Like many in this country, Fatima's family had had to go without during the Great War, his mother later explained, and she is a little anxious about the future.

'A boy at school said we're all going to starve,' Fouad said. 'Is that true, *mama*?'

She pulled him to her, gentle fingers smoothing back his hair, her sweet breath permeating the air around him.

'No, *habibi*, of course we're not going to starve. This war is a long way away, after all, and it has nothing to do with us.'

But things did change, after all, Fouad becoming more aware of the French soldiers who roamed the streets and manned barricades around the neighbourhood and of the bitterness people felt at their constant presence.

One afternoon, walking home from school with Marwan, he looked on in horror when a passing French officer pulled out a gun and pointed it at his brother. What did you say, you rascal, the officer shouted. Marwan grabbed his hand and pulled Fouad behind him as they ran through familiar streets, back to the safety of their home.

'What happened?' Fouad asked once they were standing at the front door.

Marwan grinned.

'I just told him what I thought of him,' he said.

'What's that then?'

Marwan shrugged and turned away with a look of disgust.

'You're such a baby, Fouad. Don't you know anything at all?'

Two years later, the Vichy government in France finally defeated, Allied troops began to arrive in Beirut, British soldiers who spoke English with a quick, clipped accent that was difficult to understand at first until one became accustomed to it, and Australians who became known for their fondness for beer and pretty girls. More French soldiers came too with troops from their colonies in Africa.

When the YMCA set up a dormitory and canteen for the newcomers from Britain at the American University, Fouad and a few of his classmates volunteered their services, selling luncheon vouchers at the canteen on weekends as well as helping with a variety of other tasks to make the soldiers' stay more pleasant. He would arrive on a Saturday morning, bright eyed and full of enthusiasm, his cinema days well behind him, eager only to learn more about these men who in many ways seemed out of place here but who also promised something better for Lebanon, the autonomy he had heard spoken of so often, a future filled with opportunity.

Before long, he had made friends with a number of the soldiers who came to stay at the dormitory during their leave, was secretly pleased at having gained favour for being quick and efficient and speaking better English than the other volunteers. And during the many evening performances staged by the officers and their men at the university's West Hall, plays and musical concerts and the like, he would stand watching from the back of the theatre and listen for the audience's laughter, for their occasional shouts and cheers and that breathless moment when a complete hush took over the room.

At a café by the water that was crowded with Allied soldiers, Fouad sat one afternoon with *jiddo* and Marwan, Beirut's lighthouse perched on a hill behind them and the Mediterranean washing over the rocks by their feet. While

63

jiddo puffed at a *nargileh*, occasionally handing the pipe to Marwan who drew on it gingerly only to cough noisily afterwards, Fouad watched a group of Australian soldiers eating and drinking at a nearby table, their voices and laughter growing louder by the minute. They were tall, beefy men with fair skin that was burned red from the sun and they spoke a version of English that no one was familiar with, though it was usually easy to tell what was on their minds just by the manner in which they said it.

'Look,' Fouad nudged his brother. 'There's a French soldier from the table up there coming towards them.'

The two boys watched as the Frenchman stopped to talk to the Australians.

'What do you suppose he's saying?' Fouad asked.

Moments later, he gasped as one of the Australians stood up and grabbed the French soldier by the collar.

'There's going to be a fight,' Marwan shouted, getting up from his seat with Fouad following close behind.

It was not long before the whole café was plunged into chaos, men knocking each other down and a group of local boys, Fouad and Marwan among them, handing plates and bottles to the Australian soldiers which they then broke over the heads of their rivals. Fouad stepped aside for a moment and noticed the owner of the café arriving on the scene and begging the men to stop. Looking behind him, Fouad saw his grandfather smile. This is what it feels like to finally be on the winning side, he thought to himself, heat rushing through his body at the sudden realization.

Overhearing a conversation between his father and the American professor from upstairs a few days later, Fouad felt confused about the situation once again. The two men stood on the landing outside the front door. The professor, tall and thin with shoulders that stooped a little and bright blue eyes, had one foot on the stairs and a slender hand on the balustrade. He smiled and nodded at Fouad's father as he spoke.

'It's not as if the British themselves haven't been brutal colonizers elsewhere,' *baba* was saying. 'How can anyone overlook that fact?'

A sad look came over the professor's face.

'It's not unheard of for people to use the strength of one occupier in an attempt to rid themselves of another without being aware of the dangers involved,' the professor said quietly. 'And now that America has also joined the war, it's likely that we'll take a position on what's going on in your country as well.'

Father shook his head.

'It's almost as if we have no real say in our own destiny,' he sighed. 'This is the inevitable fate of a small country, I suppose.'

Yet there were days when nothing seemed to have changed at all, when the family went about its business as usual, *sitto* and *jiddo*, who unlike the rest of the family were Christian, going to church on Sunday morning and returning just before noon to sit with the children round the wireless in the living room as mother oversaw lunch preparations in the kitchen and father wandered around the garden or lounged on the terrace on his own.

They listened to a regular broadcast of popular American songs, Bing Crosby crooning *I'll Be Seeing You* and Marlene Dietrich's *Lili Marlene* in that unmistakable, husky voice, Fouad humming quietly to himself and his sisters nudging him to be quiet every now and then.

Oblivious to distractions, he would picture America as he listened, wide thoroughfares, stocky, clean-shaven men walking through them, smiling women in hats and high heels at their side, something about them, about that independent air that seemed to surround them, so appealing that he secretly dreamed of going there one day to see for himself. Then, seeing his grandfather lean forward in his chair to switch off the radio, he would shake himself awake, stand up abruptly and, pinching Afaf and Samia on their arms, run out into the garden laughing so that they would follow him, past rose bushes, his grandfather's pride, and weaving in and out of rows of vegetables and herbs, the smell of watered earth and green wafting around them. For a moment, the world was once again a safe and tranquil place and his home and family an enduring part of it.

Baba was a trader like his father before him, travelling regularly to the city of Tripoli in the north, east to Damascus and Amman, or south to the countless towns on the road to Jerusalem, trading in the raw silk cloth made in villages in Mount Lebanon and finally returning home to tell stories of his wonderful journeys without borders.

On those nights when he was home, father would sit on the terrace that overlooked the garden, his feet in slippers and his legs stretched out, a *nargileh* pipe in one hand while the other rested on the coffee table next to him; and one by one, the rest of the family would join him, grandparents sitting beside their son-in-law and *mama* standing behind his chair, her slender arms resting on his broad shoulders, the children arriving and hovering around him like honeybees. Fouad especially looked forward to hearing about his father's adventures, imagining himself in his shoes, in a swiftly moving train perhaps or an elegant automobile, or riding on horseback where roads were nonexistent and hills were dangerously steep.

'What did you bring us this time?' Afaf, the youngest, asked.

'Hush, baby,' said *mama*. 'You're father's tired. Let him rest now.'

Father puffed on the *nargileh* and the water inside it

made a loud bubbling noise. Samia giggled and ran down the steps and into the garden with Afaf following close behind.

'Did you go on the coastal road this time, *baba*?' Fouad asked.

Father nodded.

'All the way to Damascus and back.'

'Any trouble up there, Ameen?' *jiddo* asked. 'We heard about what the French troops did in Bar Elias.'

'It was over by the time I was making my way back.'

'It might prove to be the last straw,' *jiddo* continued. 'Those soldiers had no business storming the village and mistreating its inhabitants. We're supposed to be an independent country, for heaven's sake, not another colony of theirs.'

Fouad was surprised at the anger in his grandfather's voice.

'They're not going to give up their hold on Lebanon easily, we all know that,' father said. 'But the problem is that the longer these troubles go on, the more difficult it will be for the country to recover afterwards.'

'They've been here for two decades, ever since the Ottomans left, and now that the Americans have entered the war, the allies are trying to divide the region up again in their favour,' said *jiddo*. 'Why did they promise us independence if they had no plans to carry it through?'

Baba raised his eyebrows and blew smoke into the air above his head.

'What did the troops do, *baba*?' Fouad asked after a pause.

'It's not something you need to worry about, son. It's already been sorted out.'

'Why don't you tell him the truth?' Marwan interrupted loudly. 'Things haven't been sorted out at all. *Jiddo's* right. It's time the French stopped interfering in our affairs. We can't go on letting them do that.'

'Marwan,' *mama* said quietly. 'You may be a young man now but I will not have you speak to your father like that.'

Marwan turned abruptly away and walked back into the house.

Father reached up and grabbed hold of *mama*'s hand.

'It's alright my dear,' he said softly. 'The boy has a right to feel the way he does. After all, he's only expressing what we all know to be true.'

Fouad heard his mother sigh.

'It's time for the girls to go to bed,' she said, turning to Fouad. 'Fetch them from the garden, *hayati*, will you?'

Fouad woke up to find Marwan pulling on his shirt and trousers.

'Where are you going?'

Marwan looked at him and continued to dress.

'Has something happened?' Fouad insisted.

'The French arrested our President and the Cabinet during the night.'

'But why?' Fouad asked horrified.

'They're angry because Parliament has passed a law declaring Lebanon's independence from the French mandate. They're trying to stop us from finally getting our freedom.'

'So what happens now?'

'Another general strike has been called and I'm meeting up with some of the guys.'

Fouad jumped out of bed.

'I'm coming with you.'

'Alright, but try to be quiet. We don't want *mama* to hear us and ask us where we're going.'

They walked through deserted streets, Fouad saying nothing and Marwan not offering any further information, greeting a group of university students gathered on Bliss

Street with a firm handshake and a nod of the head and ignoring his younger brother as he did so.

A young man pulled away from the main group.

'*Ya shabab*, give me your attention for a moment,' he said in a loud voice.

Everyone turned to listen.

'The bus will be here in a few minutes,' he continued. 'You know what to do when we get there. If the Senegalese soldiers arrive and come on the attack, disperse and make your own way back here. Above all, avoid being arrested. Good luck.'

'Where are they going?' Fouad asked his brother but Marwan did not reply.

Moments later, there was a scramble for the bus. When Fouad stepped forward to get on it, Marwan pulled him back.

'They won't let us on the bus, silly,' Marwan whispered in his ear. 'They think we're too young to fight. Just pretend you're only watching and wait for my instructions.'

Once all the students were more or less settled in their seats, Marwan led Fouad to the back of the bus and pointed to the ladder that led up to the roof. They climbed up it and lay flat on their stomachs, clinging to the top of the now moving vehicle. Fouad strained to turn and look behind him. Three other boys had joined them. Where are we going, he wondered?

The bus made its way down to Bliss, to the tramway stop at Graham Street and moving in the direction of downtown Beirut. Although Fouad's hands had begun to tire he was afraid to let go even for a moment in case the bus lurched and he fell off. A breeze blew over from the sea behind them and ruffled his hair. He smelt the familiar scent of salt and damp air and took a deep breath, his heart beating hard and fast.

'Hey, Fouad. Sit up.'

Marwan took his hand and tried to pull him up.

'No!' he cried, feeling himself slipping.

'Don't worry. I'll hold on to you. Just hang on to this railing and you'll be fine.'

Fouad carefully lifted himself up to a seated position and looked around him. Marwan gestured with one hand towards the road and nodded.

'We're going to the French boys' school on Jemaizeh Street,' he shouted. 'They're not observing the strike like they're supposed to. We're going to make sure they do.'

Fouad heard one of the boys behind him laugh. He turned to look at him.

'I've brought a stick with me,' the boy said, lifting the stick high above his head. 'We'll bash those foreigners' heads in.'

For the first time, Fouad began to think they might be headed for trouble.

'Marwan,' he turned to his brother. 'Are you sure we should be doing this?'

His brother frowned.

'If you're scared, you can run back home as soon as we get there. I'm staying and joining in the fight.'

Fouad felt his face redden with shame.

'No. No, I'm staying too.'

'Good boy,' Marwan smiled and turned away again.

When the bus finally came to a halt, they quickly climbed off the roof and joined the others at the school gates. Fouad felt himself being pushed ahead with the crowd and he struggled hard to keep up. He looked for Marwan but his brother was nowhere to be found. I'll just have to manage by myself, he thought, the pull of bodies around him moving him inexorably forward.

'Open those gates,' someone shouted. 'Don't you know there's a strike on?'

He felt the crowd heave as if with one breath, one, two,

three and the gate finally came open. The crowd surged forward, into the school playground and to confront the men waiting there.

'Down with the colonizers! Long live a free and independent Lebanon!'

Fouad stood still for a moment, uncertain what to do. He watched as one of the university students was attacked by a tall, foreign-looking man with a beard. Suddenly Marwan appeared as if from nowhere and grabbed the man by the legs.

'Come here and help!' Marwan shouted to him.

Fouad grabbed the man by the waist and tried to pull him back. The man dragged him for a moment, before tripping and falling to the ground.

'That's the French headmaster,' Marwan hissed at the fallen man. 'That'll teach them to defy the call to strike. Let's go help those guys over there.'

Fouad looked up to see young boys in blue pinafores on the balcony overlooking the courtyard. A few of them were cheering and clapping when a teacher approached and motioned for them to go back inside. One boy didn't move, leaned over the balustrade instead and looked straight at Fouad, his hands gripping the railing, his dark head straining forward. That was me once, Fouad found himself thinking. Then he turned back to the commotion around him. Not anymore, though. Not anymore.

On the day of Lebanon's independence in 1943, *jiddo* brought the new flag home, a cedar tree on a white background with two horizontal bands of red, one above and one below it. The children gathered round to take a closer look at it, taking turns to touch the delicate cloth with their fingertips before grandfather attached it to the pole which he nailed to the balustrade on the terrace . From that day on the sound of it flapping in the evening wind lulled them all to sleep.

*   *   *

71

The summer Fouad turned seventeen, the war in Europe had already been over for two years and Lebanon, basking in its now well established independence, had a booming economy and was attracting people from all over the region and beyond.

The Ras Beirut he had grown up in was fast disappearing, buildings going up at great speed, eating up the fields of gorse bush and cactus that had once surrounded the family home. Foreigners appeared on the newly paved streets, the employees of international companies that had set up shop in the city, in his own Beirut, future gateway to the rest of the Arab world.

Stores also began to materialize on Hamra Street, bigger and better than those of yesteryear, the family-owned grocers or single-storey haberdashers. Clothes shops, shoe shops and even a small department store; cafés where men and women sat talking, sipping coffee and eating cakes; a general air of freshness and audacity about the city that, rather than embracing the past, seemed to dismiss it: there is no going back now, Hamra was saying to whoever stopped to listen, I am the Lebanon of the future.

There were changes too within Fouad's own family. Marwan, who had announced to his parents on leaving school that he would not attend university, was now engaged to be married and was working alongside father in an increasingly profitable business that took up more and more of their time. Fouad thought the fervent concerns that had dominated his older brother's life when they were both younger had somehow dissipated, not because Marwan was now without passion but because he had directed his attention elsewhere, towards following in his father's footsteps as first-born sons were wont to do and creating a family of his own. Somewhere in the back of his mind, Fouad suspected also that in conceding as he had to the more traditional role,

Marwan was paving the way for his younger brother to go beyond it.

Jiddo, was also a different man, grown increasingly frail, and leaving the care of the garden to a man who came in to tend it every morning, diligently supervising the gardener's work and deriving more pleasure from this role than the rest of the family had expected. Grandmother remained the same, for the most part, caring for the household with her usual fastidiousness, her voice perhaps a little less brusque, the bend in her back a little more pronounced. And the girls, still at school, were growing into a world of their own, intensely feminine and now difficult for Fouad to understand, though he remained fiercely protective and kept an eye out for them from a distance. Only mother remained the same, in a strange way becoming more beautiful as her youthfulness began to fade, her skin, in glowing less, looking softer still, the once sparkle in her eyes diminishing to reveal another kind of deepness, the gradual lifting of her soul.

This was the summer also when Fouad fell in love. He stepped out the front door one day and saw a young girl going up the stairs to the apartment above. She had loose golden hair that curled softly at her shoulders and her bare arm, leaning lightly on the balustrade as she moved, was lithe and fair of skin and seemed to him at that moment like grace itself.

She must have felt him watching her because half-way up the stairs she stopped and turned to look down at him, her eyes, luminous and green, meeting his own, her face glowing in the light and shadow that played on the walls of the stairwell. He noted also the delicate pout of her lips, a translucent pink colour, and her small nose, set perfectly in the centre of her face, reminding him of the fairytale princesses in the illustrated storybooks his sisters still liked to read.

He swallowed hard as she continued to gaze at him. Then she blinked, turned away and made her way up the stairs again. Fouad stood still for a moment longer, uncertain what was happening to him, a slow heat stealing over his body and his heart beating so hard against his chest that he placed a hand over it in a vain attempt to calm it. And then it came over him, a sudden, certain knowledge that things would never be the same again, that with this beginning there was also the end of a journey for him, one that he had not even been aware of taking, the necessary meeting of minds.

It was some time before he saw her again, then on a bright Saturday morning she stood outside the gate that led to the house and appeared to be waiting for someone, her arms curled around a bunch of books clutched closely to her chest.

'Can I help you with those?' Fouad asked quietly.

Her eyes opened wide as if in alarm, then she smiled and shook her head.

'I'm fine, thank you,' she said, her voice light but composed.

He remained by her side, nonetheless, his nervousness abating, her mere presence soothing him.

'My name is Fouad,' he began. 'I live here.'

She looked at him and nodded.

'What's yours?' he continued.

'I'm May.'

They fell silent. He thought he could discern the faint scent of orange blossom in her hair.

'I come for English lessons with Mrs Johnson,' she said, gesturing towards the flat upstairs.

'The professor's wife?' he asked.

She nodded again and he only just managed to stop himself from reaching out and touching her face. Her name was May.

'There's my father,' she said, waving at a car across the street. 'I have to go now.'

She ran to the car and, just before getting into it, she looked up to smile at him. She mouthed the words silently: I'll see you again.

He became a lifeguard at the American University beach, gaining his certificate following several days of intense training and ensuring free entry into the swimming club for the entire summer, a few months of relative freedom before he would enter the university as a student.

Early every afternoon, he would pull on a pair of shorts over his bathing suit, put on a T-shirt emblazoned with his school emblem and run down to the rocky strip of beach at the lower end of the university campus where dozens of students and faculty lay baking in the sun or bobbed up and down in the blue sea.

Throughout his two-hour shift, Fouad would walk along the beach, looking out at a floating platform fifty meters out where swimmers paused to rest, his eyes resting momentarily on a figure standing up, arms stretched outwards, diving in and coming up again, then moving away to scan the breadth of the water for any sign of trouble, the voices of those around him rising and falling in waves until he felt himself enveloped in the completeness of his surroundings, the pulsing, insistent energy within him mirrored in the world outside.

Once or twice that summer, he heard a cry for help and found himself responding without thought, plunging into the sea and moving swiftly to his target, the sound of his splashing limbs ringing in his ears, his breathing blowing strong and steady through the water, until he reached that person in distress, pulling this other body towards his own and swimming with it to shore and safety. This is the man I am become, he said to himself with pride but also, he hoped, with a measure of humility.

Returning home one day, he saw mother and Mrs Johnson on the terrace drinking Ceylon tea into which Fatima had placed fragrant green leaves from the garden. It was a quiet afternoon, *baba* and Marwan away on another business trip, *sitto* and *jiddo* lying down for a rest and the girls doing something or other in their bedrooms.

The two women made a pretty picture, *mama*'s small, dark head bending forward as she poured the tea, Mrs Johnson moving almost in unison with her, grey hair and glasses over a long, fine nose that twitched whenever she smiled.

Fouad sniffed and *mama* turned to him with a start.

'Fouad, you're back from the beach,' she reached up to touch his head. 'Your hair is still wet, *habibi*.'

'Mrs. Johnson,' Fouad pulled away from his mother and reached out to shake the visitor's hand. 'It's good to see you again.'

'How are you, Fouad?' Mrs. Johnson asked in her soft-spoken English. 'My husband says you're doing a great job as a lifeguard. We're very proud of you.'

He smiled, pulled up a chair and sat down, mother looking on with surprise. She would wonder why he was taking such an interest in her guest, he knew.

'Are you joining us then, *habibi*?' she began.

'*Mama!*' Samia suddenly called from inside the house.

Mother stood up.

'Will you excuse me for a moment?'

Fouad watched with relief as his mother went into the house.

He pulled his chair closer to Mrs. Johnson.

'I'm glad you're here,' he said after only a second's hesitation. 'There's something I wanted to talk to you about.'

'Of course, Fouad. What is it?'

'Well, you know I'll be starting classes at the university this autumn.'

'Yes, of course. Have you decided on a major yet?'

'Most likely it'll be engineering, but I'm not really sure.'

Mrs. Johnson nodded knowingly.

'You'll have plenty of time to make up your mind, dear. The important thing is that you do something you enjoy.'

He cleared his throat.

'I've been thinking, though, that I should probably work on my English beforehand.'

'But you speak very good English, Fouad.'

'Still, it'll need to be better if I want to do well at university, don't you think?' he hoped he sounded convincing. 'I wondered if you would be willing to give me some lessons. I'd pay you, of course.'

Mrs. Johnson laughed and placed a hand on his arm.

'You wouldn't need to pay me, Fouad. Of course, I'll help you if you feel you need it. Just come upstairs one day when you have some free time and we'll see what we can do.'

'I . . . You have other students already, don't you?'

'Yes, I do.'

'There's one young woman, May, I think her name is . . . I bumped into her the other day and we talked for a bit.'

Mrs. Johnson looked at him and frowned.

'Yes,' she said slowly, before smiling and pressing her lips together.

'May goes to a French school and wants to enter the American University when she graduates in a couple of years,' she said. 'I'm helping her with her English.'

Mrs. Johnson paused.

'It might be a good idea if you joined us at her lesson next Tuesday and I can show you then what we've been working on,' she continued. 'It would give you a good idea of what you need to prepare for as well.'

When *mama* came out to join them a little later, Mrs. Johnson did not mention her conversation with Fouad, kissing him goodbye as she got up to leave and wishing the family well as she always did. He thought he saw her wink at him, almost imperceptibly, a twinkle in her eye to show that she had understood him perfectly.

Besides her obvious beauty, May was just as he imagined she would be: clever, kind and wise, something of the princess about her, an only girl in a family of boisterous boys, determined too and clear about what she wanted for herself, an education first and foremost, this was what her family expected of her. Later perhaps a career and a home of her own.

Sitting in the dining room of the professor's apartment, books strewn across the table before them and Mrs. Johnson in the kitchen making tea, she had suddenly reached for Fouad, placing her small hand over his, saying nothing but looking at him as though she too was aware of the import of this meeting, of what was to come for them, and like him, accepting and taking comfort in this fact.

He discovered soon after that their families were, in fact, well acquainted, May's parents attending the same church that *jiddo* and *sitto* did, belonging to that loose network of closeness among all the families in this part of Beirut, a mixed community of people from all of Lebanon's sects woven into the colourful and intricate designs of the carpets they displayed in their homes, everyone playing a part, entwined and deeply conscious of their connections.

Fouad eventually brought May home, introducing her to his parents and grandparents, then taking her into the garden as *jiddo* looked on from the terrace, watching her touch the roses that were now in full bloom, deep pinks and yellows like the sun rising and setting, her face lighting up as she bent down to take in their scent, imagining he too could smell the sweet fragrance because he felt so close to her in that moment, his love for her overflowing.

'I've never seen you at church,' May said, looking up at him.

'No,' he shook his head. 'My grandparents go, though. They're Christian.'

She waited for him to continue.

'My father is Muslim and my mother converted to Islam when they got married.'

'A marriage based on true love, then?' May asked.

He nodded.

'They went to the same evangelical school as children and have been in love ever since,' Fouad said shyly.

'And their parents didn't object?'

He watched a bee hovering above one of the roses for a moment.

'It wasn't easy at first but my parents were determined to get married,' Fouad continued. 'My mother says they even thought seriously about eloping at one point.'

He wanted to tell the story as he imagined it should be told, how love had managed to overcome seemingly insurmountable obstacles, how his family was borne of the triumph of that love, but seeing May with that sweet, quiet look in her eyes and his own heart sighing, he knew he would just tell her the truth.

'My father's family comes from Damascus. They're devout but have always been very open-minded and my mother's parents are the same. I guess both families were hesitant to give their approval at first because they worried about how their communities would react. Then my grandfather came up with the idea of *mama* converting, so it solved the problem.'

He paused and looked at her.

'Does it matter to you, May, that I'm a Muslim, I mean?'

'No, of course it doesn't. It's just curious, that's all, and makes you even more interesting ...'

He laughed and leaned over to grab her hand but she moved away suddenly, then looked back and waited for him to chase after her. In some ways, she reminded him of his sisters, Fouad thought as he followed her round the garden, their innocence and the intensity of his love for them.

He asked his mother what she thought of May.

'She's lovely,' *mama* said gently. 'Clearly intelligent too, and that's just as important.'

'She is, isn't she? Her father's a doctor at the American University Hospital and her mother used to be a nurse. They know *sitto* and *jiddo* from church. That's why they don't mind May coming here to visit.'

'I'm sure they're a very nice family, *habibi*.'

'Why don't we invite them all over for lunch one day? Get to know one another.'

Mama sighed.

'She's still very young, Fouad,' she finally said. 'You need to give it time. There'll be plenty of opportunity to make a commitment later and you've both got university to get through first.'

It was May's accommodating nature, her tolerance and level-headedness, as much as the love he felt for her that made him so sure they were meant for one another, but he knew it would be some time before they could begin to think of marriage, that first they would each work towards a degree, Fouad eventually finding the kind of work that would provide him with a good income, allowing him at last to approach May's parents.

They decided to keep their feeling for each other to themselves for the time being, May telling only a female cousin about it and he intimating something to Marwan, but they were good friends and saw one another often, Fouad satisfied with this for now, his thoughts only occasionally looking to the future because there was too much life to live still and so much more to discover.

He knew the campus well, had walked and wandered and raced through it as a boy, loved its green expanses and flowered paths, its buildings in yellow stone and their wooden doorways painted green, the elegant covered arches that ran between them and the sense always that chaos could be kept at bay here, that calm would always hold sway. He felt, as soon as he began attending classes, that his whole life had been leading up to this moment, those sometimes troubled years when he had been unsure of himself, when his brother's actions and thoughts directed much of what he believed and did. All this had turned in his mind into instances when Lebanon, like himself, seemed to be growing into something greater than it had ever been before, man and country together shaping a less circumspect world.

He was aware of the university's history also, that it was set up in 1866 by American missionaries with funds collected from private benefactors and that since then it had educated thousands of his countrymen and women and many more from all parts of the Arab world. He had often heard his father praise it not only for its role as an educator offering greater opportunities for the region's youth, but also as an institution that had created a legacy of openness and freedom that could not now be undone; history, father always said, would provide ample evidence of this fact in the years to come.

He took a variety of courses in his freshman year, both

81

in the arts and the sciences, literature and history because they intrigued him, physics because it had always been a personal favourite, and chemistry and biology because they would help him make a decision about an eventual major. And whenever he sat down to study at a well-worn table in the university library, enveloped in the hush of ideas in the making and surrounded by books, he sensed the significance of the collective effort of which he was now a part, his own story slowly unravelling as he grew more aware of it, Beirut a repository of dreams still to be fulfilled.

His routines began to change, home becoming less a focus for his attention as he spent more and more time with his fellow students. He rarely ate breakfast with his family, preferring instead to stay in bed until the very last moment, then rushing out to make it to class with only minutes to spare, his hunger to be assuaged sometime around noon at a table at Faisal's, a small restaurant on Bliss street where students congregated over nourishing and affordable peasant fare, bowls of *foul* and *hoummos* doused in olive oil or plates of chicken livers cooked in lemon and garlic sauce that they dipped their bread into.

Fouad and his friends sat at a table by the window facing the university's main gate and watched arriving female students as they ate and talked of anything and everything that came to mind, revealing themselves in measured bits and pieces, their pasts and backgrounds, their hopes for the future and also their fears. The table was never empty, received a constant stream of diners who came and went only to come back again a little later, in one form or another remaining in attendance at all hours of the day and often into the night. There were Lebanese, Syrian, Jordanian and Palestinian young men among them, as well as students from further afield, from Egypt and Iraq, from North Africa and the Arab Gulf, and though they all spoke Arabic, their accents and stories, their perspectives on life were so different that Fouad began to feel everyday as though he were embarking on another journey, deep into the mysteries of the self, until what he had once thought of as the outer limits of his world suddenly seemed immeasurable.

He brought his new self home, a bit shyly at first because he imagined the family might be surprised by how much he had changed, and then boldly when he realized that growing up was, in fact, expected of him, a son of whom they could be proud. On Sundays, he sat with Marwan and *baba*, sometimes *jiddo* too, on the terrace with *nargilehs* and cups of heavily sweetened tea, and talked of all the things that mattered, the family business, Fouad's studies and the increasingly worrying situation in Palestine.

'There will be a war with the Zionists, I'm certain of that,' father said one day in early spring of 1948.

Jiddo nodded.

'If they allow them to set up their Jewish state, there will be hell to pay for all of us,' *jiddo* said slowly, in his old man's voice.

'The problem is that a war will be no contest.' Father frowned and shook his head.

'Why is that, *baba*?' Fouad asked quietly, still a newcomer to these adult gatherings and anxious not to put a foot wrong.

Marwan stopped puffing on the *nargileh* and turned to him.

'Because the West is giving military, economic and political support to the Zionists and we don't have a decent army to stand up to all of them, that's why,' he said quietly. 'What chance do the Palestinians have of hanging on to their country now?'

'The Soviet Union is supporting the Zionists too, son,' father said. 'They're all making a mistake about what the outcome of setting up a Jewish state on Arab land will be. But you're right, it does seem hopeless at the moment.'

'The British and now the Americans are doing this deliberately,' *jiddo* interrupted, his voice louder and more forceful. 'It's hardly a mistake they're making. They want to create conflict in this part of the world.'

Father sighed.

'I don't know that they're thinking that far ahead,' he said. 'I think this is just a way for them to assuage guilt over the terrible things that happened to the Jews in Europe during the war. The fact that we had nothing to do with what happened in Europe seems to have escaped them.'

'But how can they create a state when there is already a country there?' Fouad protested. 'What about all the Palestinians who have always lived there?'

His Palestinian friends had talked about the troubles in their country, the conflict that had been brewing there for nearly thirty years, ever since the British promised the Jews of Europe a homeland in a Palestine already populated by Muslims, Christians and Jews whose ancestors had lived there for centuries, and just last year when the United Nations decided to partition the country into two states and then turned a blind eye to the brutal suppression of protests by the local inhabitants against that decision.

'All this interference in our affairs, it will all come to no good, I tell you,' *jiddo* muttered to himself. 'It's an injustice that can never be forgiven.'

Some weeks later, following the defeat of a hastily assembled Arab army in Palestine, tens of thousands of refugees from *Al-Jaleel*, with nothing but the few belongings they could carry with them, began to arrive in Lebanon and were welcomed into the homes of families from all over the south. Those who came from the cities around Palestine sought refuge in Lebanon's cities, Sidon, Tyre, Beirut and Tripoli in the north, and with the money they had brought with them set up homes and attempted to start over as their hopes of returning to Palestine slowly faded. It would be some time before the vast majority of Palestinian refugees were made to settle in camps around Lebanon and elsewhere in the Arab world, in the bitterness and despair of a diaspora.

At their usual table at Faisal's, Fouad's friends decried the fate of hundreds of thousands who had been expelled from their homes and spoke of their anger at the West and at the ineptitude of Arab leaders. Listening intently to these conversations, Fouad chided himself for having been so naïve in the past, in the days when he had thought of the British as champions of Lebanon's independence against the French, when politics, like everything else in life, had seemed so straightforward to him. Rather than engineering, he decided to study towards a degree in history and international relations, subjects which he believed would make him better informed about the world around him and allow him to form opinions of his own.

He saw how Lebanon's stability in a region otherwise increasingly troubled resulted not only in its economic prosperity but also helped to make it more viable as a nation made up of a mix of communities with differing interests. The borderless Middle East that his father and grandfather had known had changed for ever, this was clear, but it was not yet apparent what would become of peoples that had until a few years before thought of themselves as separate communities living comfortably together under the same sky, their identities not in question, being human and God-fearing definition enough of who they were and what they hoped to be.

This was their favourite time of day, sunset in *jiddo's* garden, Fouad and May side by side on the stone steps that led down to it, whispering not just because they did not want to be overheard but also because it seemed only fitting in this blissfully quiet place. Their elbows touched inadvertently from time to time, their hands, though, clasped each other with more purpose and their lips also met lightly whenever they were certain no one could see them.

'I love you, you know that,' Fouad said softly, pushing the hair from May's beautiful eyes.

She sighed.

'I know you do. I feel the same way about you, Fouad.'

More and more they thought the same thoughts, had the same fears and anxieties, and he sensed that she was worried.

'I won't be gone too long, *habibti*,' he continued. 'I'll be back in time for your graduation, you'll see.'

She lifted her head up to the sky. The sun was almost completely gone and she was intent on making a silent wish that would coincide with its leaving.

'May, May,' he said softly. 'What are you thinking?'

'I understand you have to go because this wonderful opportunity has come up for you,' she said, shaking her head. 'But I will miss you.'

He leaned forward and looked into her eyes.

'We'll get married as soon as I get back, *habibti*.'

In a matter of weeks, he would go to England to study for a post-graduate degree and return to work for a foreign company that planned to set up offices in Beirut. It had all happened so quickly that Fouad's mind was still reeling, the chance meeting with the company's director at the professor's house a few weeks after his graduation and the subsequent offer of work as a liaison for the rest of the Arab world. He was hesitant to accept at first, how could he leave Beirut, after all, his family and May? But sitting down with his father and Professor Johnson, talking of what the job might mean for his future in Lebanon, Fouad had begun to look at things in a different light.

'This country,' the professor began, leaning forward in his chair to emphasize his point, 'is moving into an era of expansion and development, Fouad. It's a question of whether or not you wish to play a role in its eventual success. Taking up this opportunity is not just about you getting a well-paid job that will give you the security you need. It's a great deal more than that.'

Baba smiled and then turned to Fouad.

'The professor is right, son,' he said. 'Getting a higher degree and taking this job will open many doors for you in this country and elsewhere. Things are changing fast, *habibi*. Remember that.'

The truth was that Fouad already recognized this as a turning point in his life, not just because he had gained a degree, but also because he'd long felt the pulsating energy that was moving Lebanon and his generation forward and he was anxious to be a part of it, to make his mark in some way. Looking at *baba* now, his *tarboosh* on the table beside him, his bare head appearing more vulnerable as a result, his always distinguished features drooping a little with age, Fouad understood that something significant was being handed over to him, the chance to make real a new vision not only for his own life but for his community and country as well. He was twenty years old, yet in that moment of discovery, he had felt ageless, the possibilities open to him limitless.

He took May's hand and stood up, pulling her up with him. It was dark in the garden now, the lights inside the house making shadows around them, and the air somewhat cooler. He felt her shiver and leaned down to wrap his arms around her.

'I can see it, May,' he whispered in her ear. 'I can see our happiness coming.'

*   *   *

More than anything else, it was lonely.

He was staying in a bedsit a few minutes' walk from the university, a small room on the third floor of a semi-detached house just off the Euston Road with similarly drab dwellings on either side. A brown shag carpet covered the floor of his room so that he could not see the creaking boards beneath and the ceiling was stained with patches of damp that let off a faint smell when the window and door were closed. There was a single bed in one corner, a sink with a mirror above it in the other and, by the window overlooking the street, a large armchair in which he sat in the evening feeding coins into the gas heater and watching the world go by.

His landlady was polite and businesslike, had welcomed him on his arrival with the detached concern she had probably shown all her students over the years, showing him around the house on his first day, the sitting room and kitchen to which he would have access only at certain times of the day, the ground-floor bathroom and the separate lavatory beside it, and handing him clean sheets and towels which she explained would be laundered once a fortnight along with his clothes, though he would be expected to do his own ironing. Breakfast and dinner would be served promptly at eight in the morning and at half-past six in the evening, the same fare that she prepared for her husband and herself and which, she assured him, he would become accustomed to in time.

Two other young men roomed in the house, a third-year medical student from Nigeria who came in and out at odd hours and had little time to make conversation, and another man, just arrived from Pakistan to study engineering, who like Fouad was somewhat bewildered and not ashamed to let show in his eyes a yearning for home. They met at mealtimes, exchanging a few words under the watchful eye of their landlady and then rushing off to class or retreating to their rooms, feeling still too vulnerable to take their acquaintance any further.

The rain when it fell was very different from Beirut's unruly storms, a constant drizzle and an accompanying grey sky that hung overhead and made Fouad listless, a biting cold seeping into his bones despite the many layers of clothing he wore, his fingers and toes icy to the touch. At night, he found himself putting on the woollen socks that his grandmother had knitted for him and which he had not wanted to bring along and lay the huge, camel-haired *abaya* that his father had given him over the blanket on the bed to try and ward off the cold, thoughts of Beirut's warming sunlight lulling him to sleep.

Sundays especially depressed him, the city gripped by a forbidding stillness, its streets empty of people, shops closed and his lone footsteps echoing along the pavement. He would walk aimlessly for an hour or two, trying to acquaint himself with different parts of the city, and return to the house to sit in his room and read or write letters home which, despite the sense of isolation that haunted him during those first few weeks, he filled with descriptions of his surroundings and his hopes for the months ahead, with an excitement that he did not yet feel.

Things were better once courses began, his mornings taken up with lectures and tutorials then, following a quick snack at the university canteen, making his way to the library where he would work with satisfaction for several hours, often missing the evening meal back at the house and going to bed with a gentle gnawing in his stomach.

This was also when he began to make friends among the other post-graduate students, faltering friendships at first that quickly developed into a kind of boisterous camaraderie, evenings spent in public houses in the university area, sipping lemonade because he could not abide the

taste of beer and feeling himself surrounded with warmth, his heart beginning to thaw at last.

It was during one of his Sunday walks that he first saw Margo. The sun was out that day and Fouad had decided to venture further than usual, north and into Regent's Park to breathe in the crisp, green scents of mown lawns and leafy trees. He found her sitting on a bench by the pond, her dark hair like a cap that fit snugly over her head, her feet crossed neatly beneath her. She was so still that he thought for one moment something might be the matter with her. Approaching slowly, he was startled when she turned to look at him, her grey eyes calm and unquestioning.

'Are you alright?' he asked.

She continued to look at him, saying nothing.

'I'm sorry, I thought . . .'

She shook her head.

'I'm watching the ducks,' she said, pointing to the pond.

There were several of them moving on the surface of the water. He watched as one duck suddenly dived down, sticking its tail up in the air before coming up again and shaking itself vigorously, its grey and green feathers now glistening in the light.

'Ah!' Margo exclaimed, bringing her hands together in front of her and turning to him with a look of pure delight.

It was the first time since leaving home he had felt truly included in anything.

Beirut was in his dreams now, appearing in those moments before he finally fell asleep and in the early hours of the morning as he emerged into wakefulness. He saw the Mediterranean as he had always known it, an even blueness undulating in the seas of his heart and the sun above warming the streets of the city and all its neighbourhoods, images that would never leave him. He smelled the flowers in *jiddo*'s garden, saw himself sitting on the terrace in his father's favourite chair and looked up at the night sky as if the stars would sparkle only for him. On those days when the emptiness he felt around him threatened to seep into his skin, he glimpsed his life back in the days when things had followed naturally one to another: the boy he had been and his parents' undying devotion, the taste of *sitto*'s cooking and his sisters sitting side by side, their dark heads bent over a picture book, Marwan in a newly pressed suit and mother absently brushing at his lapel with her hand, and May when first he saw her, glowing in her yellow dress, his eternal captor.

He waited anxiously for letters from home, galloped down from his room as soon as he heard the postman's knock on the front door and stood patiently on the steps as the landlady sifted through the day's mail, willing her to turn to him with an envelope in her hand.

Mother sent long letters with detailed descriptions of that week's events, no matter how small, telling him something about every member of the family, never admitting how much she missed him but implying it nonetheless, her stories hinting at something gone missing so that the picture of life they had all been accustomed to was no longer complete.

Sitto and I have been busy preparing for Marwan's wedding next month. There will be a great deal of cooking to do, of course, besides the stuffed sheep that Abou Taleb (remember the butcher at the top end of Sadat Street?) will do, though your father is taking care of all the other arrangements, thank goodness, and Fatima's sister will come up from the village for a few days to help. We will have a party in the garden once the marriage contract has been signed in the sheikh's presence – that is the one part I am somewhat nervous about given my tendency to say

91

the wrong things at times – something fairly small as both Marwan and Alia have sensibly decided they would rather save the money that might have been spent on the wedding to get their own place eventually. I'm still not sure what I will wear for the occasion, although baba has kindly bought me a beautiful fabric in blue silk from Damascus that he wants me to have made up. He loves me in blue, he says, but I'm not sure that particular colour will be appropriate for the mother of the groom. They will move in here after the honeymoon, as you know, so I have had to clear your things out and put them in the box room, your books and bits and pieces (do you want to keep that old bicycle with the broken chain or should I give it to the scrap man next time he comes round?) and what you left of your clothes, there's that good coat that you refused to take with you, a decision I'm sure you now regret given how cold it is over there. Would you believe that I have worn it since you left, not out, of course, but around the house in the early morning when it's been cold, and on the terrace of an evening when your father sits down for a smoke and asks me to join him. It brings you home to me for a brief moment, and that is something at least . . . Otherwise, your grandparents are both well and looking forward to the wedding. Jiddo says he hopes he'll live long enough to see a great-grandchild and although I sympathize with him, I'm not sure I'm ready to be a grandmother. Can you imagine it? A little baby in the house after all these years. Perhaps it wouldn't be so bad after all . . . Your father is as busy as ever with work and says he may open offices in Hamra soon. You've only been gone a few months, habibi, but things are moving fast here and Hamra Street is almost unrecognizable, all these tall buildings going up and the cactus fields diminishing. I miss the backwoods somehow, walking through the brush on my way to get the groceries each morning and kicking up the dirt with my feet. Instead, there is construction now and new shops and people I've never seen before, though they do greet me as I go past so that at least has not changed. The company you're going to work for has already taken two floors in a building at the other end of Hamra, not far from the new university medical centre. I hope they give you a decent office with a view of the main street. I shall visit you there from time to time and you can take me out for a coffee. Wouldn't that be nice? But I haven't asked you about your studies yet, sweetheart. How's it going? It seems from your letters that you are happy and well. I am glad of that. I am glad that you are adjusting well and enjoying this great adventure. There are moments when I even envy you a little. All that newness and freedom . . . May comes round from time to time. She is lovely and I have grown very fond of her. We always have a great deal to say to one another, it seems. She is mature for her age and so sure of what she wants. She is confident also that you will return to us. I know you receive letters from her and get all her news so be sure to write her back, no matter how busy you get with your life over there . . . All my love to you always, my darling son. I'll write again very soon.

Margo was not pretty like May nor as sweet, but she was capable of radiating such quietness that he felt immediately at peace in her presence. She was older too and vastly more experienced than he, though it was some time before she told him the details of her past, the great love she had lost in the war and the fate her parents and many in her family had suffered.

They spent Sundays together, meeting at the park early in the morning then wandering through its green expanses before eventually making their way to her tiny flat over-looking the canal where she would prepare their midday meal, an omelette that was slightly runny in the middle and a green salad with vinaigrette sauce, or small filet steaks fried in butter and served with sautéed leeks garnished with lemon and olive oil. They always had wine with their food, Margo expressing surprise the first time when he told her that he had never actually tasted the drink, then becoming amused because he grew to appreciate it so.

Sometime towards the end of the afternoon, they would drift towards the bedroom and fall onto Margo's bed, making love awkwardly the first few times, eventually becoming so familiar with one another's bodies that the act became almost purely functional, as though no day together could end without it, an efficient means for relieving life's stresses and strains.

Once back in his bedsitter, Fouad would sit down to write his weekly letter to May, filling it with his longing for her, surprised that he should feel entirely guilt free about his affair with Margo. There was no question of his having fallen in love, after all, and the same, he knew, was true for Margo. This was something else, something to do with his being here and feeling himself growing older and perhaps less sure of himself. He often thought that if he were to allow himself to think he was betraying May in any way, then the same would be true of the whole experience of being away from home because being in London was so unlike anything he had ever known, so far from the reality that had once belonged to him.

When he told Margo about his musings, she laughed.

'My darling boy,' she said, ruffling his hair as they lay in bed. 'You are in the process of losing your innocence, that's all.'

'What do you mean?' he asked.

'It had to happen, you know, Fouad. You had to learn to be adept at duplicity at some point in your life.'

'But that's not what's happening here, Margo,' he protested, sitting up.

'What is it then?'

She sounded tired.

'I . . . It's difficult to explain. It's strange, but I feel sometimes as though my life here were happening to someone else and not to me. Do you know what I mean?'

It took her a moment to reply.

'I think I do, yes,' said Margo.

'There are times when I'm not really sure who I am anymore, you know?' Fouad continued. 'Beirut, my family and even May, seem so far away.'

He gestured at his surroundings.

'This city makes me feel . . . I feel so disconnected from the world at times. What is it about this place?'

He hung his head.

'Maybe you should ask yourself what it is about Lebanon that makes you feel the way you do.'

He looked up at Margo again. What is it indeed, he suddenly thought to himself?

'You're just missing home, that's all,' Margo put her hand on his shoulder. 'It's not a complicated thing, really. You can at least be thankful that home will still be there for you to go back to when the time comes.'

She did not turn up at the park one Sunday, Fouad pacing back and forth as he waited then resting momentarily on a bench in view of the pond before eventually becoming concerned that something might have happened to her.

He decided to walk towards her apartment in the hope that they might come across one another on the way, but despite keeping an eye out for a small figure moving towards him in the distance, he arrived at her front door without having seen anyone.

He knocked on the door and waited, then knocked

again a little louder. He was about to turn away when he heard stirring inside. He tried the door again and was surprised to find it unlocked. The door opened into Margo's living room which she had furnished with a two-seater sofa and a coffee table made from an old door that she told him she had found in a skip somewhere.

Fouad stepped inside, his eyes slowly adjusting to the darkness and gasped when he saw her lying on the floor between the sofa and the table.

'Margo, are you alright?'

Fouad bent down and tried to lift her up.

She moaned and tried to shake him off.

There was a large stain on the carpet by her head. He got up to fetch a towel from the bathroom and placed it over the cut on Margo's head, lifting her up onto the sofa at the same time.

'Go away,' she said, her voice slurring.

There was a strong smell of alcohol on her breath and when she finally opened them he could see her eyes were bloodshot.

'Leave me alone!'

She leaned against the back of the sofa and closed her eyes.

'You must have hit your head on the table when you fell,' he said gently. 'It's bleeding a little.'

She tried to shake her head but stopped half-way, got up quickly and ran to the bathroom, slamming the door behind her. She came out some time later looking subdued.

When Fouad went into the galley kitchen for some water, he noticed several empty wine bottles in the sink. He led her back to the sofa and handed her the glass.

'You need to drink this, Margo.'

She sipped slowly and avoided his eyes.

'I missed you at the park today,' said Fouad, trying to smile. 'What happened?'

'Is it Sunday already?'

He took a deep breath.

'We need to get you to a doctor, Margo. You may be suffering from concussion.'

She reached up and took the towel off her head, looking at the patch of blood that had soaked into it.

'I don't remember it happening, Fouad,' she whispered, turning to him with an anxious look. 'I don't remember any of it.'

Then she leaned forward, put her face in her hands and began to sob, her thin shoulders heaving. Fouad was unsure what to do. Margo had, until then, always been the stronger one and he had never before seen her cry.

'Don't Margo,' he said, patting her on the back, surprised to discover that he was feeling irritation rather than sympathy.

He got up and went to a small window at the other end of the room. He pulled the curtain back, opened the window and took a deep breath. When he turned around again, Margo was huddled on the sofa, her legs pulled up beneath her and her head bent low. She looked totally without defences.

Through the window behind him, he heard the beginnings of rainfall and for the first time the sound was welcome to his ears. He walked over to the sofa and sat down again, wrapping his arms around her and rocking her gently back and forth.

'It's going to be alright, Margo dear,' he murmured quietly. 'You're not alone. Hush now, I'm right here.'

From Margo, he learned about friendship, not the coincidental kind that hovered on the periphery of one's life, but rather true companionship that brought with it emotional sustenance, the certainty of unrelenting trust. And while he had sensed these things in Margo's feelings towards him very early on, it was only after he'd seen her at her most vulnerable that he encountered them in himself also, an understanding of deep relationship that he had previously associated only with his family.

That he should discover this truth when he was so far from home and in a place that had failed to capture his heart astonished him now, though he would always remember it afterwards as the point at which his priorities had shifted, challenging him to act where he had once only observed, encouraging him to create his life rather than merely respond to events within it.

They saw more of one another now, spending several days together at a time, revealing to each other the details of their everyday lives as only those who have faith in one another can. Though they had ceased to be lovers, they now thrived within the embrace of a more profound closeness, feeling at times as though they had known each other all along, as siblings do, through the pain and wonder of their growing years.

She met him most days just as he came out of the library, a smile of recognition lighting up her face, her arm half-raised in greeting, and Fouad, his heart warming at the sight, nodding reassuringly, descending the steps two at a time then stopping to put an arm round her shoulders, steering them both towards home. They would prepare the evening meal together, Margo a deliberate and consummate cook, welcoming his help and teaching him skills that he would employ later in life, using only good wine in sauces and cooking meat to succulent perfection. After eating, they would sit together on the sofa that would later serve as Fouad's bed, listening to the radio that was propped up on the mantelpiece or talking late into the night, their voices growing softer as the hours passed, their eyelids drooping.

The stories she told him about herself seemed almost

like fables with magic in them and villains and heroes, memories of a childhood where grown ups were larger than life and children lived enchanted lives, and praise for the men and women she had admired as an adult. But there was sadness as well, sometimes so intense that Fouad felt himself being pulled into it against his will, discovering truths that he would have preferred to remain ignorant of.

He tried to determine a place for himself in the history that she spoke about: while Margo and John conducted dangerous missions in occupied France, Fouad thought, I was still a boy kicking at the shins of foreign soldiers; just as men were prepared to die for independence in Lebanon, so too the resistance fighters in Europe had been prepared to die. It seemed to him then that even as the world appeared broader in his own eyes, it had somehow grown infinitely smaller too, its details more visible and its colours more subtle, individual lives surrendered and also happily lived.

Once Fouad had completed his studies and was preparing to leave for home, Margo suggested that they spend their last Sunday together wandering through the city as they had always done. She prepared a picnic lunch for the park, boiled eggs and sandwiches and crisp apples that they ate sitting on a damp bench beneath a chestnut tree, soft drizzle falling, then just as the sun made a cautious appearance, they set off to Piccadilly and across the Mall, all the way to the bank of the river where they stood watching the murky water rush and breathed in its odours, their thoughts running with it like the rain.

'I shall be going to America again soon,' Margo told him as night began to fall.

'Oh?'

They were only a few streets away from home now.

'I don't know how long I'll be there for this time,' she continued.

He stopped and looked at her.

'You mean you might stay there?'

She shrugged.

'I'm not really sure. It all depends . . .'

They walked in silence for a few moments, eventually arriving at Fouad's front door.

'I'm glad Margo,' he said. 'That you'll be starting again somewhere new. After I'm gone, I mean.'

He put his arms around her and they stood in that embrace for a moment, saying nothing, until he felt her shiver and pull away from him.

'Make sure you write me and let me know,' he said. 'Please, don't forget to tell me what you decide to do.'

She looked up at him and smiled.

'I won't. Goodbye, Fouad.'

'Goodbye.'

Then he watched her turn and walk away.

PART THREE

Kamal

He knows he has always looked at things differently from most. But if he allows himself to think of what it has meant to his life, of what it has been like to carry the weight of absence on his shoulders, to have the sense, always, that some essential part of him has gone astray, he realizes that displacement has made him understand that certainty, no matter how solid it might seem, is transient.

Being Palestinian continues to define every aspect of his existence, even after all these years of being settled in one place. He carries the same identity papers given to his parents when he was born which describe him as a refugee with special dispensation to reside in Lebanon, though not to work or gain citizenship, and which serve to remind him that he is a man in transition even if neither the starting point nor the end of his journey are clearly discernable.

When Kamal became a writer, it was not because there had never been any other choice for him but because as someone with a fluid identity that was more a matter of perspective than physical presence he felt he possessed the right measure of detachment to record the irony and splendour inherent to the human experience.

In music, for example, he is just as appreciative of the pauses between notes, the absences of melody, as he is of the tune itself, so that the magnificence, for him, is in how the composer brings it all together, the separate body of each part integral to the whole. In works of art also, he sees first the individual colours, the way they swirl around defiantly in their own brilliance, independent of the images around them, and feels astonishment at the singular audacity of it, at the beauty in oneness.

With people, he is able to exercise composed disinterest, not, he hopes, with the indifference of one who is self-absorbed but with a kind of gentle concern that is almost fleeting, like the touch of silk on the skin or an image of birds in flight. He likes to think that it is this trait that has always directed his writing, this inner compulsion to view the world as being somewhat off centre, askew, a picture that can only be looked at once before it is altered forever, a story that changes with every telling.

Often he senses that this ability to stand apart without judgment, even in matters that relate to his own life, makes him more open to compassion. At other times, only his determination not to take himself too seriously as well as his love for words offer the solace that he needs, help him bring order to the uncertainty around him and make sense of things.

He has written nearly a dozen books, two of non-fiction on the histories of Palestinian villages before 1948, four novels, one volume of poetry, a play, and two novellas of children's tales retold with an adult voice. Some of his books have been successful, read relatively widely in the Arab world, in whole or as excerpts in newspapers, and, in some cases, translated into other languages and sold abroad.

His new novel is based on the idea that all human tragedies are inter-connected. The continuing tyranny against his own people, the systematic murder, both past and present, of millions with apparent impunity, natural and man-made disasters, poverty, disease and injustice, all these he believes are linked in one way or another, through time or association, so that the conclusion has to be that if one could find a means of dislodging these associations there would be an end to cruelty, a flight away from madness.

There are moments when the characters that populate his stories, the men and women he tries so hard to understand, elude him, disappear into their fears and disparate longings. And as he struggles to find them again, to bring them out of the shadows and into the light, he sometimes wonders if he shouldn't simply abandon them to their fate, move on with his own life of days and nights and being, without the dogged deliberation that the writing process demands of him.

It is past midnight. Kamal is lying in bed with the light on and the window open. He hears a sound on the stairwell and lifts his head to listen further but all is quiet again. He lies back against the pillow and closes his eyes. There will be no sleep tonight, he knows, just the roaming and rambling of his fragile thoughts.

His family moved into the building where he now lives in the early 1960s, he the youngest of three sons, his mother fragile and prone to bouts of illness, his father a frequent traveller to the Arab Gulf where he worked. His parents and older brother had come from Palestine when Israel was created and hundreds of thousands were expelled with no prospect of imminent return. Though not yet born when it happened, the stories Kamal would later hear of the family's flight, of aunts, uncles, grandparents and cousins leaving everything behind them and fleeing towards the unknown, have become memories of a sort for him too, the makings of a history that he would later explore and try to assimilate.

As a child, he was told about an attractive one-storey house with a front garden planted with rose bushes and jasmine where his mother would stand waiting for her husband to come home; about the sea, a distant but definite presence, a reminder of a larger world beyond. These pictures were of Yafa, their hometown, and of the house in which they had lived in a newly constructed complex in a verdant suburb. His father had worked as a director in the factory set up by Kamal's grandfather and money was plentiful in those days, the future filled with hope.

His mother also recalled poignant details of the escape, of men staying behind to try to safeguard the land, many of them killed for it, of being lifted onto a boat already over-full with women and children clearly in distress, and later, of the sand hills of Gaza on which the children played, tumbling down into the warm earth while the smell of summer hovered in the air about them.

Carrying his older brother on one arm and a bag of belongings in the other, his mother had made her way with relatives to Lebanon where his father eventually joined them by way of Jerusalem, Amman and Damascus. The family settled in the mountain town of Aley where there was already a sizeable community of displaced Palestinians living in a variety of houses, small, confined spaces in summer when rents were high, and for the rest of the year, once all the summer residents had departed, in more spacious homes with wood-burning stoves for warmth and high ceilings that let in the light even when it was scarce. As the years advanced, two more sons were born, Kamal somewhere between his parents' unspoken longings to return to Palestine and the eventual realization that this would not be.

As he grew older and the world around him began to diminish, he became aware of the truth about the endless movement that defined his life and that of his family. It had to do with constantly feeling that he was meant to be elsewhere, that there was something else waiting for him, as though he were always holding his breath in anticipation of relief that was a long time in coming.

He must have been seven years old the day his mother thought him old enough to go along with his older brother to fetch the family rations from the United Nations base in the centre of t7own. There, he had seen men standing around in small groups and taking turns to enter a small stone hut that his brother told him had the words 'Relief and Works Agency' emblazoned on its door. Once inside, he watched as his brother handed a piece of paper to an official who in turn loaded sacks filled with flour, rice, sugar and powdered milk onto the cart that they had brought with them.

As the two boys clambered up the hill heading for home, he had finally asked his brother what the words on the door of the hut meant. It means that we are refugees, his brother had retorted. Now be quiet and help me with this blessed cart.

Although the word had been unfamiliar to him at the time, Kamal had sensed there was something fearful about it and knew that he must not ask his brother for further explanation. He felt himself blush and attempted to hide his confusion by pulling even harder on the cart until it nearly tipped over. When not long after this incident his father moved the family from the mountains to Beirut, Kamal had mistakenly thought he would finally be able to shed this feeling of dislocation and start anew.

In Arabic, there are many words that rhyme with the word 'refugee', *'laji'*, both in its feminine and masculine forms, several that he has used in his writing. Still, all these years later, even in the quiet certainty that he has finally found a place for himself in the world, the forced secrecy that pervades his childhood memories and the vague sense of shame associated with it continue to haunt him.

On Saturday mornings during Kamal's adolescence, the women in the apartment building in Beirut went on a cleaning frenzy, flooding the landings and stairwell with hot soapy water, those in the top floor flats pouring out overfull buckets in front of their doorsteps and expertly sweeping the water with straw brooms towards the staircase, down the steps and onto the lower landing, where the next group of women would take over. Whenever his mother was not feeling well, he would take on the task himself, removing his shoes and rolling up the hems of his trousers to avoid getting them wet. The women would smile at him and mutter to each other what a good boy he was and he, broom swaying back and forth in hand, would frown in silence.

Although the walls between the apartments in the building were thin, there was always a sense among the tenants that privacy was essential, maybe because it was so difficult to get. When his family first moved in his mother had insisted on curtains for the front room which were pulled back during the daytime and drawn again at night as the boys and their father, whenever he was home, sat talking or reading. And whenever his mother felt poorly and had to lie on the sofa with her books and a cup of tea during the day, she would pull the curtains half-shut, allowing in a little of light while keeping safely out of view.

The building was an insular world where strange things sometimes happened, gatherings in the building's entrance late at night of two families from the top floor flats who believed there was a hidden treasure in the alleyway next to it and who whispered conspiratorially, one of them occasionally letting out a shout that woke the other residents. When he wondered out loud about what was happening, his father had told him they were waiting for a *djin*, a spirit endowed with magical powers, to appear and reveal the treasure to them. Father smiled and shook his head as he said this, though this did not stop Kamal from feeling intrigued by the idea of mystery in their midst, a notion that stayed with him long after he had grown and should have known better.

In summer, Kamal remembers a young woman and her brother who lived in one of the ground floor flats dancing to music from a record player outside their front door, kicking up the dirt with their feet while children gathered round to watch them. Once, the young woman grabbed Kamal's hand and pulled him towards her and although he had stood transfixed beside her, unable to move, his embarrassment was alleviated by the pleasure he had felt at being chosen like this.

When it rained, the alleyway, which did not get much sun because of the buildings surrounding it, took on a musty smell and the earth, damp and darker in colour, felt more pliant beneath his feet. That is when the neighbourhood children would abandon their customary football games and play hopscotch or marbles instead, oblivious to the mess they were making of their clothes and shoes. Reluctantly, Kamal and his brothers would make their way back home, where their mother sent them straight to the bathroom, then the inevitable fighting over the hot water and soap and later, while sitting at the kitchen table for dinner, Kamal going over the afternoon's events in his mind and feeling contentment spread through him as he ate.

Kamal sits in a café on Hamra Street watching the mid-morning traffic of people and cars. His table is by a floor-to-ceiling pane of glass that allows him a view of everything and everyone both inside and out. Remaining quiet here, at the centre of a hustle and bustle of which he is not a part, fills him with an inner vigour that often seeps out of him when he stays home too alone and for too long. He does not carry paper and pencil with him – attempting to write today would be a mistake, he knows – but is content instead to observe what is going on around him.

An old man, shoulders hunched over with age, comes to sit at a nearby table, taking off his grey tweed cap with gnarled, arthritic hands and placing it on the table. There is a strong scent of a familiar cologne about him, a fresh smell that reminds Kamal of his father and makes him smile.

Outside, a car toots its horn. Hamra is a wide one-way street lined with boutiques, cafés and shops occupying the ground-floor level of the commercial buildings that stand on either side of it. It is lively and noisy during the day and still never sleeps at night. Kamal remembers coming here as a teenager, wandering up and down the street, occasionally going into a café to eavesdrop on the conversations going on around him, and then, as he got older, as a young man, meeting up with friends and going to the cinemas and nightclubs that used to be located here.

The old man next to him clears his throat.

'Could you help me, please?' he asks Kamal.

The man points with his stick at something on the floor.

Kamal bends down and picks up a blue bank card and hands it to him.

'Thank you.'

'*Ahlan.*'

'It would have taken me too long to do it myself,' the old man chuckles.

He places the card in a wallet and puts it into his pocket. Then he picks up his newspaper and reaches out with it to Kamal.

'Would you like to see this?' he asks.

Kamal shakes his head.

'I think I'll take a break from the news this morning. Thanks anyway.'

'You're right,' the man continues, replacing the newspaper on the table. 'Nowadays, it's probably better not to know what the politicians in this country are up to. The news is bound to be bad.'

The old man attempts a shrug but his shoulders are clearly too stiff. Kamal feels a sudden surge of sympathy for him.

'Still, perhaps we should keep ourselves informed of what's going on,' Kamal says. 'One way or another, the political situation always affects our lives.'

'Things were very different when I was a young man, there was a lot more tolerance,' the old man shakes his head. 'Sometimes I think I'm not living in the same country any more.'

Kamal feels himself momentarily transported to the Beirut of his youth when the outer edges of his horizons seemed limitless and there was strength inside him that would not be defeated. He nods in agreement with the old man.

'There was a point in my life when I had dreams for this country too,' he tells him. 'But somehow or other they were all dissipated. I'm not sure how that might have happened.'

The old man smiles.

'You're a great deal younger than I am but I suspect many of us felt that way about Lebanon at different moments in the past,' he says. 'Still, it seemed easier to be certain then of who we were, and of what we wanted to become.'

There were instances of quiet in Kamal's childhood, moments when he thought he heard the air whistling through the gaps in the sounds of his life. They appeared as he and his brothers grew older and began to fend for themselves, dressing silently and eating their breakfast with little fuss in the morning, then rushing off without slamming the front door behind them; and later, as they made their way home from school, walking slowly, pausing to scrutinize the world around them and feeling a secret delight at their separateness.

They attended an evangelical school not far from their home, where other Muslim children like themselves sat patiently through morning assembly and diligently recited the Lord's Prayer alongside the Christian children on the benches beside them. Theirs were the same neighbourhood families that shared the rituals and bounties of religious feasts, eating together in the hours before daybreak during the holy month of Ramadan or enjoying special sweets at Christmas or on All Saints Day. As Kamal grew into adolescence, he began thinking of belief in god as a presence that defined only certain aspects of people's lives while leaving others to chance and imagination.

Walking to school with his brothers one morning, he had felt the earth tremble beneath his feet and emit a deep, rumbling sound that filled him with fear. He looked up to see terror and disbelief in his brothers' eyes. From a distance, he heard his mother shouting and saw her running towards them, her flowered dressing gown flying open to reveal a flimsy nightdress beneath, ancient slippers on her feet. Soon, dozens of people were fleeing to the top of a neighbouring hill to find safety from the earthquake, waiting there for further tremors to finally subside.

I had completely forgotten about that earthquake, he suddenly thinks. He looks towards the living room sofa and, for a moment, imagines his mother lying there, her slim body covered in a dark green shawl, her head against the cushion behind her and her eyes closed, dark wavy hair framing a pale and delicate face.

What would she say to all these musings, he wonders? He sniffs loudly and shakes his head. Does it really matter now?

The first time Kamal visited a Palestinian refugee camp was with a friend from school whose relatives lived there. The two boys were met on the outskirts of the camp by a young man who led them through a maze of dirt paths and narrow alleyways to a two-room home with an outhouse at one end and a grape vine growing on a trellis on its roof. Once inside, sitting with Hisham and their hosts on a thin mattress with their backs against a damp wall, Kamal had wondered how a family of six could live in so confined a space. Turning to whisper disbelief into Hisham's ear, he was shushed into silence. They'll hear you, Hisham had said. They're poor, that's all. There's nothing wrong with that.

Kamal had waited until his father returned from a trip abroad, a week after the visit, to ask him the question that had occupied his mind ever since.

'How come we don't live in a camp with other refugees?'

'We're fortunate enough not to have to,' his father had replied.

'But we're . . . we're Palestinian too, aren't we?' Kamal was still confused.

'Yes, we are.'

113

'So why aren't we living in a camp like those people I met the other day?'

'It's a question of being able to afford to live better than they do, that's all, Kamal. In reality, we're all in the same boat, waiting for the chance to go back home.'

They were sitting on the sofa in the living room, his mother moving around in the kitchen behind them and his brothers somewhere outside . Kamal looked around anxiously, wanting his father's reassurance.

'But *baba*, I thought this was our home. This apartment is our home, isn't it?'

His father leaned towards him and put a hand on his arm.

'We're only tenants here, Kamal. You know that.'

He gestured towards the front door.

'This apartment doesn't belong to us and nor does this country,' his father continued. 'We're only here until the day we go back to our own home in Palestine. You're old enough to be aware of all this, son. We've talked about it before.'

'But why do we have to leave?' Kamal insisted. 'Why do we have to be different from everyone else? I want to be Lebanese.'

His father took a deep breath and stood up.

'I don't want to hear you say things like that, Kamal,' he said with a frown before turning away from him. 'Go out and call your brothers in for their dinner. They're late and your mother will be upset.'

It seemed only natural when Kamal returned to Beirut after completing his studies abroad many years that he should search for a place in the same neighbourhood he had grown up in. He was astonished to discover that the old apartment that had served as home for his family was vacant and had undergone a renovation of sorts. His first night there, unopened boxes and disparate pieces of furniture strewn across the floor, he stood perfectly still, listening for the sound of his father's voice. When it finally came, remnants of conversation that hung listlessly in the air, Kamal heard the sadness in it that he had not heard before, the regret that had died with him.

His mother had loved American films, knew the names of Hollywood stars and their most famous movies by heart. The memory of all those names has stayed with him, Clark Gable and Vivienne Leigh in *Gone with the Wind*; Humphrey Bogart and Ingrid Bergman in *Casablanca*; James Stewart and Donna Reed in *It's a Wonderful Life*. She would repeat these titles to herself sometimes until they became as familiar to him as his own, the English sounds taking on a magical quality precisely because he did not know where each word ended and where the next began.

He remembers arriving home from school at times to find she had gone out with a neighbour from upstairs to see the latest film release. She would return looking slightly flushed with excitement, wave her friend goodbye and finally turn to speak to him. What a story I have to tell you, *habibi*, she would say before sitting him down on the sofa next to her. Oh, Gary Cooper looked so handsome, a real gentleman, and such a good actor too!

He waited expectantly, looking at the bright light in her eyes, savouring her pleasure as though it were his own, loving her more than ever during these rare moments when she was no one else but her own dear self. Were there cowboys with guns in it, *mama*? Tell me what it was about. She would laugh out loud, squeeze his arm, and lean over to describe what she had just experienced of adventure and romance and courage, all so much greater than anything either of them had known in real life.

Years later, when she was completely bed-ridden and

had only her beloved books for comfort, he found out that she had never wanted to marry, that her parents had taken her out of school and forced her into marriage at fourteen. If I had had my way, she told him, I would have continued my studies, perhaps gone on to university. But then, she continued, her hand cupping the side of his face, I wouldn't have had you boys. When she passed away, only weeks before he was due to leave to take up a university scholarship in Germany, he tried to take with him only those memories of her that were joyful, her excitement over romantic movie matinees and her carefree spirit.

Kamal puts the pencil he had been writing with down and stands up. The dining room table where he does most of his work is cluttered with papers and books but he does not attempt to clear them away even though he knows he is not likely to do any more writing today. For the first time in a long time, he does not have the heart for it.

What would I do, he suddenly thinks, if writing were to leave me? Who would I be then?

In the kitchen, he measures two small cups of water into the coffee pot and just as the water begins to boil, puts in two heaped teaspoons of finely ground coffee and stirs the mixture until it rises again.

Back in the living room, he walks to the window, cup in hand. It is late afternoon and the light is beginning to fade. He can hear children playing in the alleyway downstairs but the outside landing is empty. Moments later, he sees the old woman from two floors above climbing up the stairs. She looks foreign and is small with a shock of short, white hair. They have come across each other in the building before but they have never spoken. When she lifts her head and looks him straight in the eye, he nearly spills his coffee. She smiles and he feels himself blush with embarrassment. By the time he lifts a reluctant hand to wave to her she has already rounded the corner and is no longer looking in his direction. He contemplates stepping outside and calling her in but does not. What would they have to say to each other, after all?

In the decade before the outbreak of civil war, Beirut was a hub of activity. It was a heady time of optimism with intellectuals and artists from all over the region arriving here to enjoy the freedom of expression that did not exist elsewhere. In the crowded, smoky cafés of the city, they talked of the end of the political dictatorships that ruled the Arab world, of their desire for democracy and of their aspirations for the liberation of Palestine.

Kamal took a job as an editorial assistant on a weekly political magazine soon after receiving his school diploma. He quickly fell into a work routine, arriving at the publication's cramped office every morning trembling with anticipation, then spending most of the day running in and out, fetching newspapers and coffee for the writers or, if he was lucky, typing up their articles on an old typewriter he had been given for the purpose.

He had been at work for a few weeks when the editor, a respected Palestinian intellectual, asked him to reply to a reader's letter. The editor was so pleased with the result that he eventually put Kamal in charge of the magazine's general correspondence. Kamal soon realized that he would need to be better informed to carry out the job and began to read as never before, books, magazines and newspapers that helped him understand not only what was happening in the region at the time but also everything that had come before, the seeds of uncertainty and conflict.

With time, he began to join the editor and several of the writers to lunch at a restaurant not far from the office. They would sit at a table by the window, eating a rich *mezza* of *tabbouleh* and *hoummos*, of savoury pastries and spicy meat sausages, of stuffed grape leaves and soft cheeses sprinkled generously with virgin olive oil, and talking of the issues of the day, of their conviction that a better Arab world was forthcoming.

The editor was middle-aged and handsome and had dark flowing hair and a moustache that accentuated his striking features. He would listen carefully, smiling every now and then and speaking with an even voice once everyone had had their say.

'How's that piece on the refugee camps going?' the editor asked Lutfi, the magazine's senior writer.

Lutfi, who was Egyptian, looked up from his plate.

'Fine, I suppose,' he said. 'There are so many issues involved that every time I think I'm almost finished, something else comes up that needs to be covered.'

'But what are the most important points that need to be made, do you think?' the editor continued.

Kamal listened intently to the reply.

'I'd say the fact that PLO commandoes are becoming more vocal and more powerful within the camps is the first one, so we have to ask ourselves how that's likely to affect the Lebanese political scene.'

'What we should be asking is how far this country's politicians are willing to go in using the Palestinians to further their own political ambitions,' said Salam, a journalist from Syria.

'And to what extent is the PLO going to allow itself to fall into Lebanon's sectarian quagmire at the expense of its own refugee population,' the editor retorted quietly. 'Is the sectarianism on which this country's political system is based about to cause it to collapse? It's a complex situation and the article has to reflect that.'

Lutfi nodded.

'Then there's the growing tension between the Lebanese Maronite leadership and the PLO,' said Lutfi. 'They're worried that the Palestinian presence will threaten their influence over the domestic political scene. So where is that likely to lead? What about the Muslims in Lebanon? Will they try to use the current situation to gain political power?'

'Isn't it possible that there will eventually be some sort of confrontation?' Fouad said, looking at the editor. 'Israel is watching what's going on very closely and it's not happy with the situation either.'

The editor nodded.

'You're right,' he said. 'Although the article should not try to predict what will happen, we do have a duty to put all these factors into a wider perspective.'

He sighed and shook his head.

'Let's hope there won't be an outbreak of civil strife,' he said. 'What do you think, Lutfi?'

Lutfi smiled.

'I think young Kamal here might have a future as a journalist ahead of him,' he said, and they all laughed.

When he finally left the magazine to study abroad, Kamal did so reluctantly, walking out of the office for the last time with a heavy heart, conscious that the experience of Lebanon he was leaving behind might never appear the same to him again, that his own sense of identity, as complex and country-bound as it had so far been, was about to change.

He spent the first few months after his arrival in Germany studying the language and living with a family in a village outside Munich, feeling almost as though he had never left home. The warmth of the reception he was given surprised him. He had always imagined that people in the West would be cold and indifferent.

Slowly, his view of the world began to acquire new dimensions, widened until he saw how events integral to his own life had also invariably touched the lives of others beyond Lebanon. The devastating loss of Palestine had come after the murder of millions in the holocaust, was followed by the debilitating guilt and bewilderment he encountered in the people he met in Germany, continued even now in the anguished lives of Palestinian refugees and those in the occupied territories, in the violence and turmoil that would not end until the cycle itself was stopped, the thread finally broken.ᴵAs the civil war in Lebanon raged on, Kamal's concern for family and friends there and for his beloved Beirut developed into an under-lying sense of anxiety , reminding him that whatever refuge he had discovered in being so far away would not last. It felt sometimes as though he were really living two half-lives, one present and the other just out of reach, each important in its own way but neither allowing him to be completely himself .

And then he had fallen in love. Christina was a few years younger than he, an intense and darkly pretty architectural student from Czechoslovakia who helped strengthen his growing belief that boundaries could be broken if he only made the effort to understand them. Soon, life away from home acquired a momentum of its own and the possibility of a future in the West, in this corner of the world that had seemed so alien to him at first, began to seem real to him.

When the time eventually came, however, Kamal could not quite imagine himself remaining. He had completed his studies and had been teaching at a university in Munich when Lebanon's civil war began to abate. Since his brothers had left Lebanon before him, they were already well settled in Europe, and his parents were no longer alive. He knew that in Germany his life would always be comfortable though largely uneventful, and something in him wanted more. Returning to the only country that had been home to him seemed the obvious choice. Perhaps there, he thought, his presence might have a positive impact, no matter how small. By the time the civil war came to an end in 1990, he had been back in Beirut for several years, had published two books and was well on his way to a very successful writing career.

Now, when memories of those first few months back in Lebanon come to him, it is not the difficulty in re-adjusting he had experienced nor the regrets he sometimes felt about having returned that he remembers most, but rather the absence of indefinable longings, as though in coming back he had bravely taken a new path and broken a thread of his own.

I am officially middle-aged, Kamal thinks to himself, smiling, as he gets dressed one morning, putting on his left sock and left shoe first, then the right before standing up to comb his hair in front of the mirror. I have become a stickler for routine, choosing ritual over spontaneity. Even the way I lay the table for dinner, he muses, is structured, placemat and cutlery, then a plate placed precisely in the centre with a glass a few centimetres above it and to the right.

He is exacting in the way he works also, keeping a notebook on his bedside table in which he puts down ideas for work before eventually writing them down in long-hand on the unlined, loose leaf paper he has in a pile on the dining room table. Only when he has had a chance to completely digest the ideas and let them gestate in his mind, will he make a decision on whether or not to type them on his computer.

He likes to think that in making rituals out of everyday routines he is imposing order on his inner life also, his concern about the political situation in the country growing, rivalries between different religious factions threatening to get out of hand and the assassinations of politicians and journalists continuing with impunity. For all his political cynicism as he gets older, the thought that another civil war might be in the offing horrifies him.

He knows he has also made the mistake of neglecting his friends, many of whom have gone abroad over the past year as the situation has worsened. Those still here telephone him every once in a while, asking how he is getting along, their conversations drifting into an eventual silence, Kamal unwilling to delve further into despair with someone who would understand it only too well. Whenever he does meet with friends, at a restaurant for a meal or in their homes for a visit, he finds himself gradually withdrawing into the quietness defined by his solitude, that far-off place of peace.

On the morning that his neighbor Layla arrives with a book for him to sign, Kamal is annoyed at the interruption and has every intention when he opens the door and sees her there to refuse her request and simply send her away. But he stops himself from doing this, perhaps prompted by something as mundane as politeness or maybe something more, curiosity about the possibility of connection, a desire to experience once again the uncertain longings of youth.

He is immediately attracted to her. As she stands there looking at him, clearly flustered at his refusal to respond to her praise, he feels suddenly ashamed of himself. He reaches for the book and signs it carefully, hoping that the short message will somehow make amends. Moments later, shutting the front door behind her, he wonders if he has inadvertently brought himself to a point of no return, to a moment when he is no longer able to extricate himself from an eloquent interior world of his own making.

※　　※　　※

'Kamal? Is that you?'

He is sitting at his usual table at the Hamra Street café. He looks up from his newspaper at the man leaning towards him over the table, a middle-aged man with sharp features and short, greying hair.

'Ghassan? It's Ghassan isn't it?' Kamal asks quietly.

The two men embrace, Kamal surprised at the sudden and deep emotion that fills him.

'My God, it's been too long. Where have you been all these years?'

'Sit down, sit down,' Kamal says, taking his jacket off the back of the empty chair beside him. 'I'll get you a coffee. How do you like it?'

'No sugar, thank you, *habibi*,' Ghassan replies shaking his head. 'I thought I'd never see you again. How have you been?'

Kamal goes up to the counter, orders coffee and pastries and brings them to the table.

'I'm doing well, thanks. I thought when you left for America years ago you weren't planning to come back ever again.'

'That's what I thought at first but you know it's impossible to keep away from Beirut for long,' Ghassan says with a chuckle.

Kamal nods and looks closely at his old friend. He is dressed in a beautifully cut suit and has an air of ease and comfort about him. Kamal can hardly believe that this is the same, troubled young man he had known all those years ago. At one point, Ghassan had become involved with a radical political group and had come very close to being imprisoned. Kamal had managed to persuade him to leave Lebanon before it was too late, to go to the United States to join an uncle who had been there for many years.

'Wasn't it Detroit that you went to?' Kamal asks.

'Initially, yes,' Ghassan replies. 'I moved to LA some time

ago, though. I have my own business now, as well as a wife and three children.'

'Congratulations!' Kamal says, trying not to appear too surprised.

'Don't look so shocked, *ya akhi*. I learned my lesson all those years ago.'

'You were really something then,' Kamal smiles. 'I'm glad things have worked out so well for you. I really am.'

'And you? I think I've read everything you've written over the years. I heard you were in the US for a book tour at one point but I didn't get the chance to attend any of your events.'

Kamal nods.

'My work is going well, which is something I'm very grateful for.'

'What about your family, Kamal. Your brothers and your father?'

'Both my brothers are overseas with their families. My father passed away some time ago.'

'I'm sorry to hear that.'

The conversation stalls for a moment. Ghassan picks up his coffee and sips at it slowly.

'What about you,' he eventually asks. 'Do you have a family of your own?'

Kamal shakes his head.

'I live alone.'

Ghassan shrugs.

'Maybe it's better that way,' he says. 'A family is a big responsibility and I'm sure being alone gives you more time for your work.'

It occurs to Kamal as Ghassan continues to chat to him that he too must appear very different now, a long way from the idealistic and confident young man he had once been. Where has the passion gone, he asks himself? Swallowed up by the chasm of my own mind, I suppose.

'Being here brings back so many memories,' Ghassan is shaking his head. 'Good and bad, of course. So much has changed, though, that I feel sometimes as if I'm in a totally different Lebanon.'

'That's it, isn't it?' Kamal agrees. 'I returned thinking things would be the way they had been before the civil war but I was wrong, of course. It wasn't easy to adjust at first but one does eventually manage somehow.'

Ghassan looks at him closely.

'Who is still around of the old crowd? Do you see much of them?'

'To tell you the truth, I haven't really kept in touch with anyone.'

'Keeping to yourself, is that it?'

'Something like that, yes.'

Kamal feels slightly irritated at the tone in his friend's voice. Is there an implied criticism there?

'I met up with Nasser the other day. Remember him?' Ghassan asks. 'He seems to know the whereabouts of some of the guys. How about if I arrange a get together for all of us before I leave next week? It would be great to see everyone again.'

Kamal says nothing.

'Give me your number, *habibi*,' Ghassan continues. 'I'll contact you once I know the details.'

He takes a phone out of his pocket and records Kamal's number. Then he gets up and the two men shake hands.

'See you soon, OK?' says Ghassan as he prepares to leave.

'*Inshaallah*,' replies Kamal.

Ghassan laughs.

'You don't fool me, old friend. Saying god willing usually means no, and I'm not taking no for an answer.'

Kamal feels suddenly duty bound to be honest with his friend. He reaches out and places a hand on Ghassan's arm.

125

'I'm not very good around people, these days,' he says gently. 'It's not you. It's just that I've become rather insular in my old age. I really don't think I'd be able to do it. I'm sorry.'

'Your old age?'

Kamal pulls his hand away.

'I feel grey and tired and alone most days, so what else would you call it?'

'You have too much time to think, that's what it is, *habibi*. You need to get out more.'

'I'm sure you're right,' Kamal says with a sigh. 'Perhaps that's what it is.'

'Look, I can't force you to join us, Kamal, but it will do you good to see the old gang again. Remind you of your youth and vigour. What do you say?'

Ghassan chuckles and pats him on the arm. It occurs to Kamal that he might have embarrassed his friend with his confession.

'You always were a bit of a loner, *ya akhi*, and you always made up your own mind about things,' Ghassan says gently. 'This is a hole that you'll manage to get yourself out of once you decide to do it. I'm sure of that.'

What has happened to me, Kamal wonders. I have become so solitary that even the prospect of renewing once precious friendships seems too daunting to bear.

Kamal tells himself to go about it step by step, taking more notice of his neighbours to begin with and venturing further into the community of people that immediately surrounds him. He begins by asking after the health of those he sees on the stairwell every day, then goes on to speak at greater length to the butcher and the grocer down the street whenever he goes by. Eventually, he finds himself stopping in mid-stride to exchange pleasantries with other tenants of the building or to comment briefly on the latest news.

It seems to him that in getting this far he is also re-capturing that part of himself that he had thought lost since his return to Beirut. There are no subtle shades of grey to one's existence here, he knows. Short of sequestering himself in his apartment, as he has done over the past few years, there is no opportunity to blend quietly into one's surroundings. Rather he finds himself now plunged into a social whirl of invitations, not only to please come in and stay to have a bite to eat but also of coaxing to express his emotions and to share the concerns of others almost as though they were his own or at least as if he, in one way or another, had a hand in their making.

Still, he cannot quite bring himself to approach Layla directly, to knock on her door as she had done, and invite himself in. On the few occasions that he does see her, either on the stairwell as she is walking up to her apartment or on the street, he smiles and says hello and hesitates for a moment, hoping that she will stop and talk to him but she does not. Until the day he finds her at the entrance to the building, struggling with bags of groceries and a large bouquet of flowers that slips out of her grasp and falls to the ground.

'Let me help you with those,' he ventures, grabbing the bags with one hand and the bouquet with the other.

'Thank you,' she says, following him up the stairs to her apartment on the floor immediately above his.

He stops on the landing and waits for her to open the door.

'I'm actually taking the flowers up to Margo,' Layla says, looking somewhat flustered. 'You've been very kind, really. We can just leave the bags in the hallway and I'll take care of them later.'

He tries to think of a way to prolong their conversation.

'Is Margo the lady with the short white hair I see on the stairs from time to time?'

Layla nods.

'You can't miss her, can you? She's so unlike anyone else.'

'I've been wanting to say hello to her but have never quite dared to do it,' he says.

'Yes, well, writers can be notoriously shy, can't they?' says Layla.

There is such kindness in the way she looks at him that he finds himself laughing nervously.

'Look,' she continues. 'Why don't you come up with me and I'll introduce you? I'm sure she'll enjoy meeting you.'

They continue up the stairs and find Margo's door open.

Layla shakes her head and smiles.

'When I tell her it's not a good idea to keep the door open like this, she says this way whoever wants to can just walk in without knocking.'

She knocks on the door nonetheless and calls out Margo's name.

'Ah!' Kamal hears the older woman reply, and then sees her slowly step into the hallway from the living room.

'Margo, I've brought someone to meet you,' Layla says, bending down to give her friend a hug and kiss.

Margo looks at Kamal, her deeply lined faced lifting as she smiles. She is even more striking up close. She is diminutive and clearly less than steady on her feet, yet he feels something much stronger than her physical presence fill the room and surround them so that he is both attracted as well as made somewhat nervous by it.

'Hello,' Margo says reaching out to shake his hand. 'We've come across on another on the stairs before, haven't we? It's good to finally meet you.'

'Hello,' Kamal replies.

Her hand feels larger than he expected and rougher too. He looks down to examine it further and hears Margo laugh.

'I'm an avid gardener, you see, with the hands to prove it,' she says as if reading his thoughts. 'Please go in, you two, and I'll go make us some coffee.'

She looks at Layla with a smile.

'Thank you for the beautiful flowers, sweetheart. Let's just put them in the sink for now. How lovely to have unexpected guests like this!'

They spoke openly when he visited her on his own for the first time, Kamal surprised to have felt relief afterwards as though in just releasing the words and hearing them said out loud their weight had finally been lightened. Margo remained mostly quiet but he sensed understanding in her silence, reassurance that this opening up of his deepest self would not expose him unduly.

'You live alone?' Margo began.

'Yes, I do.'

'It's unusual you know, for an Arab man to be alone.'

He laughed nervously.

'Yes, I suppose it is. But that's how things have worked out for me.'

It was then that he felt a sudden urge to talk to her about the why of it, why he should find himself alone and virtually friendless at a time in his life when he needed companionship most.

'It's my work, you see. Writing's a solitary occupation and it takes up most of my time.'

She nodded. He suddenly noticed how large her ears were and how they stuck out so that her face seemed almost comical.

'I suppose it doesn't really have to,' he continued. 'Perhaps it's a choice I have made. The problem is now I don't know how to get out of this situation.'

'You want to stop writing?'

'No, I don't,' He felt himself shudder at the thought.

'But I would like for it not to always overwhelm my life as it does.'

'Are you missing someone in particular?' she asked so quietly that he was not sure he had heard right.

'Someone?'

She paused, waiting for him to continue. He took a deep breath and could feel his face heat up.

'I . . . It's been years. I haven't seen her for so long sometimes I can't even remember her face.'

Margo offered him a cigarette, took one herself and then handed him the lighter. They smoked in silence for a moment or two.

'I met her while I was studying in Germany. She was Czech, an architecture student.'

He shook his head and smiled.

'I left and never got in touch with her again. I wonder sometimes what might have happened to her.'

'She was important to you?'

He shrugged.

'Perhaps not, but maybe she represented something important. I mean it would have been so easy to stay with her, especially since I was fairly certain of loving her. But I still chose to come back here.'

'And be alone?'

'Not necessarily,' he said. 'To come back and be here, either way.'

Margo put out her cigarette, picked up a plate of biscuits off the tray and handed it to him. Her hand touched his momentarily and he felt the warmth emanating from it.

'It's strange, isn't it, how important place can be at certain points in one's life?' she asked. 'Just when you think you have overcome the idea of attachment to one place or another, you suddenly find yourself drawn to it again. And that it should be more important than people at times. How is that?'

'You are also an exile?'

She gave a little laugh, lifting her head up slightly and hunching her shoulders.

'That's too fancy a word for it, I think, and perhaps too negative also. I like being here. It's exactly where I want to be right now.'

'But you must have family somewhere?'

She shook her head.

'Layla tells me your family came from Palestine,' she says. 'Yet you still made a life for yourself here.'

'I grew up here. This city has important associations for me. It's difficult for me now to imagine being anywhere else.'

He suddenly realized how true this was.

Margo spoke quietly.

'But you know, the real truth about most of us is that we can probably manage to be just about anywhere at all, don't you think?'

He waited for her to continue.

'It all depends on how willing we are to overlook certain truths about ourselves.'

'What do you mean?' Kamal asked.

She shrugged.

'Maybe what we think of as our connection to a country is only our fear of being somewhere less familiar. Maybe a real sense of home is meant to come from somewhere within us.'

'Here?' he asked, pointing to his heart.

Margo looked at him, saying nothing further. She was so still that he suddenly thought she might have stopped breathing. He began to move towards her then paused, and in that moment between his anxiety and thoughts, he finally understood. They were already there, the two of them, together.

*　　*　　*

Kamal and Margo speak of the past as though they could relive it through words, pulling it apart and deliberately studying its contents, seeing in this probing answers to previous discontent, and when not that then at least a certain appeasement of regret.

There is much that she does not tell him about herself, he knows, though he cannot fault her in this because he finds himself also unwilling to reveal all. He suspects their motives for these minor deceptions are different, he because so much that has happened to him seems insignificant to the man he has become, and she perhaps because she appears to have lived her life in phases, renewing herself, both in her own eyes as well as in the eyes of others, at every turn.

It is not that he is not curious about Margo. He often imagines what she must have been like in her youth and what she might have gone through. But it seems to him that there is so much she can offer him right now, such an unexpected and daring view of things, the idea that he should look at himself honestly and without judgment, that he cannot bring himself to ask for more. Perhaps, he thinks, there is also a part of him that feels too much empathy for this newfound friend to dig further into her past. Some sorrows, he believes, should be left to rest, his own as well as those belonging to others. Still, at times he is astonished at how much she is prepared to disclose, telling him of past indiscretions as though she might shock him into understanding her more deeply.

'I had a lover once who was a sculptor,' Margo says as they sit together one evening. 'He was tall and strong and beautiful and would wake up in the middle of the night to make sketches of me as I slept.

'We were out walking one day and bumped into a woman he seemed to know. I watched her as she smiled with her eyes half-closed and rubbed her hand back and forth along his thigh and knew then that he had been cheating on me for some time.

'When he finally decided to leave, he simply handed me the keys to my flat and walked out the door without saying another word.'

She shakes her head.

'People can be cruel,' she says.

Kamal nods, surprised at his reaction to the story. I would like to hold her close for a moment, he thinks, gently so that she might be comforted out of her hurt. When he looks up at Margo again, she is smiling knowingly at him and for a moment he imagines she has read his thoughts.

'I'm sorry,' he mutters with embarrassment.

'It's alright. It's so long ago now it really feels as though it happened to someone else.'

The impression that Margo is sometimes mocking him crosses Kamal's mind but it is not long, as he comes to know her better, before he realizes that she is merely laughing at herself. Perhaps, he realizes, she is also urging me to do the same with myself.

Thoughts of Layla seem always to hover in the air whenever they meet, not only because she is the link between them but also because, he now understands, the young woman's presence is so strong in Margo's life. Layla is, Margo tells him, the only expectation she allows herself these days.

'But she is too sensitive, of course, as well as unable or unwilling to learn how to protect herself,' Margo waves her hand in the air as she speaks.

'She is fortunate to have you to guide her,' Kamal says.

'Yes, but I will not be around for long, you know.'

She looks at him, her expression seemingly untroubled.

'I . . . I don't know her very well, as you know Margo.'

'Not yet, but perhaps you will sometime soon.'

*   *   *

133

He takes along with him a copy of his children's tales published several years earlier and knocks on Layla's door.

'Kamal, how nice to see you,' Layla stands at her front door and smiles. 'Please come in.'

He hands her the book and steps inside, feeling happy that she seems pleased to see him.

'I thought you might be interested in this for your literature class,' he says. 'You asked me once what I would recommend for your students.'

'Yes, of course. Oh, yes, I've looked at these stories before.'

They sit down in the living room and he is struck by how plain everything is, a sofa, a coffee table and two armchairs and an almost total absence of decorative objects. He does not know why but he had expected her home to be somewhat different, more feminine perhaps and more welcoming.

She leafs through the book and looks up at him with a smile.

'I think this one might just be the perfect choice. I'm sure the students will enjoy it.'

He is not sure what to say next.

'How's your writing going?' Layla asks.

'Not too well at the moment, I'm afraid,' he shakes his head. 'I don't know where all the ideas have gone.'

'I suppose that's bound to happen at times. Maybe you should just stop trying so hard.'

An image of days not filled with writing and the thoughts that accompany it suddenly comes to mind.

He stands up.

'I'd better get back to work,' he says.

Before he steps out the door, he turns to Layla once again.

'I hope I'll see you again soon,' he says quietly.

'I hope so too,' she nods and smiles.

*　　*　　*

They arrange to meet on the landing outside Margo's front door, sitting on plastic chairs, drinking beer and munching on nuts and fresh fruit. They speak haltingly at first, commenting on the beautiful weather and the many stars that illuminate the sky, Layla smiling nervously at her two friends and Kamal clearing his throat before every sentence, while Margo looks on with apparent satisfaction.

They sense, all three of them, as the evening advances and conversation begins to flow more easily, that this is a moment they will always remember, the cool, bright night, the simple pleasures they are enjoying, and this effortless camaraderie, a bond they weave and sustain together.

'There is so much I want to say,' Layla begins after a pause in conversation. 'But I don't know exactly where to start.'

Kamal leans forward in his seat and smiles.

'All this,' he gestures at the night, 'is impossible to describe, isn't it?'

'Even for a writer?'

A sudden breeze makes him shiver.

'Especially for a writer,' Kamal laughs. 'I often lack spontaneity and tend to analyse things too much. Anyway, some things are better left unwritten.'

'We already know what you mean, sweetheart,' Margo says gently, placing a hand on Layla's arm. 'Don't we Kamal?'

What is it about female compassion, he wonders, that can bring down a man's defences and compel him to re-direct his journey? Margo and Layla lead him beyond the confines of his mind, gently pull him forward so that he feels himself slowly expanding into the world around him; rather than being defined by his absence from it as before, he is once again a part of its fabric.

135

I am Beirut's ears, he whispers to himself whenever he overhears the conversations of strangers; I am its eyes, he calls out to the blue sea; I am the smell of morning and the velvet smoothness of the sky at night. He laughs too at this newfound confidence and reminds himself that strength also comes from the want of expectation. We grow only in moving past false hopes and towards the lives that we were meant to lead, Margo has told him.

Slowly, an image of himself as a man without definite purpose emerges in his mind. He is for the most part as he was before but less bound by former goals, more inclined to meet days with wonder, the sense that anything is possible and even more that he is capable of meeting it.

It is not that I am a changed man, Kamal would say if anyone were to ask him. It is bliss that has unexpectedly crossed my doorstep.

Kamal suggests that they all go to visit the ancient ruins in the southern city of Tyre and is amused that both Margo and Layla express surprise when he tells them he owns a car.

'It's not in the best of shape,' he says with a smile, 'but it will get us there. What do you say?'

'Are you a good driver?' Layla asks and they all laugh.

'What do you say, you two?' he asks again.

On the day of their excursion, the sun is shining, as it will on the Mediterranean, and the air is fresh. They set out early, Layla insisting that Margo sit in the front seat where she can see better and Kamal supplying each of them with a small bottle of mineral water and apples for the drive.

Instead of taking the new inland highway to the south, Kamal takes the old, coastal road which is narrow and often bumpy but, for the most part, runs close to the

136

beautiful shore. At one point, he stops to buy *mana'eesh* for their breakfast, flat bread covered with olive oil and a mixture of thyme, sumac and sesame seeds. They sit in the car by the bakery and eat in silence looking out at the sea. Once they're done, they rinse off their hands with the mineral water before setting off once again.

'I can't wait to see the ruins,' Layla says. 'I haven't been there in years.'

It takes just under two hours to get to the coastal city of Tyre. Kamal drives into the parking lot just outside one of the sites of the city's main ruins and they step out of the car with relief. Margo has brought her walking stick and begins to make her way slowly up the paved roman road that leads to the ancient hippodrome further ahead. Grass and wildflowers cover the ground beyond the paving and a magnificent stone archway appears before them.

They pause for a moment. There are aqueducts on either side of the paving and beyond that rows of sarcophagi, in different stages of dilapidation, line the ancient avenue, the remains of a Roman and Byzantine graveyard.

'This is so beautiful,' Layla says, her voice only just above a whisper.

They continue walking slowly, pausing every now and then to observe their surroundings more closely, tall columns and additional stone arches and other structures of indeterminate function. One by one, they all stop when they reach the hippodrome, rectangular and vast and built for chariot races.

Kamal and Layla help Margo onto one of the huge stones that lie around the edges of the hippodrome and sit down either side of her.

'It's wonderful, isn't it?' Layla says.

Margo nods and pulls out a cigarette which Kamal helps her light.

'Devastating grandeur,' Layla stands up and points

137

towards the stands that surround the arena. 'I'm going to climb up there. All the way up to the gods.'

She smiles.

'Go ahead, sweetheart,' says Margo. 'We'll be fine over here.'

'Be careful,' Kamal calls out after her. 'Some of those stones can be unsteady.'

Margo turns to Kamal.

'The opportunity won't be around forever, you know,' she says, pursing her lips to blow out smoke.

Kamal is puzzled.

'Opportunity?'

'Layla. She'll eventually find someone else if you don't do something soon.'

He feels himself blush.

'What are you waiting for?' she continues, irritation in her voice now. 'Why are men so slow to understand?'

'You're angry with me.'

She sighs.

'No, not angry exactly, just frustrated that you can't see how little time there is.'

Kamal shrugs.

Margo stands up abruptly and drops her cigarette to the ground.

'For heaven's sake, Kamal, stop behaving like an intellectual wimp and look around you. What more is there do you think? Do you expect some kind of fanfare for your effort and suffering in life? Is that it?'

'You're upset now,' Kamal says nervously, reaching out to touch her arm.

'My friend, can't you see how fragile life really is?' Her voice is quieter now.

He helps her to sit down again.

'I don't know how Layla feels about me, Margo,' he says hesitatingly. 'Besides, I'm so much older than she is.'

'What does it matter if you're right for each other?'

'Are we that, Margo? Are we right for each other or is it simply that we're both so alone?'

She frowns and looks up, pointing towards the ramparts. 'Do you see her?' she asks.

Layla stands on the top level of the crumbling stone structure facing the sea. Her body is slight and straight and her hands shield her eyes as she stares into the distance. She leans forward, over the wall's edge, as if to look closer at the view and then straightens up again, her back arching slightly, her head held back for an instant. The movement is fluid and easy, like the bend of a long corn stalk in a passing breeze. Even from here, Kamal realizes, the stillness that envelopes her is perceptible. She seems anything but helpless.

'Yes, I do,' Kamal replies, turning to Margo once again. 'I do now.'

He sits at the table in front of his laptop and wonders if he will ever write another useful word. For several days he has tried settling down with his first cup of coffee in the morning and going over earlier work to try to recapture the threads of his thoughts, and for several days he has written words only to want to delete them very soon after. He suspects that the urge to impart some kind of message to his readers has gone the way of the doubts of his recent past.

His reason tells him that most writers experience this problem at some point or other in their careers, though he himself had not felt it so intensely before now. Rather than get rid of everything he has written, he promises himself to wait a little longer, to sit at the table once again and anticipate that former eagerness. Maybe it's just a question of patience.

He takes his coffee out on the landing and looks down

at the alleyway below. It is early morning. All is quiet and he is surprised to find he is feeling disappointed at the lack of activity. *Who would I have wanted to see now anyway?*

As if on cue, Margo appears above him, descending the stairs slowly, one step at a time, one hand on the stone banister and the other holding a stick.

She stops to look at him.

'Ah, it's you,' she says.

Then she smiles.

'Good morning,' he is feeling suddenly cheerful. 'Are you out for a walk?'

She comes up to him and looks closely into his eyes.

'I needed to get out of the house for a bit,' she says. 'Would you join me?'

'Yes, of course.'

It is so early that the streets are almost empty, with no sign of even the children who wait on corners for their school bus.

'Where would you like to go?' she asks him.

He shakes his head. Watching her move, her head bent low a little as she shuffles forward, he is suddenly aware of her age. Then, looking down at the ground, he is surprised to see that she is still in her slippers and feels instant regret at having noticed that.

'You seem preoccupied, Margo. Are you alright?'

She stops and sighs.

'Perhaps we can find somewhere to sit down,' she says with a wan smile. 'These old legs tend to give out on me after a while.'

He leads her to the ledge of a low wall at the front of one of the new buildings on the main road. They sit quietly for a few moments. Then Margo takes a packet of cigarettes and a lighter out of her pocket. He helps her to light up.

'That's better,' she finally says, blowing a thin wisp of smoke in his direction. 'You wouldn't think someone as old and decrepit as me could be so silly, would you?'

'Why, what's happened?'

'Sometimes I wake up and feel so alone that I think I simply cannot bear it,' her voice trembles.

He looks down and realizes that she has been flicking the ashes from her cigarette onto his shoes. He tries to move his feet away without her noticing it.

'Oh, I'm so sorry. Look what I've done.'

'Please don't worry about it.'

She reaches into the cuff of her sleeve, takes out a folded tissue and bends down to wipe away the ash.

'Let me do that,' he says, gently taking the tissue from her hand.

'And look at me. I'm still in my slippers!'

He looks into her eyes. She is grinning, the folds of skin on her face suddenly lifted up towards her eyes.

'I didn't even notice,' she says with a chuckle. 'You must think I am going senile.'

'It does get difficult sometimes,' he says. 'Being alone, I mean.'

She drops her cigarette onto the ground and he puts it out with his shoe.

'Yes, it does,' she says softly, as though she were speaking to herself. 'But there's no way out of it now, is there?'

He shares her sadness so deeply for a moment that he feels compelled to reach out and place his hand over hers.

'It was like this when the war finally ended, you know,' she says. 'It was a while before I could believe that it was really over. I was relieved, of course, everyone was, but there was also the fact that I wasn't sure quite what would come next. What could possibly follow all that and still mean something?'

She pulls her hand away.

'But you could at least look towards a better future once that terrible violence was over,' says Kamal softly.

'You mean that it was a just war?'

Kamal nods.

'Don't you think so, Margo?'

'Yes, I suppose I do. By the time everyone woke up to what was going on in Germany and elsewhere, it was too late to do anything but retaliate. But that's not the situation for you, is it?'

'Nor for all the other troubled places in this part of the world,' Kamal says with bitterness. 'It seems there will never be an end to the violence. How does one live with that?'

She frowns and shakes her head.

'I don't have an answer for that, Kamal.'

'Did you ever go back, Margo?'

'When I returned home to Prague my sister wanted nothing more to do with me. And my parents . . . Well, they were already long dead.'

'Killed?' Kamal asks cautiously.

'In a Polish ghetto, with tens of thousands of others.'

'I'm sorry.'

Margo has never spoken of this before and he is not sure he understands what she means nor what it is that he is meant to say.

'Ah!' she suddenly exclaims, pulling herself up on her stick. 'Why are we talking about such things? It's never any use to dwell on the past, anyway.'

She slips a hand through the crook of his arm.

'Are you sure you can make it back on foot, Margo? It would be very easy for me to hail a taxi.'

'No, no. It'll do me good to walk. Come on, let's go back home and have a cup of coffee.'

* * *

As the weather begins to get warmer, Kamal goes to his favourite Hamra café and sits outside, at a table on the pavement facing the road. This way he can enjoy the sun and the bustle around him without having to fit the conversations of his neighbours into the scheme of his own thoughts.

Out here there is the noise of oncoming traffic and the general hum of a busy Beirut morning that in being so familiar becomes almost soundless, easy to switch off and just as easy to become aware of again.

It's possible that she will come to love me with time, he thinks as he sips his coffee and takes note of passers-by. It's also likely that if I were ever to declare myself, Layla wouldn't know what I was talking about. She can seem so undecided at times and at others so determined. I'll be careful what I say at first. I'll sit her down and reach out to touch her hand and she'll surely recognize where I'm leading her. But what then?

He reaches up to smooth his hair back and knocks the coffee cup off the table. He leans down to look for it and is surprised to find that it is still in one piece. He picks it up off the ground and places it in its saucer. When he sits up again, he becomes aware of his surroundings, of the smell of car fumes, of the sun warming him and the certainty that were he to will it, love would be his for the taking.

Kamal stands on the landing and hesitates. Layla should be back from work by now, he knows, but he does not relish the idea of telling her what has happened.

He knocks on the front door and waits.

'Oh!' Layla exclaims when she opens it. 'Kamal, hello.'

He clears his throat.

'I hope I'm not disturbing you.'

'No, of course not. Would you like to come in?'

He nods and steps inside.

'I was just sitting down to a cup of tea,' Layla says, motioning him towards the sitting room. 'Will you have some?'

He takes her hand in his. She looks somewhat startled.

'Layla, I have something to tell you. I came here earlier but you were out.'

'I was at work,' she says.

'It's Margo.'

She looks puzzled.

'I'm afraid I have very sad news, my dear. Margo died during the night. She's gone.'

'Gone? What are you talking about?'

When he doesn't respond, she lifts her hands to her face and bursts into tears. He moves forward and puts his arms around her. She holds her fists against his chest and sobs so hard he is taken aback for a moment. When she lifts her face and pulls away, he leads her into the living room, sits her down and reaches for a box of tissues off the coffee table.

'This can't be true,' Layla's voice is almost a whisper. 'She was fine when I saw her yesterday. We were planning a trip to the mountains to see Fouad. I . . .'

'I'm so sorry,' he says softly.

'How did it happen?'

'It must have been sometime during the night. Her next door neighbor said she saw her standing outside on the landing just before midnight.'

'I know,' Layla nods through her tears. 'She always liked to gaze out at the stars before going to sleep.'

'She must have gone to bed after that and passed away in her sleep. I was supposed to have coffee with her this morning and when she didn't answer the door, I went inside to check on her. The door had been left unlocked.'

She looks at him and frowns.

'I want to see her.'

'She's not here, Layla. The ambulance came and took her away this morning. You had already left for work by then.'

She wipes her eyes with a tissue and he notices that her face is flushed.

'I can't believe it,' she says. 'I just can't believe that I won't ever see her again.'

She bends her head down and shields her eyes with her hands.

'I know what you mean,' Kamal says. 'I keep expecting her to climb up the stairs and turn to smile at me.'

They hear children shouting and laughing in the alleyway.

Layla stands up.

'I want to go up to her flat.'

'I have the keys right here.'

They climb up to the third floor and Kamal unlocks the door to Margo's apartment.

Layla points at one of the pots on the landing.

'There were baby birds in here a few weeks ago. She was so thrilled with them.'

They step inside.

'I've already started going through a few things,' Kamal says. 'I needed to find out if there were any relatives we needed to inform.'

'You went through Margo's things?'

Kamal hesitates.

'She made me executor of her will, Layla.'

'Oh?'

He nods.

'Some weeks ago, she asked me if I would be willing to do it and I agreed. She said she didn't want to trouble Fouad with it and it made her feel better that there was someone to take care of it. She told me where I would find all her official documents and I've already had a brief look at them.'

Layla frowns.

'She tried to broach the subject with me on several occasions but I wanted to avoid it,' she says. 'Anyway, Margo had no family left.'

'That's what I thought too at first. But actually she did. Come in here and I'll show you.'

They go into the living room and except for a large cardboard box on the dining table everything looks exactly as it always had.

Kamal takes out a sheaf of papers from the box and hands it to Layla.

'Her birth certificate is here and there are also death certificates for members of her family.'

Layla looks at the papers and shakes her head.

'I don't understand. I can't read this.'

'It's in Czech. I'm familiar with the language.'

'Czech? But she was born in Paris.'

Kamal shakes his head.

'According to these papers, she wasn't even French.'

Layla sits down in the armchair, her face flushed.

'What do you mean?'

'It seems Margo was not her real name. She came from Czechoslovakia and lost most of her family during the war. She was also Jewish.'

Layla looks at him in astonishment.

'That's impossible,' she finally says. 'She told me she was French and that her parents were practicing Catholics.'

'That's what she said to me too although I did begin to suspect not long ago that some of the things she told us about herself were not necessarily accurate. It doesn't really matter either way, does it?'

'Why wouldn't she tell me anything about all this?'

Kamal pulls out one of the four chairs tucked underneath the dining room table and urges Layla to sit down.

'I never really asked her about anything important, not really,' Layla continues. 'I was too busy talking about myself and just accepted whatever she told me.'

'I don't think she expected you to ask, Layla. I don't imagine she needed you or any of us to know about her past.'

Kamal rummages inside the cardboard box once again and takes out a small notebook.

'I found a name and address in Prague in here this morning. I telephoned but there was no answer. It's a woman with the same last name as Margo's mother which is on Margo's birth certificate. She must be a relative of some sort.'

'But Margo told me that her sister had been the only family she'd had left.'

Kamal shrugs.

'It could be a cousin or a niece.'

'Her sister didn't have any children,' says Layla. 'Margo would have told me about a close relative like that. Wouldn't she?'

She stands up and walks to the window.

'I don't think you should take any of this personally, Layla. Margo was a private person and she clearly wanted to keep the details of her life to herself. She probably had her reasons.'

'I don't understand,' Layla says, tears welling up in her eyes. 'Why would she want us to believe all these made up stories about her? Did she think we wouldn't understand? Did she think that just because we're Arab, it would upset us to know about her background? Surely she knew us better than that, Kamal.'

He walks up to her and puts an arm around her shoulders.

They watch the children playing in the alleyway for a moment. Then Layla turns to look up at him.

'I loved her, you know,' she whispers. 'No matter who she really was.'

There are those who find comfort in calling upon the spirits of the dead, Kamal knows, although for him the thought of closing his eyes now, of falling deep into himself and appealing to Margo's wisdom makes him feel more anxious than calm. What is she likely to tell me, he wonders?

He is saddened at her death in a way that he had not thought possible, as though in disappearing from his life so soon after she had entered it Margo had been meant to make a lasting impression. She had been, if briefly, both friend and confidant, and had managed, seemingly without effort, to help restore his confidence and sense of self worth.

Yet try as he might, he cannot quite grasp what it is he is now meant to understand. Is it to do with love, with finding happiness and a sense of calm, or is it something more elusive, something like finally un-covering his life's purpose, the significance of finding himself here at just this moment, of being adrift and bewildered?

There is the job of comforting Layla which he under-takes with a sense of dedication that surprises him, not because he is unable to feel compassion at her grief but because in taking her hand like this he is also leading himself into the unknown. He understands that there is no substituting doubt for sadness here, everything is as it should be, after all, clear in remaining undefined, true in being untouchable.

Down in the alleyway late one night, flustered because its geography has changed so much that he has to struggle to see his younger self at play here, Kamal attempts to stand perfectly still. Here is that little boy he once was, arms wide, head held back and palms open to the sky. Here is recognition at his fingertips.

PART FOUR

Prague

It is raining the day I arrive in Prague. In the taxi from the airport, I look out at the wet, grey streets and wrap my coat closer around me. At the hotel, a late nineteenth-century building in the old town, the small lobby smells of over-boiled vegetables and strong disinfectant and is crowded with a group of tourists and their suitcases.

Later, standing in my tiny third-floor room, my suitcase open on the single bed, I look out of the window onto a narrow cobbled street where people are bundled up in coats and scarves and rush past with their heads bent low. It is all so unfamiliar, so unlike anywhere I have been before, that I am suddenly overcome with loneliness. For a moment, I wonder what might have possessed me to come here and realize that the feeling I have in Beirut of never having to wander too far from home to be somehow refreshed has made me too insular, too inward looking.

I open a guidebook to Prague that I have brought with me and which I examined at length before coming here. The map inside it refers to the city as Praha, the Czech name for the capital. I mouth the word silently and imagine Margo saying it, her lips forming the 'ah' sound in that slow, sighing way she had.

It was still dark when Kamal drove me to the airport earlier this morning, and we were in the car for some time before he finally spoke.

'Did you manage to get through to that telephone number in Prague?' he asked.

'No. I'll try again when I get there.'

'What if you don't get a reply? What will you do then?'

I sighed.

'I know you don't think this trip is a good idea, Kamal. But I need to go, regardless of what I do or don't find out while I'm over there.'

He glanced at me for a moment before turning back to look at the road. We were only minutes from the airport by then and there were very few cars on the highway.

'I just hope you won't be disappointed,' he said. 'You might not find out any more than what we already know about Margo.'

He stopped the car outside the departures lounge and prepared to get out.

'I'll fetch my bag from the trunk and go straight in,' I told him. 'You don't need to come in with me.'

'Alright. If that's what you'd prefer.'

I reached out and hugged him.

'Thank you for driving me here so early in the morning.'

'You'll call me to let me know how things are going with you?'

'Yes. Give me a day or two, though.'

He nodded and smiled.

'Have a safe trip, then, Layla. I'm already looking forward to your return.'

Beirut and Kamal seem a million miles away now. I put my coat back on and leave the hotel, guidebook in hand. I will go for a walk. Perhaps in wandering a little, I will also manage to clear my head.

There are many things Margo would have preferred not

to remember but still they made their way into her thoughts, in the late afternoons just as it was getting darker and she, in her usual place on the floor with her back against the armchair, flinched as the light lifted itself off her shoulders and slowly faded. Enveloped in darkness, with nothing but distant noises for company, she sank into the depths of herself and dared not close her eyes; and just when she thought her breath might stop for having nowhere further to go, something would stir in her again, the sound of someone on the stairs or a sudden shift in the air, and she would heave a sigh of relief. I am an old fool, she would mutter to herself as she reached for another cigarette.

That she had dreams in her youth of lasting love was inevitable, but to hope at such a late stage that this utter loneliness, this leaning, wrenching pull towards the dark, would somehow end with someone else's constant presence was ridiculous; a sign, perhaps, of what she had come to in her old age, of frailty and her fear.

As a very young child, Margo's grandfather, a large, rambling old man with a thick white moustache and a bulbous nose, would put her on his cart and take her with him on his daily inspection of the farm. She sat back in her seat, her hands placed palms down on either side of her in an effort to stay upright, and strained to see above the rump of the enormous horse that pulled them forward. Eventually, feeling secure enough to look around her, at the trees lining both sides of the road and the vast fields beyond, Margo would sense a gradual but unmistakable joy seeping into her and filling her lungs and heart. Then, she would laugh out loud and, forgetting herself, attempt to stand up in the cart before falling back with a bump.

She remembered the sound of her grandfather's voice as he called out to the labourers or muttered quietly to himself, a surprisingly gentle voice in so large a man.

She would look up at him and wait until he glanced towards her before turning away again with a distracted air. Every little while, he would reach a big, roughened hand out to pat her head or touch her shoulder, or would stop the cart under a tree with a pull of the reigns, lift an arm up and pick a fruit, a ripened fig or a firm apple, which he would hand to her with a smile. Eat up sweetheart, he would say softly, maybe you'll grow a little taller. Later, when they arrived home, grandfather would stop the cart, jump off and lift Margo up, holding her close to him, their faces almost touching so that she could see into the light behind his dark eyes and smell his powdery skin, before putting her down abruptly and giving her a gentle push towards the house. She ran for all she was worth then, her small feet unsteady on the uneven gravel of the drive, turned at the front door to watch him leading the horse and cart towards the stables, and felt a sudden, crushing despair.

It is not as cold as it had been earlier. I loosen the woollen scarf from around my neck and glance at the map once again. Then I cross the street and decide to head for the main square.

Although I read one or two things about recent Czech history before coming here, it was only basic information about the communist era, the repression that had occurred then and the end of Soviet rule. But I know very little about what has happened since, except for being aware of the story of Vaclav Havel, the dissident poet imprisoned by the communist regime and made president after liberation.

I suddenly remember Margo saying that she had met President Havel once, had, in fact, had a beer with him at a pub in the countryside just outside Prague. He had made her laugh, she said, and confided in her about a reluctance to embrace the trappings of political life.

Goodness, how could I have forgotten that Margo did come back here at one point not too long ago? Did she tell me any more about the visit? I shake my head but nothing further comes to mind.

This part of Prague is very much as I had expected, a city out of old Europe, small and attractive in its smallness, cobbled streets and picturesque buildings that are quaint and well preserved. There is nothing in what I see here of the brashness of Beirut, rather there is a kind of reticence that in its way is also charming. Walking through these streets, I am reminded a little of Paris, although this city is less flamboyant, more intimate somehow and displaying a fragile beauty.

Is this how Margo herself had felt about her home town? She told me she'd spent several years in Prague as a young child because her father had worked there, about how she had loved it and would like one day to bring me here for a visit. If we had made a trip here together, would she have told me the truth then?

I make my way into a shopping arcade that the guidebook says is from the art nouveau period. It has a marbled atrium and hanging from the ceiling is a sculpture of a knight in armour astride an upside-down horse. The arcade also houses a cinema, what appears to be a theatre and a handful of shops, although the electric lights do little to lift the outside gloom and it is difficult to see clearly.

I spot a café and decide to go inside. I find an empty table on a raised platform in the centre of the room and sit down, looking out through the glass façade. This is the sort of place Margo and I might have come to together. She would have ordered our coffee and cakes in Czech and smiled at the waitress so that I would have felt at home rather than like an object that has been misplaced and is unlikely ever to be found again.

I open my bag and take out the two black and white

photographs of Margo that Kamal and I found in the apartment. In the first one, she could not have been more than twenty years old. Her hair is curly and dark and swept back off her face, skimming the tops of her ears so that they do not appear too large. Her eyebrows are beautifully-shaped arches that frame heavy lidded eyes and as she smiles shyly into the camera, her teeth look white and even and there is a hint of lipstick on her lips. She is wearing what looks like a crepe dress with three quarter sleeves and a button-down collar and her arms are folded neatly one over the other in her lap.

In the second photograph, she appears perhaps ten years older. Her hair is cut short and is covered with a cap worn at an angle on one side of her head. Although her brows are as neatly shaped as they are in the first photo, her eyes seem to be looking further into the distance, and rather than a smile, she has a quiet look of confidence on her face. She is wearing a military uniform of sorts, but since this is only a shot of her head and shoulders, it is not really clear what army she might have belonged to.

What had happened to this young woman in the interim period between these two photographs? Where were the places that she lived and breathed and perhaps feared for her life?

The waitress arrives with coffee and I look up to thank her. Who are you, I say out loud instead and gasp at the mistake.

The apartment was small but pleasant. Margo loved the way the light came in through the kitchen window in the mornings, warming the living room and the bedroom later in the day just before the alleyway and the building's stairwell filled with the sounds of people coming home so that she could sit by herself in the light and in silence.

When she first arrived in Beirut she had furnished it simply with a few pieces she had found in antique shops.

The rest she had shipped to Lebanon when her sister passed away and left her all the family's old furniture.

There were two deep armchairs which she had upholstered in royal blue and her father's Morris chair that reminded her of home and which she liked to lean against as she sat in her spot on the carpeted floor. She had placed the folding table and chairs that during her childhood were used only when guests came to dine in one corner of the living room, at an angle to the wall. The table was made of shiny beech wood and was engraved on its outside edges with a dainty pattern in red and gold; and the chairs, the seats of which she had covered in a deep gold material, were carved on their backs with a delicate leaf motif. Her sister had put all these things away for safe-keeping when their parents had been deported in the hope that they would eventually return to them.

Against the main wall, facing the door, was a large chest of drawers in deep cherry wood with ornate brass handles. It had once stood in the guest bedroom at her parents' home and was used to store fine linens that were brought out only on special occasions. Margo put all her bits and pieces in it, papers and money and magazines, whatever she could not find a permanent place for and things that she wanted to keep from view.

The overall effect, Margo hoped, was understated and elegant. Her aim, after all, had been to create a haven where both she and those she valued most could seek comfort. In this she believed she had succeeded.

Although she had grown to love being surrounded by exquisite objects, as a girl and later as a young woman she had been too preoccupied with herself to value the finer things in life. But as the intense passion of youth began to fade and was replaced by something more profound, a tendency towards reflection that she had not thought she could ever possess, a love for splendour surfaced within her and began to direct her life.

It had everything to do, she was certain, with her sudden but nonetheless predictable appreciation for her dead mother, a fragile woman whom she had never really tried to understand while she was still alive. She was everything that Margo – who took after her father – believed she would never be: beautiful and gentle and so refined in spirit that she sometimes appeared ethereal, as if she might vanish into thin air at one's touch.

Coming home one day to find *maman* standing in the dining room, a large swathe of cloth covering the table, and the flowers that she loved everywhere, in buckets on the floor and on the sideboard next to her, which she was busy arranging into a tall crystal vase, a pair of gardening secateurs in her gloved hand, Margo was struck by a new vision of her mother. She watched her pick out two yellow roses from a bunch, snip off their ends and then place them carefully in the vase, her movements slow but confident, her eyes, and clearly her heart, focused entirely on what she was doing. For a moment, she appeared in a completely different light, not as the wife who refused to stand up to her husband's philandering, nor as the mother who displayed weakness when she gave in to her children's demands, but as an independent being, someone who was capable of strength and who possessed distinct desires.

It was resilience, Margo realized, that must have helped her mother endure towards the end when hope had abandoned all those around her and she had been their only solace.

Margo sighed and reached for her cigarettes. In the descending darkness, she breathed in, feeling the smoke penetrate deep into her lungs like a thick, burning liquid, and then swallowed hard.

Her mother had not known she smoked and would have thought it unladylike. Yet she could not have stopped me from doing what I wanted no matter how hard she might have tried. I was too stubborn, too wild. It's just as well she didn't know, then. Just as well she never had the opportunity to see how far I would stray.

We held the memorial ceremony at Margo's flat a few days after her death, Kamal and I receiving guests as they came in, most of them unfamiliar, some I recognized from the neighbourhood or from the building. It was more of a social occasion than anything else, an opportunity for Margo's friends, who for the most part had not known of each other's existence, to get to know one another.

Fouad arrived dressed in a dark pin-striped suit and brought along with him a large tray of Arabic sweets.

'I'm so sorry,' he said, wrapping his arms around me.

I introduced him to Kamal and the two men shook hands.

'Oh, Fouad,' I said, tearful again. 'How could she be gone?'

'I can hardly believe it myself,' he said.

'I think I secretly believed she was immortal,' I said, wiping my eyes. 'That she would always be there for me. Selfish, isn't it?'

He placed his hand on my shoulder.

'There's always a bit of selfishness in our grief, my dear,' he said quietly. 'It's perfectly understandable.'

When everyone had gone, Kamal and I sat at the small table in the kitchen and marvelled at how good Margo had been at keeping her friends in separate compartments, for the most part making certain they did not meet and perhaps reveal aspects of her life that she wanted to keep hidden.

'She was clearly a very clever woman,' Kamal said with a smile of amusement.

I shook my head. 'I don't understand you.'

'What do you mean?' Kamal lifted a hand to his chin and stroked his beard.

'Doesn't it upset you that she kept so much of her life secret from us when we were supposed to be her closest friends?'

He stood up and placed an empty cup in the sink.

'I think we should start to clear up before it gets too late, don't you?' he said quietly.

'Or is it just that you don't really care what she thought of you?' I continued, following Kamal into the living room.

'What are you saying, Layla?' He swung around and looked at me. 'Is the fact that there is so much about Margo you did not know more important to you than the reality that you have lost someone you loved? How is it that this is now all about you?'

'That's not what I meant. I . . .'

'What is it you're trying to say then?' Kamal momentarily closed his eyes. 'What is it, Layla?'

I could feel my lips tremble as I tried to answer and had to pause for a moment before speaking.

'It's just that I'm not sure anymore,' I finally said. 'I mean if she felt she couldn't confide in me about the most important things in her life, then I can't have been a true friend, can I?'

On mornings when she could not bring herself to sleep much beyond dawn, Margo would get up, dress and go on the outside landing to tend her plants. She had pots filled with basil, mint, thyme and rosemary which she used in cooking and also shared with her many neighbours. There were flowering plants and evergreens, her favourites, which were in pots hanging on a white trellis attached to the outside wall, and a beautiful kumquat tree that she had placed to one side of the front door.

She bent down next to the tree and dug into the dirt with her trowel, breathing in the smell of damp earth and savouring it. These were the moments when she felt most at ease with herself, when she could lose herself in the immediacy of her surroundings and find a temporary peace.

Her first love had been an itinerant gardener who had worked for her parents one summer. A small young man with dark, curly hair and light eyes that looked away every time she tried to approach him, he eventually ventured into conversation with her, speaking hesitatingly and looking anxious as he did. In time, he seemed to look forward to her visits to the garden. They had their first kiss by the garden wall, late one night where they would not be seen, grass and trees in leaf around them and the scent of summer flowers and baked earth too with the sound of crickets in their ears. A few days later, Margo had persuaded the young man that they were meant for each other and they planned to elope at the first opportunity.

It made her laugh later, the sweet innocence of it, though the memory of *papa*, pointing a rifle over one shoulder pointing at the gardener as the two of them tried to make their escape, could still send a shiver down her spine. Her father had dismissed the poor man and marched her back to the house without saying a single word. It was her mother who told her she would be confined indoors for the rest of the summer before being sent off to boarding school. There, she would be expected to behave. She had looked at Margo for a long moment and then bent down to kiss the top of her head. My little rebel, she whispered before leaving the room.

But in those two years away from home, Margo had not learned much about discretion. She had found herself falling in love with the oddest people, the cheerful boy who rowed the boat on school trips to the lake, the middle-aged teacher who taught French literature at her school, and the handsome brother of one of her classmates who came to visit one weekend and stole the hearts of all the other girls.

Feeling more confused than ever, Margo at first attempted to contain the passion that surged within her by keeping to herself but this had not worked, and it was not long before she had caused a mini-scandal over which her father had been summoned to take her away.

My long-suffering parents, Margo thought quietly to herself, blinking back the tears. How could I have put them through so much?

Standing up again, her backbone creaked and her knees shook a little and she felt suddenly irritated with herself. She shuffled slowly to the other side of the front door to tend to the geraniums, her slippers grating against the rough ground, and began to lift her small trowel to the rectangular pot just at eye level. Inside, she found a small nest of fine twigs and moss and four tiny, speckled eggs. She gasped with delight, put her arm down and stepped back gingerly, looking around for signs of the mother. Then she turned towards the sun rising over the top of the building opposite. Even this far away, she could feel it warm her face and her shuddering skin.

Back in the hotel room, I pick up the telephone and dial the number in Margo's address book.

'Hello. Is that Anna Velka?'

'Hello. Yes, this is Anna speaking.'

I am relieved to hear her reply in English.

'I hope I'm not disturbing you. My name is Layla. I'm a friend of Margo's from Beirut and I'm in Prague for a short visit.'

'Ah, yes. How is Margo?'

I hesitate.

'I just wondered if we could meet in the next day or two, if it would be convenient for you.' I decide not to reply to the question. 'I'm pleased I finally got through to you. I tried to call before I flew over but I was told you were away on holiday.'

'Yes. I only got back on the weekend.'

There is a pause.

'Where are you staying?'

I give Anna the location of my hotel and we make arrangements to meet the next day.

'I'll come to your hotel and we'll go somewhere from there.' Anna's voice is abrupt but not unkind. 'I imagine you have something to tell me.'

'I'll see you tomorrow then? Thank you very much. Good night.'

I hang up, get into bed and run the conversation through my mind once again in the dark. Perhaps I should have told her, I think as I wrap the blanket more tightly around me, but what could I have said without knowing exactly who this woman is and what kind of effect Margo's death is likely to have on her?

Margo believed she had not done enough; not enough good to placate the demons that vexed her, nor enough to change anything in this weighted, beleaguered world. And though she had no illusions about life owing her anything, a brighter future perhaps or a more forgiving past, she felt something like anger at times, at the futility of an inner struggle that refused to abate.

Where am I going with these musings on the past, she often asked herself? It will all die with me and perhaps that might be for the best, after all.

Life in England after the war had been relatively easy,

nothing like the strain and hopelessness of previous years, although at times, even as the pain over what had happened to her family became less acute, the prospect of total defeat threatened to overwhelm her. And there had been feelings of guilt too, that after all the horror, after the violence and the unspeakable loss, she should have survived it like this, relatively intact, physically well if emotionally fragile and able to experience longings and pleasure, wanting, in fact, to revel in them, to forget and even dismiss the deprivations of the past.

When she had felt the urge to travel again, she went to visit friends in America and the West Indies, to the Far East, then to Lebanon, Jordan and Syria, finally making the unexpected decision to remain in Beirut because it seemed the one place in which she could forget who she had once been and remain anonymous enough to ensure a future of sorts for herself.

She had made friends everywhere she travelled, some close enough to confide in and others she privately referred to as 'intimate acquaintances' who suddenly came into her life through one circumstance or another and then just as quickly disappeared.

There had been a number of men after John, some whose names she could no longer remember and others who had touched her in a way that even now allowed her to recall, if not their faces, then the feel of them against her, the scent of each body becoming familiar until it had made way for someone else, another body and a new adventure.

Her love for John had been different because there had been no question of introspection then, no time to examine the wisdom in giving herself so completely to a man, in sacrificing so much for him. Still young and unable to completely control her impulses, she had seen in this Frenchman everything she had looked for since she had left home, physical splendour and strength and, once the war came along, an unwavering determination to fight the good fight regardless of the consequences.

Yet he could also be severe and unsympathetic at times, unable or unwilling to show her the gentleness she longed for and not always allowing her to make her own decisions. They had, in some ways, managed to bring out both the worst and the best in each other, lingering in resentments that Margo knew would have eventually torn the relationship apart. At the time, she put any difficulties they had down to the harshness that surrounded them. After John's death, she lamented his absence not only because she had loved him so completely but also because she had not had the opportunity to see him in a more forgiving light, away from the violence and the misery that had devastated so many lives.

But it was some time later that Margo realized that romantic love, the burning kind that left her reeling at first and then eventually settled either into a warm satisfaction or into growing contempt, was not meant for her; for good or bad, she would never have either the will nor the strength to keep it going. Perhaps all her passions had already been spent in her love for John and in the confusion that followed his death, but she came to see this was too simplistic an explanation.

Later in her life, there would be many meaningful encounters as well as long and significant friendships that would help sustain her faith both in herself and in others. Yet, throughout, she would maintain a measure of detachment, would nurture the ability to stand back and observe, though always with compassion, the complicated bonds that bound people together as well as those which tore them apart.

As she grew older and could finally entertain thoughts of her own death, the end of a remarkable journey, she found herself longing for closeness again, not the intimacy of physical love, but a certain degree of comfort in relationship, the privilege to take someone for granted at least part of the time, an undertaking to honour love right to the end. And while she was not afraid that her friendships might go amiss – she always had a facility for alleviating perceived wrongs – she became simply tired of having to try so hard, of having to constantly chip away at that shell of loneliness, only to find her obstinate, bemused self standing on the other side.

During more lucid moments, she knew it could never have been any different, realized that she had long ago made a choice to linger in her solitude and to find there, hidden behind the pretences of permanence and gratitude, an almost imperceptible joy, momentary yet forever repeating itself, until the music within it, the notes and pauses that met and parted in a light, syncopated rhythm, could finally be heard.

Margo watched the ash from her still lit cigarette drop into her lap and sighed. Pinching her thumb and middle fingers together, she attempted to remove the dirt and place it in the ashtray on the floor beside her. Her hand, large and covered with liver spots, shook as she moved it slowly back and forth. When she looked down at her trousers a moment or two later, she realized that the ash had not diminished in the least, that she had, in fact, been displacing nothing but the empty air. She put her head back and laughed out loud with no one there to hear her. When did I become so wise, she asked herself? And how long would it last?

Anna is a pretty young woman with fair hair and very light blue eyes that look at me with open curiosity. We shake hands and Anna leads the way out of the hotel lobby and towards the river. It is late afternoon and the sky is clear, the sun shining somewhat weakly onto the now dry pavements. We walk silently through back streets and for a moment I lose my bearings, until the river appears up ahead and I realize where we are.

'Would you like to go in here?' Anna stops by some steps leading up to what looks like a French bistro.

Inside is a very large L-shaped room with a glass façade that is   directly facing the water. A waiter leads us to a booth, one row from the front. The room is crowded and in the far corner, a pianist is playing waltzes. The lilting music and the noise from people's conversations are harmonious and discreet rather than loud. I feel instantly at home.

'Has something happened to Margo?' Anna asks as soon as we have sat down.

I nod.

'I'm sorry,' I say. 'I'm afraid it's not good news.'

Anna frowns.

'How long ago was it? Was she ill?'

'She died in the middle of the night, in her sleep. It was very peaceful.'

I cannot read the expression on the young woman's face.

'It happened three weeks ago, on the fifth of the month.'

I pause.

'How were you related to her?' I finally ask.

'She was my mother's cousin.'

'I'm so sorry. We tried to call you several times to let you know.'

Anna shakes her head.

'I didn't know Margo very well, you know. I met her a few times when I was a young child and then saw her one last time when she returned to Prague some years ago. My mother was still alive then.'

The waiter arrives to take our orders. I realize that

during those first few moments of our conversation, the noise in the room had faded into the background. It is back again now.

'We lived in the same building,' I continue. 'She was a very dear friend.'

Anna smiles.

'She had a way with people, didn't she?' she says. 'She was quite the family legend, you know. Everybody was curious about her.'

'Oh?'

'I mean there is a period in her life that she refused to talk about even to her own sister.'

I shake my head.

'I found some documents in her apartment after she died.' I'm not sure quite how I should put it. 'It seems there was a great deal she hadn't told me about herself.'

'About what happened during the war?'

'She always told me, along with all her other friends in Beirut, that she was French. And her real name wasn't Margo, was it?'

'No, but she apparently insisted that she be called that when she came back to Prague after the war was over.'

'I don't understand.'

The waiter brings our lemonades. I watch as Anna empties two packets of sugar into her drink and stirs it vigorously.

'She left Czechoslovakia early in 1939, just before the Nazis took over. She told her parents she was going to England to study English. They did not hear from her again after that.'

'But where did she really go?'

'Well, my mother said Margo told her afterwards that she spent the first year in London, though she didn't specify what she was doing there. But it's likely she had made contact with the British secret service even before she left

Prague because she was eventually recruited by them, the family is pretty certain of that.'

'One of the documents we found after her death showed that she was being paid a pension by the British government,' I say. 'She always told me that she was living off her inheritance. How did you find all this out?'

Anna smiles.

'Several years ago, I thought I might attempt to record the history of my mother's family,' she tells me. 'So many of the older generation were killed during the war that I felt it was important to remember them in some way. My parents somehow managed to escape detention, although the Nazis did deport my grandmother.'

'I'm sorry.'

Anna frowns.

'Anyway, I was very intrigued when I started to look into Margo's past, and decided to find out more. Later, I even took some courses at university on the history of World War Two, specifically about those who spied for the allies.'

'And Margo herself didn't tell you anything about her experiences?'

'No, but I looked up another cousin of hers, Carl. He was a university professor and was the only one who seemed to know anything at all about those "missing" years in Margo's life. He said she was trained in England by the Special Operations Executive of the British secret service and then was sent out to work undercover in occupied France.'

'But why Margo?' I ask in astonishment.

'Her father's family was from a region near the German border, so Margo and her sister grew up speaking German like natives. They also learned to speak French from their nanny and had also learned Russian. Language skills are crucial in intelligence work, so she would have been a valuable agent.'

I wrap both hands around my glass and frown.

'Did you ever confront her with all this information?' I ask.

She shakes her head. 'I only saw her once after I had spoken to Carl,' she says. 'That was the last time we met and somehow I couldn't bring myself to say anything to her. It occurred to me that there was no point in doing that. It was all long over and done with anyway.'

But I am not finished with my questions.

'She told me she had been in the French resistance and spoke to me often about her husband John,' I say. 'She said he was a French pilot and that both he and his brother were killed while on missions over Germany.'

Anna looks puzzled.

'That can't be true. The French air force was pretty much disabled after the Vichy government took over and most of France was under Nazi occupation.'

I take a deep breath and look out at the view for a moment.

'You mean John might never have existed?'

I am surprised at how upset I am at the thought that Margo might not have experienced that great love she had so often told me about.

Anna shrugs.

'When Margo came back here, she told my mother there had been a young man, a Czech lawyer, whom she had been engaged to and who was arrested by the Germans just after she left here. She said he later died in a concentration camp.'

'There would have been other men in her life after that though,' I say softly. 'Maybe she met John in France, while working with the resistance.'

'Yes, that's possible I suppose. But he could also have been a member of the Free French forces. Some of their pilots were based in Britain during the war and flew British and American planes.'

'So Margo might have met John in England during her training.'

Anna nods.

'And what about her immediate family?' I continue. 'What about her sister Emily and her parents? What happened to them?'

'Emily died only a few years back. Margo returned here to see her at the end of the war.'

'And Margo's parents?'

'They were taken to a Jewish ghetto in Poland in 1942 and died there shortly after. Emily was spared of course because she had been married to a Christian.'

The pianist switches to a livelier tune, a polka or a mazurka, and the murmurs coming from the tables around us fill my ears. I feel almost overcome with sorrow at the thought that Margo had suffered so much loss. I drop my head and weep quietly.

'I'm sorry,' I say moments later, finally recovering my breath. 'Margo was very important to me, you see, and this is all a bit overwhelming. It's difficult for me to understand why she felt unable to tell me all this herself.'

'I don't think she ever discussed it with anyone.' Anna reaches out to touch my arm. 'Not even with her family. Perhaps she felt it would serve no purpose to go over the past every time she met someone new.'

'But why maintain all the secrecy about her work in the secret service once the war was over?'

'Maybe she felt the danger of being found out was still there,' Anna says. 'I know that when she first returned here, she was concerned the communists would arrest her for being associated with the British and American forces during the war years. Besides, I think old habits die hard, isn't that what you say in English? Margo had been taught to conceal the truth about herself for so long she didn't know how to do anything different.'

'Did she not want to return to live in Prague?' I ask.

'She apparently left again very soon after coming back.'

'Then it must be true that she and Emily had a disagreement.'

'My mother told me Margo had hoped to live with Emily for a while after her return, but her sister was adamant she wouldn't. She was furious with Margo for leaving the country just before disaster struck and their parents were deported.'

Anna sighs and sips at her drink.

'But Margo was the only surviving member of her immediate family. You'd think she'd be glad to have her back after all that had happened.'

There is so much that I still do not understand.

'She went to live in England after that, didn't she, before she eventually moved to Lebanon, I mean?'

'Yes,' Anna replies. 'When we saw her that last time a few years ago, she told us she had fallen seriously ill at one point when she was living in London and her Lebanese friends took her back with them to Beirut. She told my mother later that she was very happy there.'

'You know, hearing all this, there's a part of me that feels as though I never really knew Margo,' I tell Anna.

'But isn't that true to some extent of all the people we come across in our lives?'

'Yes, perhaps you're right,' I say with a nod.

'Look, we've only just met and I don't know you very well, but do you think it would really make a difference if you were to find out more about the details of her past?'

I recall once not long ago seeing Margo in a restaurant on Hamra Street. She was sitting at a table by the window with a young man I had never met and could not see me watching her from the pavement. The two were talking animatedly, Margo putting her hand to her mouth and laughing every now and then and her companion gesturing and reaching out to lightly touch her as he spoke. They seemed on very intimate terms. That is when it occurred to me that no matter how much one loved someone and how familiar they seemed with time, there would always be something private and mysterious about them.

'I suppose not,' I reply. 'Perhaps some things are meant to remain secret.'

I look at Anna and smile.

'Still, I wish I could have found out more about her,' I say. 'This is what I came all the way to Prague for, after all.'

'Why don't you pay Carl's wife a visit? I know they were good friends. She still lives in the house she and Carl lived in before he died. It's about two hours outside of Prague. She might be able to help you.'

'Would she be willing to talk to me, do you think?'

'I'm sure that if I telephoned and told her about you she'd be happy to see you.'

'Would you do that for me?'

Anna nods and reaches out to touch my hand.

She had met the British secret service agent through Alex, the young lawyer she was engaged to. They had been sitting in a café overlooking the river one night when the Englishman had walked past and greeted Alex as though her were an old friend. When he joined them at their table, they had sat, all three of them, in silence for some time, Margo stealing glances at the stranger every now and then, annoyed at his apparent indifference but intrigued, also, by the tension his presence seemed to engender.

Later that night, Alex confessed that the meeting had been arranged beforehand. He told Margo he had been working with the British secret service for some time, and because of her intelligence and her languages they were interested in recruiting her, too. 'You could be very valuable,' he said.

'You work for the British secret service?' Margo was astonished.

But Alex had made no secret of being alarmed at what was going on in Europe and had spoken to her of his feelings about it before.

'The Nazis have plans to go far beyond Germany and Austria, Margo, there is no question of that now. We can't just sit back and watch them set up their concentration camps in this country too.'

Margo eventually saw this as an opportunity to gain the direction and excitement she had always sought in her life. There was no question of being fearful, there never had been for her, even when she heard, once in England, that Alex had been arrested and probably killed while on assignment in Germany. If anything, Alex's death had only served to strengthen her confidence.

It was early morning and Margo had left the front door to the flat open to let in some fresh air. At the kitchen table with a cup of coffee in her hand, the radio propped up on the windowsill switched on to the BBC world service news, she sighed at the memory of those days now long gone. As usual, nothing good was being reported. She reached for a packet of cigarettes and muttered angrily to herself about the terrible ways of the world.

Suddenly, she heard a scratching sound in the entrance hall and just as she prepared to get up to find out what it was, the mother sparrow from the nest on the landing appeared in the kitchen doorway. Margo watched the four baby birds who had up until then never left the nest, hop closely behind their mother, through the hallway and then towards the sitting room. Their tiny bodies were no longer bare but were covered with soft brown and black feathers.

Margo stood up very slowly, switched the radio off and moved into the kitchen doorway. For a few moments, she could hear a cacophony of chirping noises coming from the living room. She tiptoed out into the hallway and stood perfectly still as the birds reappeared and stopped only a few inches from her feet. The mother turned to the youngsters and seemed to be talking to them as they hopped nervously around her, answering back with twittering of their own.

Margo scarcely dared to breathe, her lips pressed closely together with excitement and her body, for once, free of shaking. Moments later, apparently satisfied that her babies were at last prepared to do what they were told, the mother bird hopped back out onto the landing and up onto the ledge, with her youngsters in tow. They all formed a line, standing on the concrete ledge with their delicate, twig-like feet, their tiny chests puffed out against a gentle breeze that was blowing in from the sea. Then, the mother bird suddenly leaped off the ledge, opened her wings and soared up into the sky. Margo let out a gasp as one by one, the tiny sparrows followed, flapping their wings furiously and lifting themselves higher and higher.

She watched the birds disappear into the distance, her heart hammering loudly against her chest and her ears tingling, and in that moment, the sun appearing like a soft glow on the horizon, Margo was certain that she too was capable of flight.

'Kamal?'

'Layla? I've been worried about you.'

'I . . . I needed to talk.'

'I'm here, Layla. Is everything alright?'

I sigh, not quite knowing what to say next.

'How is Prague?' he asks after a pause.

'It's beautiful, Kamal. Just as I knew it would be.'

'I'm glad.'

His voice is gentle and calming.

'I've spent most of my time walking around, trying to get to know the city. There's so much history here, and so much sadness too.'

'I can imagine that, yes.'

'I've been doing a lot of thinking too,' I laugh nervously. 'Is this the point at which I admit to you that you were right after all?'

'What about?'

'I finally got through to Margo's relative. I met her earlier today and had a long chat.'

'Yes?'

'There are moments when I can see her here clearly, Kamal, and others when I wonder why I'm delving into a past that she kept from me, from all of us. Did she really think of us as friends, Kamal, or were we simply people she came across at a certain point in her life?'

Kamal clears his throat.

'Perhaps we should wait and talk about this when you get back,' he says. 'It's a lot for you to have to take in all at once, Layla. Just stop thinking about it too much and try to enjoy the few days you have left there.'

I hear someone walking past my door and pause for a moment.

'Are you alright?' Kamal asks.

'Sorry. I was just thinking. Anna, the young woman I met with today, told me that Margo kept her past a secret from everyone, including her own family. In England, after the war, she used an assumed name and fabricated a background for herself long before she came to Beirut.

'It seems she lost most of her family in concentration camps. She only escaped because she was out of the country when they came for them.'

We relapse into a long silence.

178

'I'm not surprised she wanted to conceal the truth then,' Kamal finally says.

'What do you mean?'

'I don't think Margo wanted to forget what happened. How could one forget anything so terrible?'

'What is it then?'

'She must have felt that telling the truth would stop her from starting a new life. If she had revealed the truth about herself, it would have clouded all her future relationships. I'm sure the last thing she would have wanted people to feel for her was pity.'

'But wouldn't she have realized that not telling the truth about herself might have a negative effect on her friendships? Aren't we supposed to trust those we love with our true selves?'

I hear him sigh.

'Yes, of course,' Kamal says. 'But things aren't always so straightforward, you know. Margo was a very complex personality and her relationships reflected that. Besides, she never professed to being perfect, did she? You're the one who wanted her to appear blameless, Layla. She tried to make you see that she was vulnerable and riddled with faults and uncertainty just like the rest of us but that's not the picture you wanted to keep of her.'

The window in my room is open and through the inky darkness outside, the lights of Prague flicker and fade.

'Margo loved you, Layla,' Kamal continues softly. 'Regardless of what she might or might not have told you about her past. We all have different ways of dealing with our sorrows and perhaps by keeping the truth from us, she was only trying to cope with her own. Why can't you bring yourself to give her the benefit of the doubt, Layla?'

'I . . . I just don't know what to think anymore,' I say, feeling more confused than ever. 'I'm going to meet with another relative of Margo's tomorrow. Perhaps she'll be able to tell me more.'

'Who is she?'

'Someone Anna told me about. I'll call you in a day or two, Kamal.'

'Alright. Take care of yourself until then, Layla.'

'I will. You take care too.'

The house appears behind a horizontal line of tall trees whose leaves flutter and glisten in the rain. As the taxi winds its way down the gravel path towards it, I lean forward to get a better look. The one-storey structure is painted a deep, mottled grey and has large rectangular windows all along its front façade. The front door is made of some kind of heavy, dark wood and there are pot plants filled with greenery on either side of it.

I pay the driver and get out of the taxi with my suitcase in one hand and handbag in the other. I will stay the night, at my host's invitation, and go straight to the airport from here tomorrow morning.

The front door opens just as I reach it. A woman with a pleasantly round face, light eyes and blonde hair tied back in a bun appears behind it.

'Layla?' she says. 'I'm Patricia. Please come in.'

'Thank you.'

I put my suitcase down and we shake hands.

'Was the drive down alright?' Patricia asks in clear, slightly accented English.

I nod.

'Yes, thank you. I'm very glad you insisted on speaking to the driver before we left Prague, though. I don't think I could have made myself understood otherwise.'

She smiles and gestures for me to follow her. We turn left and go down one step into a long living room where a log fire is burning.

'It might be spring but the weather is still cold and damp,' she turns to me. 'I thought it would be nice to have our meal by the fire. Please make yourself comfortable. I won't be long.'

She walks away, towards the far end of the room where I can now see an open-plan kitchen and dining area. I sit down in an armchair by the fire and look around me. Not for the first time since my arrival in Prague, I wonder just what I was expecting to find out about Margo here that I didn't already know. I look up to see Patricia making her way to the sofa opposite me.

'Just a few more minutes and it will be ready,' she says with a smile.

'I . . . You are really very kind to go to all this trouble and let me come here and talk to you,' I tell her. 'Despite the fact that I'm a virtual stranger to you, that is.'

'Please,' she says, shaking her head. 'You are a good friend of Margo's and that's all I needed to know. Besides, it's nice to have company from time to time. It's been too quiet here since Carl died.'

'I'm sorry about that.'

'My husband had a long and rich life, thank goodness, but I do miss him,' she says looking straight at me.

I turn my head to look at the fire and let the flames warm my face for a moment.

'Margo confided in you?' I finally ask.

Patricia puts her head back and laughs.

'We were good friends and she told me some things about herself, yes. Not everything, though. She liked to surround herself with a bit of mystery, I think.

'I met Margo when Carl and I got married in the mid-sixties. I was here studying, from Switzerland where I come from originally, when I met Carl. I was his second wife, of course, and he was a great deal older than I was. I guess you could say I was young, very

181

much in love and also very naïve. Margo was a great support to me.'

'She would have been living in England at the time,' I say. 'Did she visit here regularly?'

'She did come and stay with us a couple of times but I really got to know her during my trips to London. I went there for my painting exhibitions, you see, usually without Carl, so Margo and I had the opportunity to spend a lot of time together on a regular basis. She was serious and still capable of having fun and I loved that about her. She influenced my thinking in a way that no one else did and really helped me understand myself better. I missed her terribly after she left England.'

'I know exactly what you mean. Margo had that kind of effect on me too. There was a purity about her, I don't mean an absolute goodness or anything, but a kind of simplicity that gave me comfort. It's difficult to explain.'

'I understand.'

We pause for a moment. I look at the paintings on the walls around us.

'Are these yours?' I ask.

'Most of them, yes.'

I point to a painting just above the fireplace. Four bold strokes of red, green, orange and purple fall against a dark, nearly black background. The colours are vivid and the feeling is compelling.

'It's beautiful,' I say, turning to Patricia.

'Thank you.'

'Anna told me you're a well-known artist and that your work has been shown in galleries all over Europe.'

Patricia bows her head slightly before looking up again.

'Not so much these days, I'm afraid. I produce a lot less work than I used to when I was younger. But I suppose it's also because I'm not so interested in exhibiting any more.'

'Why not?'

She shrugs.

'I don't really know. Perhaps recognition from the art world is no long so important to me.'

She stands up.

'I'll just get our food. Let me show you to your room first, Layla, and you can freshen up if you need to.'

We eat by the fire, potato stew with rice and fruits and a variety of breads and cheeses for afters. I feel comfortable here and conversation comes easily. I tell Patricia about my life in Beirut, about how my friendship with Margo helped me cope with the difficulties I encountered soon after my return there and the sense of loss I have felt since her death.

'I realize now that in many ways I didn't really know her, you know?' I say at the end of the meal. 'I was too preoccupied with myself to give her a proper chance to tell me about it.'

'You're assuming that she would have been willing to tell you,' Patricia says, somewhat abruptly.

I look up in surprise.

'We were close friends, I told her about everything that was important to me . . .'

Patricia puts her coffee cup on the table between us and shakes her head.

'Maybe Margo thought her past was no longer important,' she says.

'But we all bring our pasts into relationships,' I protest. 'How else would we be certain of being wholly accepted?'

'Margo felt the need to compartmentalize different aspects of her life, I think. Besides, she didn't think she was special just because of what she'd gone through during the war. Millions of people suffered as a result of it and she knew she wasn't alone in losing people she loved.'

'So why did she feel the need to keep it all secret?'

183

'She just didn't want the past to continue to dominate her life and chose not to dwell on it by talking about it constantly. Surely that wasn't wrong?'

'No, I suppose not,' I sigh. 'You must think I'm foolish, coming here and making a fuss about stories that Margo herself was probably no longer interested in.'

'Don't be so hard on yourself, Layla. I always thought there was something very romantic about Margo's past too. Whenever she came to stay with us, she used to come out to my studio in the garden and sit and smoke and talk while I worked. She told me about her years in the secret service, about the man she fell in love with and lost.'

'So John really existed?' I ask, my heart skipping a beat. Patricia gets up to stoke the fire.

'She told me they had been on mission together in France when he was arrested by the Gestapo. She never saw him again.'

'It's so sad. They can't have been married long when it happened.'

She sits down again and looks at me with a frown.

'But John was already married,' Patricia says. 'He sent his wife and children to America very early in the war, some time before Margo met him.'

I shake my head.

'It's difficult to work out what among all the things she told me was actually true,' I say.

'His family stayed on in the United States after the war. Margo eventually travelled there to see them.'

'But why?'

'He had apparently made her promise to make sure they were alright if ever he was killed, so she followed them to America and went back again to visit them a few times after that.'

'His wife knew Margo and John had been lovers?'

184

'Margo didn't tell her but she figured it out for herself, told Margo that it hadn't been his only extra-marital affair.'

I open my mouth in surprise.

'Why do you look so shocked?' Patricia laughs.

'But whenever she spoke about him, she sounded like they'd been very much in love, that she had been the love of his life and he hers.'

'They did love each other very much, I'm sure. I just think relationships were much more intense, more urgent at that time. People didn't know whether or not they would survive the war and so they threw caution to the wind when it came to love.'

'What did Margo tell you about John's family?'

'She spoke a lot about the children, there were two girls and a boy. She grew to love them, the boy especially because he looked so much like his father. I suppose she felt they were her only link to John.'

'Did she keep in touch with them?'

'Yes, for a while. They wrote and she telephoned them from time to time, sent them presents for their birthdays and so on. But once they grew up and found out about her relationship with John, that she had managed to escape arrest while their father ended up being murdered, they were less inclined to be friendly. Their mother was already dead by then.'

Patricia sighed.

'The last time Margo spoke to the son he told her he didn't want her calling him again and that his sisters felt the same way he did,' she continued. 'She took it very hard. I think that's when things started to fall apart for her. It's almost as if she didn't really grieve the loss of John until twenty years after his death, as if she didn't really allow the effects of the war to affect her until long after it was over.'

'Poor Margo.'

'No,' Patricia shakes her head. 'She made her choices and lived with the consequences. You shouldn't make judgments about her life and feel sorry for her. She was too proud for that.'

It is beginning to grow dark outside. I stand up feeling suddenly ashamed.

'You're right, of course,' I say.

'I'm sorry, I didn't intend for that to sound like a reprimand,' Patricia says kindly. 'I'm sure you don't mean to judge Margo. You were her friend and you loved her, after all.'

'No. You were right. Margo's death is not about me and my reaction to it. I've been so slow to understand.'

Later that night, standing in Patricia's guest bedroom looking out at the trees that line the edge of the front garden, I realize why Margo had kept a part of herself so well hidden from many of those who had loved her. She must have felt that every time she told her story, something in it dissipated, flew away from her and took on new dimensions, meant different things to different people, until it became distorted. Keeping it secret was the best way for it to remain intact.

Seeing John's children the first time she had visited them in the United States had been a shock, the boy especially, slim and highly strung like his father had been, his features still soft, though, his eyes liquid as he stared at Margo. Your father was my friend, she had said, bending slightly towards him. Then the sudden drawing of his child's breath, a whiff of sweetness past her nostrils, and all the sorrow at her lover's death in that instant suddenly dispelled.

Their mother had been unexpectedly kind, had welcomed news of John's last few months, pressing Margo to tell her still more as the two of them sat in the ample shade of an oak tree in a back garden that was also filled with roses and lavender and other fragrant flowers. We have lived here, the children and I, ever since we came to this country, John's wife began, and although it's time this house felt like a home, something has always been missing here for me. What you bring of him now, Margo, is a great comfort, and I can only be thankful to you for that.

Margo had not had the strength to feel humbled at the time, but later she did wonder if it was then that she began to embellish accounts of the war with her own imaginings, stories that eventually ran away from her until they dissembled and were no longer hers. That she had loved John with every fibre of her being was without question, even knowing as she did that he was not hers to keep and thought only of returning to his family once the war was over. But she also understood that there was something in her that dreamed of them staying together, that almost wished the war would last longer so that his desire for her might also endure. But that was not to be, as her babies also were not to be. These things she had learned to accept.

She went back again several times to visit John's family in America , had even thought at one point of staying on there simply to be near them. But what good would it have done, after all, to attempt to fill the emptiness with more fantasy? Attachment to others was no substitute for true connection, she knew, need was not an alternative to love, even for someone as old as she.

There were days when she remembered being young so vividly she would feel herself displaced in time, in an old, weakening body that belonged to someone else. Then, trying to get up off the floor, sitting up on one knee and grabbing onto the armchair, pulling herself up slowly to find herself standing slightly unsteadily so that she had to pause to look around for a moment, she would suddenly recall her age and smile ruefully to herself. It was time, perhaps, to let go, for there could be no question of beginning anew, of reinventing home.

She was curious about death, had come into frequent contact with it both as a young woman and later in her work in hospitals. And while she had experienced the loss of her parents at a distance she felt it still as something intimate and final, a departure from her old self and a definite step towards the detachment she had always craved.

Long after the memory of her parents had begun to fade, she had sat with the condemned children at the hospital where she worked in the same way as she did with those whom she knew would eventually get well, quietly and without intention of intrusion. The children allowed her this privilege, she knew, because in dying they had no notion of self loss and pity.

There had been one little boy in particular, a brown-skinned four year old with huge eyes, whose body had whittled away even as his spirit seemed to grow diffuse, floating into all those around him, little bits of wonder that would never fade. She had sat beside him, held his little hand and gazed into his eyes, into the deep, fluid quietness that he had become, and once he was gone, held his mother, a great strapping woman who had not until then shown any emotion, as she sobbed uncontrollably.

Yet with each death that had touched her, Margo had felt herself drift further beyond the will to fight, knowing that all things and all people must end just as they begin, alone and with no thought of the coming moment, without a history to cling to, without wish of reprieve.

She sat down on the edge of her bed, turned out the bedside lamp and lifted first one leg and then the other onto the mattress before lying back on her pillow. There was a hint of moonlight coming through the window and she was distracted for a moment by the shadowy patterns on the ceiling. She realized that if she was happy it was because she meant to be so.

She delighted in many things these days, her miniature garden, the feel of a hot mug of coffee between her hands, the company of friends and intelligent conversation; and when confronted with hope, whether in herself or within the hearts of others, only waited until it had retreated to that place where all false expectations must go. Yet she could not help but harbour a wish that the end come gently, not because she thought she deserved it, she had long given up thinking of herself as in any way special, but simply because despite her lack of faith in any kind of god, she did, after all, believe in infinite grace.

I can see you here, Margo, your small figure moving confidently down one of these narrow streets, your head held high and your feet noiseless on the pavement. You stop at a red brick building on the corner of a cobbled street, put your suitcase down and search for your sister's name on the list of tenants to the right of the doorway. When you ring the bell and hear the click that signals the unlocking of the door, you quickly push it open, feeling a shiver of excitement go through you at the prospect of this longed for homecoming.

Once inside the stairwell, you are momentarily surprised at not finding Emily running down the stairs to greet you. You shrug your shoulders, lift the suitcase up with both hands and make your way slowly up to the third floor. It is dark and there is a danger that you will trip and fall, but inside you a quiet joy seems to lift you towards the light; and in the surrounding air, in the silence that permeates it, there is a final release.

What happened next, Margo? Did Emily open the door, unsmiling and cold? Did you throw your arms about her and finally allow yourself to weep? How long was it before you became aware that she was not returning your embrace? How long before you pulled away, reached into the pocket of your handbag for a handkerchief and not finding one there, finally lifted your eyes to hers and found there the absence of love that you had always dreaded?

Afterwards, your eyes red but dry, you walk out again, to this quiet corner at the top of the street, sit on a bench in the shade of this tree and wait for calm to descend. For a moment, you savour the silence around you, look up into the leaves of the tree as they loop and flicker in the light before finally making your decision. You will leave Prague and discard a secret self that still weighs heavily on your heart and somewhere, remake yours into a more ordinary life, a life beyond expectation, beyond dreams.

PART FIVE

War

When war breaks out a few days after Layla's return from Prague, it is as sudden as it is brutal. Early on the morning after Hizbullah kidnaps two Israeli soldiers in southern Lebanon, Israeli planes bomb Beirut International Airport.

Layla hears the explosions and jumps out of bed. She rushes up to the third floor landing to watch smoke rise from the runway in the distance. In that moment between wakefulness and sleep, she feels suddenly breathless, the pulse in her neck beating hard against her skin and her mind unfocused.

Soon, other tenants join her on the landing, most, like her, still in their pyjamas, all looking dazed and anxious. She feels an arm wrap itself around her shoulders and looks up to see Kamal.

'Hey,' he says softly. 'Are you alright?'

'What's going on, Kamal? What's happening to us?'

She feels him take a deep breath.

'I think it's best if we go back inside now, *habibti*,' he says. 'Come on. We'll turn the radio on for the news.'

He steers her towards the stairs, then stops on the way downstairs to talk to other neighbours who seem to be in shock as the deep rumble of fighter jets flying overhead grows louder.

Layla hears someone say, 'If they've started with attacking the airport, then things are likely to get much worse.'

'Do you mean they might bomb the city next?' someone else asks. 'Is that possible?'

In the days that follow, they watch as Beirut quickly empties of people, car loads of them racing up the main highway, through the mountains, towards the Syrian border and eventually to Damascus and Amman and onto flights that would take them to further destinations, to the Gulf, Europe ,the United States and Australia. In the meantime, the attacks continue, again on the airport, on southern Beirut and the Bekaa region, as all over the south Hizbullah fighters and the Israeli army fight fierce battles. The bombardment destroys roads, bridges, buildings and homes, burying under mountains of rubble those not lucky enough to get away in time and making movement between different parts of the country increasingly difficult.

Layla and Kamal spend hours indoors, drinking coffee, reading newspapers and listening to the news. Their part of the city remains safe although even if it weren't, Kamal tells her, taking shelter in the basement would not be a good idea.

'When there is aerial bombing, you just get buried under tons of rubble if the building you are in is bombed,' he says.

'And that's somehow supposed to make me feel better?'

But Layla is only half-joking as she says this.

Still, it seems that most people have come to the same conclusion, either packing up and leaving for towns and villages further north or remaining in their homes in the hope that their neighbourhoods will not be bombarded.

Whenever Layla and Kamal go out, to get something

essential or simply to gaze up at the sky, they bump into neighbours who comfort one another with talk of what is to come and the likely outcome of it all. She sees the reality of what she is feeling on other people's faces. There is something about shock that makes their features appear expressionless, their eyes vacant and gestures almost robot-like.

As the fighting continues, those made homeless attempt to escape the bombing. Inner Beirut fills up with refugees from the southern suburbs of the city as well as from towns and villages in the south, hundreds of thousands of them, mostly women, the elderly and children, making their way gingerly along ruined roads towards safety, carrying what they can of their belongings and not certain of where they will end up. Any hope that other Arab countries or the United States and Europe would be able to put pressure on Israel to stop its aerial bombardment is very soon shattered. Lebanon, it seems to Layla, will once again have to bear the brunt of the Middle East conflict on its own.

One morning, Kamal takes Layla to the Sanayeh gardens, a five-minute walk from their building and where he and his brothers played as children, to see the people who have pitched makeshift tents between the trees. Dozens of volunteers are busy distributing aid to the refugees, bedding and food and drink. Layla looks on in shock, at the same time feeling almost overwhelming relief that she still has a bed to sleep on and a home as yet untouched by the bombing.

'This shouldn't be happening,' she says, gripping Kamal's hand tightly.

'I know.'

A friend moves into Kamal's apartment with his wife and two children after their home elsewhere in the city is destroyed. It then seems natural that Kamal move into

Layla's apartment for the duration of the war. At night, with the distant rumble of aircraft relentless above, the two of them fall into a pattern of intermittent sleeplessness, he stretched out on the sitting room sofa, and she curled up in bed wondering how she will find the strength to go on.

Slowly, the whole building fills up with people who have nowhere else to go as friends and relatives take them in. Still, despite their numbers, the refugees are clearly subdued, going about their days in relative quiet, their presence felt but unheard. Layla sees the men either seated on the steps or standing at the building's entrance downstairs with transistor radios glued to their ears for news of the war. The women, most of them veiled and wearing long colourful dresses, spend their time indoors cooking and doing other household chores. Occasionally, Layla gets the opportunity to greet them with a few words but that is all. They are reticent, preoccupied, and she understands that. Most of them, she knows, are aware that once they do return to their villages, there might be nothing left for them there.

Shortages begin to have an impact on people's everyday lives. Long queues appear outside petrol stations with fights breaking out every now and then. When Layla goes out to do the shopping, fresh produce is hard to find and supermarket shelves are nearly empty of essentials like oil, sugar and flour. When Lebanon's largest dairy farm in the Bekaa is bombed, fresh milk is no longer available and powdered milk also starts to disappear from the shops.

There are hours in the day when the neighbourhood goes unusually still. The energy Layla once felt every time she went out is hardly discernable. A blanket of quietness muffles the sounds of living around her so that she sometimes imagines herself in a city of ghosts. Days go by when she can no longer remember what her existence had been like before the bombing began, what joy might have felt like and where the tingling in her fingers that once signalled contentment has gone.

'I . . . I'm not holding out too well, am I?' she tells Kamal one day, a tremor in her voice.

He smiles and shakes his head.

'I always thought I was stronger than this, Kamal. I feel so frustrated with myself.'

Layla lets her head fall and squeezes her eyes shut to stop the tears from falling. Then she hears Kamal clear his throat.

'Would you like us to get out?'

She opens her eyes to look up at him again.

'Leave Lebanon, you mean?'

He nods.

During all the years away from home, despite being too young to truly appreciate the implications of a savage civil war, Layla had experienced a sense of overwhelming help-lessness. The decision to leave Lebanon had been made by her parents and she had had no choice but to go along with it.

'There is no shame in wanting to escape war, Layla,' Kamal says. 'If that is what you want to do, then it can be arranged.'

She shakes her head. There can be no question of running away from this.

'That's not what I mean, Kamal.'

Later, during a lull in the bombardment, they stand on the third-floor landing outside Margo's empty apartment. The sky is black and the air, humid and oppressive, is clear. They hear children playing in the alleyway below and for a brief moment, Layla allows herself the thought that things have returned to normal.

'There are some things at least that even war cannot change,' she says with a long sigh. Then turning to look behind them: 'You know, it's almost as if any minute now Margo might come through that door to join us, just as she used to.'

Kamal moves closer to her and lays a hand on her arm. 'I miss her too,' he says. 'Especially now.'

'What would she have made of all of this, do you think?'

They are both leaning against the balustrade now, looking out at the view, their bodies touching.

'I'm not really sure,' Kamal replies. 'I don't think she would have been as shaken by the war as we have been.'

He chuckled.

'She always said there was nothing in life that she hadn't experienced either directly or indirectly and that nothing could really shock her. I think she would have shown resilience. After all, this sort of thing had happened to her before.'

Layla shifts her body slightly so that she is looking at him.

'All those questions I had about Margo's life and the things Anna and Patricia told me about her when I was in Prague seem so far away now,' she says.

A child's squeal rises up from the alleyway and Layla pauses for a moment.

'It's pointless to care so much about things that happened in the past when dealing with what's going on right now is such a struggle. Sometimes I feel as if there is something vital I am meant to understand at this point in my life but it's always just out of reach.'

Kamal puts a hand up to her face, his eyes shining through the growing darkness, his features shaped by shadow. He pulls her gently towards him until she can feel his breath brush her cheek, then he wraps her in his arms. She is like a fragile flower in his embrace.

'Perhaps it's a lot closer than you imagine, Layla,' he whispers in her ear.

She lifts her head up in astonishment only to encounter the glow of a million stars.

Layla is unable to sleep and decides to get up and make herself something hot to drink. Kamal does not stir on the sofa as she tiptoes into the kitchen and shuts the door behind her in order not to disturb him.

Only a few days ago, while going through what remained of Margo's things, she had found an old notebook in which Margo had written an account of some of her experiences during the war.

'Look, Kamal,' Layla said excitedly as she leafed through the notebook. 'It has a title too, "Hut Thirteen". What do you think that means?'

She later explained to him, once she had finished reading the manuscript, that thirteen was the number of the pre-fabricated hut Margo had stayed in, along with several other women, during her training with the British army just before going on missions into occupied France.

'It's all about the women who were there with her. They were a disparate bunch, it seems, although she writes about them with extraordinary tenderness and there seems to have been exceptional camaraderie between them.'

The notebook brings Margo's mysterious past back to mind, although Layla is glad to discover that what she feels about it now is closer to curiosity than resentment.

She boils water and pours it over a sachet of traditional flower tea. A mixed aroma of roses, orange blossoms and herbs and spices rises from the cup.

She sits down at the kitchen table with her tea and opens up the notebook. She leafs through the pages, studying the handwriting, bold and sturdy and unlike the shaky hand that Margo had had later in her life. She comes upon a black and white photograph hidden between two pages somewhere in the middle of the notebook and pulls it out. She has seen it before but would like to have a second look. It shows a group of people, young men and women, sitting around a large dinner table where the remains of a meal have yet to be cleared away. All the diners are looking at the camera, some with their half-full wine glasses lifted before them in a gesture of salute. Margo has a cigarette in one hand and her other arm is draped over the back of the chair beside her. She looks relaxed, her smile open and warm. Layla peruses the other faces in the photograph, wondering once again which of the men might be John.

'May I join you?'

She looks up to find Kamal in the doorway.

'Oh, I'm sorry. Did I wake you after all?' Layla says.

'It's alright. That tea smells wonderful.'

'The water in the kettle is still hot.'

She gets up but Kamal gently pushes her gently back onto the chair.

'I'll do it, *habibti*,' he says firmly. 'Is that Margo's notebook?'

She nods.

'I'm just looking over that picture again. You know, the one we found of her and her friends. I'm pretty certain John is the man in the middle. The one with the deep-set eyes and the scarf wrapped around his neck.'

Kamal sits down at the table with his teacup.

'He's certainly the most impressive looking of the lot,' he says, taking the photograph from Layla and bringing it up close to his face.

John has the sharp features that she had always imagined he had and the look on his face is intense enough to set him apart from the rest.

'I wonder sometimes if he really did love her,' Layla says. 'Margo told me he could be almost ruthless at times, even when it came to his relationship with her.'

'Hmm. Maybe it was because of the circumstances that surrounded them at the time.'

Kamal puts the photograph back on the table and looks back at Layla.

'That's what I said to Margo when she told me about it,' she says. 'But since I found out that he was already married when they became lovers, somehow I feel it was more than the war that made him behave that way. I don't think he was capable of giving her what she needed.'

'Like what?' Kamal sits back in his chair and sips at his tea.

'I mean they were intimate, but he doesn't seem to have been very affectionate.'

Kamal puts his cup down.

'You don't think he loved her.'

Layla shrugs.

'She wasn't his only affair and he already had a wife and children when he met her, so maybe she wasn't as important to him as he clearly was to her. I'm sure there was passion between them, that's certainly the impression Margo gave me. But she never described him as being tender or warm towards her. You know when a man's love makes a woman feel she is cherished above all others?'

Layla pauses. The night is quiet, with no planes overhead and no rumbling in the distance. Is the war finally over then, she wonders?

'It's the kind of happiness she wanted for me, isn't it?' she says, wrapping her arms around herself.

'Fouad phoned earlier,' Kamal says. 'He wanted us to know that we're welcome to stay with him if we want to get away from the bombardment. Would you like to do that?'

Layla sighs.

'Why, do you think it's safer up in the mountains?' she asks.

'I think it probably is, yes.'

'I don't know, Kamal, I wouldn't feel too happy about leaving the apartment empty at a time like this. What if it's occupied by refugees and what if once we leave we're unable to get back?'

'There's no point worrying about things over which we have no control, Layla,' Kamal continues gently. 'Our neighbours will look out for the flat in our absence. We can go up in the car so it shouldn't be a problem returning, and I'm sure I can manage to get us enough petrol for the trip. It would be good to get away from the city.'

He reaches out to lay a hand on her arm.

'*Habibti*, we've talked before about where we might scatter Margo's ashes, and we still haven't had the chance to do it because of the war. I was thinking that maybe close to Fouad's house, which she knew and loved, would be the perfect place.'

She stands up and turns away from him.

'What makes you think this is the right time for that?' she asks, surprised at her anger. 'And why are you in such a hurry to get rid of Margo's ashes, anyway?'

'I don't understand,' he sounds hurt. 'What have I said to upset you?'

'Things are difficult enough as they are, Kamal, without our getting into this kind of discussion now. We're in the middle of a terrible war and everything is so uncertain. How can this be a good time to lay Margo to rest?'

Even as she says this, she realizes how absurd it must sound. Margo had stipulated in her will that Layla make the decision about where her ashes should go and Layla is only now beginning to understand why she might have done that. She feels her irritation dissipate. Kamal comes up behind her and wraps his arms around her.

'I know what you're going to say,' she says with a nervous laugh. 'This is more about what I feel than it is about the right place for Margo's ashes, isn't it?'

They stand for a moment, Layla resting her head on Kamal's shoulders, feeling safe and weeping quietly.

'I know it sounds unreasonable but I'm not ready yet, Kamal,' she finally says. 'Let's wait a little longer, please.'

She turns to look at him and they kiss.

They are at the beginning of everything, it seems, the start of love and the unnerving bewilderment that accompanies it. They go through each day in the knowledge that at its end, once dusk settles and darkness inches its way across the beckoning sky, everything will narrow itself down to that one moment during which they will once again meet and fall into each other's arms. They make love slowly, Layla's eyes alternately opening and closing as she moves and Kamal in constant fear of losing himself; and once they wake up after a brief sleep, when it is still night and Beirut seems to breathe as quietly as they do, they lie still and silent, gathering together the remains of unfinished dreams.

To Layla, Kamal is unfamiliar only in the most super-ficial ways. She realizes, for example, that she is not really familiar with his everyday likes and dislikes, that she could not, if she were asked, recall the exact shape of his nose nor the angle at which he holds his head when he is deep in thought. But she is nonetheless certain of the untiring gentleness in him and can feel her heart, for so long untethered and drifting, finally settling into the ease of recognition.

And for his part, there is a quiet loveliness that envelopes Kamal's otherwise fragile existence now, a kind of strengthen-ing of the soul that he dare not examine lest it suddenly abandon him. In Layla he sees beauty and grace and also an inkling of the woman she is likely to become. She is, he thinks, at once passionate and unsure, vibrant as well as at times subdued, and harbours deep within her a capacity for tenderness that has the power at times to astonish him.

The war continues and is somehow incorporated into their love and the uncertainty of their present life. The city they once knew as vibrant and untiring begins to lose its light, its colour fading, its energy sapped. The Israelis continue their relentless bombardment of Lebanon and Hizbullah fights back in the south, firing rockets into northern Israel. Everywhere, as always, civilians bear the brunt. Layla wonders how this ruthless aggression by one country against another that is so much weaker should occur. It is not naïve to wonder about the total absence of justice, she tells Kamal. How could this be happening to us? Ask the Palestinians what they think, he replies with bitterness.

When they can no longer bear to hear news of the fighting, Layla and Kamal go for long walks, crossing back and forth through different Beirut neighbourhoods, and revisit their childhood haunts one by one, the *raouche* rock that juts out of the sea and reminds Layla of long evenings strolling in its view eating corn on the cob and drinking *jillab*; the narrow byways of their own neighbourhood as Kamal recounts stories of his childhood with his two brothers; and Hamra Street once filled with the cheerful people of Ras Beirut.

Kamal tells her also about days of roses, when Beirut was bright and breezy and full of promise and he, a young man with ideas big enough to encircle the whole world, was in control of his own fate. There was nothing that could not be openly discussed, he says, no one we really needed to fear and everywhere around us, woven into the fabric of our everyday lives, was the certainty that change was within our reach.

He stops in mid-sentence and looks beyond her. He gestures at that gilded, far-flung past. It felt unlike anything else, we could not help but be touched, be wholly embraced by life in those days. Where did it all go and how will I ever manage to describe it to you as it truly was? He shakes his head. Then civil war broke out and it became clear to those of us who had dared to dream of a different Arab world that the people were not free to make their own decisions, that there was too much at stake for the West here for us to be left alone. And our own leadership was the biggest hurdle to overcome.

But Layla understands exactly, pictures fluid days, waves of time and thought that rise and abate without obstacle. Surely this is what you and those like you managed to see, she tells him, the certainty that this country, despite its fragility and history of turbulence, would always be worthy of being loved?

Later, when she thinks about how love and war are changing her, she also sees pictures in her mind's eye of Margo and John, perhaps sitting in a café overlooking a small, beautiful square in Paris where farmers once sold an abundance of produce, vegetables and fruits of all kinds, pungent cheeses and all manner of country breads. Looking casually around them, the lovers would have dipped chunks of buttered baguette into large bowls of milky coffee and, once they were done, smoked one cigarette between them, blowing smoke into the air and watching it disperse, blending in with the subdued liveliness of a city that had once been the jewel of Europe.

They would have had aliases and stories that went with them, Layla imagines, perhaps posing as husband and wife and sharing a sparsely furnished *chambre de bonne* at the top of a four-storey building overlooking the rooftops of Paris. That first night together, both weary at the thought of what lay ahead of them, John would have turned out the light, drawn Margo to him onto the narrow bed that was pushed up against one wall and made love to her, perhaps a little roughly at first, then with more tenderness, until they experienced the relief they had both been seeking.

Like those lovers from long ago, Kamal and Layla venture out only rarely at night simply because they feel themselves more exposed in the dark, as if their love might suddenly ignite sparks that will be clearly visible to everyone or the war might somehow disturb them in places where they like to imagine it cannot.

Instead, they spend evenings sitting on plastic chairs on the landing just outside Margo's flat which remains without tenants, sipping cold beers out of the bottle and picking at salted pumpkin and sunflower seeds. From their vantage point, they observe the lights of the city, only occasionally talking to anyone going past about the latest news of the war or murmuring quietly to each other so that no one else will hear them

'Sometimes,' Layla leans forward and whispers to Kamal, 'I wonder what they think of us when they see us together like this?'

He looks at her.

'Do you think our neighbours know we are lovers and somehow disapprove?' she continues.

'Why, have you noticed a change in their attitude towards you?'

She shakes her head and sighs.

'No, I suppose not. Still . . .'

They are startled by the sound of a very loud car horn in the street below.

'Do you want to know what I think?' Kamal finally asks.

Layla nods.

'I think people here are very different now from the

way they were in the past,' he says quietly. 'Their priorities have changed. Our neighbours are too busy trying to look after themselves to worry about what two social misfits like you and me might be up to.'

'They're opening up the local school to incoming refugees,' Kamal says as he comes through the front door and into the kitchen where Layla is preparing their lunch. 'They need volunteers to clear up the classrooms.'

'What, now?'

He nods.

'One of our neighbours was on his way there as I was coming up the stairs and told me about it. Do we have any cleaning supplies that I can take with me? The rooms will have to be cleaned before the refugees arrive.'

'Yes, of course we do. I'll come with you, Kamal. Fetch the bucket and mops from the broom cupboard over there and I'll just put on some shoes.'

The school is only a few minutes' walk away, its entrance on the main road that leads to the city centre. There are already a number of people there when Layla and Kamal arrive. A young man introduces himself as Ziad, the school's vice-principal. He is dressed in jeans and a white t-shirt and his head is shaven clean so that his features, an aquiline nose and large mouth, appear even more pronounced.

'Thank you all very much for coming to help,' he says with a smile. 'We're expecting the families to get here sometime tomorrow morning so there's a great deal to do before then.'

They begin by moving desks, chairs, cupboards and other equipment into a large hall in the school's basement where they will be kept for safekeeping. Then, because the school has been closed for the summer holidays for several weeks and there is a great deal of built-up grime and dust to clear away, once each classroom is emptied of furniture, the floors are swept and mopped and the windows are cleaned.

They work quietly throughout the afternoon before Ziad calls all the volunteers outside for a break. They sit in twos and threes on the wooden benches placed on one side of the playground. Layla notices that Kamal is speaking to the two women beside him. She waves to him and sits down a few seats away. Ziad is passing around paper cups and bottles of mineral water. He sits down by Layla and smiles.

'You teach at the university, don't you?' he asks.

Layla nods.

'Yes, I do.'

'I graduated from there three years ago. I never took any of your classes, though. I majored in education.'

She smiles.

'It's wonderful that the school is doing all it can to help,' she says.

'Well, government schools all over the country were turned into shelters in the first days of the war and although we're a private establishment we thought we should contribute as well.'

Ziad pours more water into Layla's glass and she thanks him.

'It's still a bit of a risk, though, since no one knows when the war is likely to end,' he continues, shaking his head. 'If people aren't able to return to their villages and their homes by the beginning of the school year, we'll all be in trouble.'

'What will happen once they get here? I mean, where are they going to sleep and cook and things?'

'It's all been taken care of. We've organized mattresses and blankets and some foodstuffs as well. Help is coming in from all over the region as well as from within Lebanon, communities everywhere are collecting aid and volunteers are helping distribute it. It's really heartening to see it happen.'

'Yes, it is.' Layla sips at her water. 'I suppose it makes people feel they're doing something useful even if we can't do anything to stop the fighting itself.'

Ziad frowns.

'I spent the first few days of the war glued to the television trying to understand what was going on,' he says. 'After a while I felt I would go crazy if I didn't get up and do something.'

In the early evening, a truck arrives loaded with foam mattresses, blankets, small gas cookers and other essentials which Ziad asks the volunteers to distribute between the different classrooms.

'That's it folks,' he says once they're done. 'Thanks for all your help. *Allah maakoun.* God be with you.'

As Kamal and Layla make their way back home, Layla realizes that for the first time since the war began she can feel her frustration lifting.

'Maybe it's because it's been several hours since I last watched the news,' she says more to herself than to Kamal.

'Hmm?'

'I've just realized how much better I feel after all that work,' she continues, linking her arm through his. 'At least we did something useful instead of just sitting around bemoaning our fate.'

'Is that what we've been doing?' Kamal is smiling.

'I want to be there tomorrow when they arrive.'

'Well, Ziad did say he could do with some help then as well. So we'll both go.'

They walk at a leisurely pace, as much because they are tired as because they want to savour this moment. As they get closer to home, the neighbourhood too seems to be coming alive, people walking in and out of shops or, like them, simply strolling down the street. We are as vital to this city as it is to us, Layla thinks silently to herself. There is no question of either one of us giving up on the other.

Sixty seven people come to stay at the school, all from the same village in the south, from the same family, and ranging in age from only a few months old to eighty two. They arrive with very few belongings, mostly the clothes they are wearing and what possessions they could carry with them as they fled.

When Layla first sees them the morning of their arrival, she is struck by how composed they seem, filing into the classrooms allocated to them without fuss, and talking amongst themselves in hushed tones as though fearful of disturbing anyone. Perhaps, she thinks, this is exhaustion that I see; although later, once she gets to know some of the families better, she will discover that their composure is more the result of a kind of determined resilience, an acceptance of whatever fate throws their way.

'Are you telling me they've simply become accustomed to displacement?' she asks Kamal when they discuss it afterwards.

'Well, it's certainly not the first time that people from southern Lebanon have had to flee because of war,' he replies.

'And you think the experience no longer traumatizes them?' she continues, feeling indignant on behalf of the refugees.

'It's not that, Layla. I believe that all it really does is make them even more determined to return home.'

She shakes her head.

'The Lebanese have become just like the Palestinians, you mean?' she continues with sadness.

He sighs.

'Yes, I suppose that's what I mean.'

They both go to help at the school as often as they can, only sometimes together. Layla likes to arrive in the morning in time to have a quick coffee with Ziad and discuss what needs to be attended to that day. He has been very efficient at organizing aid for the families and at making their stay at the school as comfortable and as trouble-free as possible. He is equally concerned about maintaining order and ensuring that school property is not damaged, and introduces a set of rules that the families are more than willing to follow. For her part, Layla marvels at Ziad's ability to distance himself from the plight of the refugees without at the same time being totally devoid of compassion. When she tells him this, he looks at her with some surprise.

'Pity is no help to anyone at a time like this,' he says, a hint of impatience in his voice. 'You do what you have to do to make a difficult situation bearable and hope things will eventually resolve themselves.'

A few days into their stay, Ziad arranges for a large-screen television for the refugees which they begin to congregate around every morning in the hope of hearing news of home.

'The talk is always about what village that might be that they're seeing on the screen and whose home might have survived the bombing,' Ziad tells Layla. 'Only yesterday, the old grandfather told me he was especially worried about his house because he had left his life savings behind there, hidden in a sack cloth in the kitchen.'

Layla feels too shy to approach the families at first, busying herself with helping Ziad, picking up medications from a local pharmacy that is donating them to the refugees for free or distributing boxes of food aid that arrives at regular intervals from an international relief agency. With time, she feels more comfortable about approaching the

women and offering to help them with the food prepar-
ation and other daily chores.

One day, Ziad suggests Layla might like to organize
some play sessions with the younger children.

'It would keep them occupied and give their mothers
the opportunity to get things done in the morning,' he
says with a smile.

'But I've had no experience with children that age,'
Layla protests.

'The older ones can amuse themselves so it's the little
ones we need help with,' he says. 'I'm sure you'll think
of something fun for them to do.'

Layla brings paper and a box of pencils from home, as
well as a large box of wooden bricks, some toy cars and
dress-up dolls that neighbours whose children are already
grown have given her. She enters the classroom where a
small group of boys and girls, all under six years old, are
waiting for her. They stare wide-eyed and are clearly
unaware of exactly how they should react to her presence.
She says nothing at first, quietly moving the small tables
and chairs from where they have been placed in the centre
of the room and putting them up against the walls. Then
she sits down on the floor with the laden bags around her
and waits.

One by one, the children approach, either sitting beside
her and looking up at her with hopeful smiles on their
faces or standing somewhere nearby, their eyes darting
between her face and the plastic bags by her side. One
tiny girl, her hair a shiny, dark helmet around her head
and her large eyes heavy with long lashes, comes up to
Layla and lays a hand on her shoulder.

'Would you like to see what's in these bags?' Layla asks,
aware of the little hand pressing into her skin.

The little girl nods.

'You'll have to tell me what your name is first, though.'

The girl looks away and says nothing.

'Her name is Fatima,' one little boy says. 'She's my cousin. She's only two and is shy with strangers but she'll get over it once she gets to know you.'

Layla laughs and one or two of the children giggle along with her.

'My name is Layla. What's yours?' she asks the little boy, pleased that one of the children is prepared to talk to her.

'I'm Ali and that's my brother Mahmoud over there.'

Layla nods and waves at Mahmoud.

'Are you our new teacher?' Ali asks.

'Not a teacher exactly, but I will be playing with you from time to time if that's alright.'

She opens the first bag, rummages around inside it and takes out a round-headed and hairless doll dressed in shorts and a halter top. Layla turns the doll's face to her own.

'I have a new friend standing right here beside me. Would you like to meet her?'

She puts her arm around Fatima and hands the little girl the doll.

'I think she likes you,' Layla says quietly and is delighted when Fatima returns her smile. 'What do you think her name is?'

'Layla,' Fatima says, her voice just above a whisper.

When Layla talks to Kamal about her experience with the children later that evening, she does not try to hide the excitement in her voice.

'It was wonderful, Kamal. We played and sang and made drawings of each other and they were warm and welcoming.'

'And you were worried you wouldn't be able to handle them.'

'I managed to capture their interest from the moment I entered the classroom,' she continues, sitting down beside him on the sofa. 'But it was only after I left and was on my way home that I realized it was Margo who taught me how to do that.'

'Oh?'

'She always said that the best way to get a child's attention was to sit quietly, look at him or her with a smile and wait for them to come to you.'

She looks into Kamal's eyes.

'Would you believe me if I told you that I sometimes feel that she's watching over me?'

'And me too, I hope,' he says with a smile. 'She cared about me too.'

Layla punches him gently in the arm.

'You too, of course,' she says, laughing now. 'Margo is with us both, always.'

A doctor arrives at the school one morning and when she comes in for her shift Layla asks Ziad about him.

'He's an old friend of mine and only down in Beirut for the day from his village in the mountains where he's working with the refugees who fled there,' Ziad tells Layla. 'I've asked him to come and check on some of the refugees while he's here. It's only a temporary measure because we won't have a regular doctor making rounds until next week.'

When they are introduced, Layla asks Bilal if she can sit in on his examination of the younger children and he agrees. The little ones are led into the classroom by their mothers, all of them wide-eyed with fear. Bilal sits in a chair so that he is at the same level as the children and begins each check-up with a moment or two of conversation. It is not long before he manages to put most of his young patients at their ease, sending them out with smiles of relief on their faces.

'They're happy because no injections were involved,' he

says, turning to Layla. 'But no one's suffering from anything serious, thanks to the excellent conditions you've all provided for them.'

'You've been places where it's a lot worse, I suppose,' says Layla.

The young doctor nods as he packs medical instruments in his bag.

'There are almost a thousand people who took refuge in my own village up in the mountains. We were completely unprepared for them, of course, because the war was so sudden. Things were very difficult at first but it's somewhat better now.'

'But where are they all staying?'

'At the local school and wherever we could find space for them.' He shakes his head. 'Some of them are sleeping ten or twelve to a room and sanitary conditions are not the best. We had lots of gastro intestinal infections and entire families falling ill with Hepatitis A in the beginning. It wasn't easy to get that under control.'

When Layla probes him further, Bilal tells her that many of the older refugees who suffer from chronic illnesses such as diabetes and hypertension had fled their homes without their medications.

'Since the country is virtually under siege with all the bombing, many medications are no longer available,' he continues. 'At the same time some of the people we've been treating are elderly or illiterate and don't even have a clear idea of what their illnesses are, let alone what medicines they take for them. We don't have the facilities to conduct laboratory tests and we've had to do the best we can with whatever medications international organizations can give us. Pharmacies in the area have very limited supplies left.'

Later that day, when Bilal completes his rounds and bids Layla goodbye before making his way back up to the mountains, Ziad stops him just as he is about to leave.

215

'I just heard on the radio that they've bombed the Damascus road,' says Ziad. 'You'll have to stay in Beirut tonight.'

'That's impossible,' Bilal shakes his head. 'I've got too much to do. I'll have to find some other way to get up there.'

'You'd have to go past the airport to get on the other road that leads to the village. You know that's not a good idea at the moment because the airport has been targeted several times. Isn't there another doctor working with you up there?'

Bilal nods.

'Yes, but the workload is too much for one person.'

'He can manage without you for one night. It's just too dangerous for you to try to drive up there right now. Look, I'm going to be sleeping at the school tonight and you can stay here with me.'

Layla clears her throat.

'Bilal, why don't you and Ziad come and have dinner with Kamal and me? Our place is just down the road and we can walk there. You can come back here to sleep afterwards.'

The electricity goes off towards the end of their meal. Layla lights candles, places them around the living room and goes into the kitchen to make flower tea. When she returns with the tray, the men are very quiet.

'Is everything alright?' she asks.

'The doctor was just telling us about one of the families he's been treating,' Kamal says. 'The mother lost a son, a brother and a nephew, all in the first few days of bombing.'

'Oh, no.'

She passes the tea around before she sits down.

'It must be difficult for you,' she finally says, turning to Bilal.

The young man looks up at her and attempts a smile.

'Many of the people I see on my rounds keep thanking me and I sense that they feel guilty for being a burden on us,' Bilal says quietly. 'I think of what they're going through, of the humiliation of being driven from their homes through no fault of their own and of becoming dependent on the kindness of strangers, and I wonder why they imagine they have to feel indebted to us for helping them.'

He lifts his cup to his lips and Layla notices that his hand is trembling.

'Yes, it is difficult,' he turns to her. 'Especially difficult when you see people who are depressed and traumatized and you know you can't compensate them for what they have lost, can't give them the same comfort they would have had in their own homes and with their families. Beyond treating the physical symptoms, there's really very little that one can do.'

Candlelight illuminates the darkness around them and the rumble of fighter planes is persistent overhead.

There is a brief cease fire and Kamal sits in the back of the small truck with several other volunteers. They are all uncomfortably squeezed in between large containers of drinking water which they are taking down to a refugee centre in the southern city of Sidon. The truck, despite its load and the unevenness of the road, moves fast down the empty highway and comes to a sudden halt a short while into the journey.

Kamal stands up and sees where the road ends and dips down into a shallow channel below. The driver turns off the engine and gets out.

'They've bombed the bridge that used to be there,' the driver says gesturing ahead. 'I'll have to check and see if we can get the truck across the makeshift overpass.'

The two men walk over to look at the debris, dirt and dust. Then they examine the thick slabs of wood placed over the area where the rubble from the bombed bridge is at its highest. In some places, the makeshift overpass rests on piles of sand and rock and looks relatively sturdy.

'It's rough and ready but whoever made this did a good job,' the driver continues. 'We'll have to empty the back of the truck, though, before I can try to get it across.'

Within minutes a relay is organized with volunteers lined up from one end of the overpass to the other at the point where the road begins again on the other side. They work quickly and in silence, passing the water containers along the line, everyone conscious that the delivery must be made within good time, before the cease fire comes to an end.

It is midday and the sun is hot. Kamal notices that several of the young men have taken off their shirts and covered their heads with them. He turns to the volunteer standing to his right, grabs hold of a container, steadies its weight in his arms and then swings slowly to the other side to hand it to the next person in the line. As he works, he becomes aware of his breath going in and out in rhythm with his movements, right, heave, then left and release. He catches a whiff of the sea directly behind him, an airy, familiar freshness, and smells the almost musty scent of the warm earth beneath. He begins to picture the scene as though he were outside it, as though the setting and the people, movement and rhythm, the surrounding aromas and the air, subtle and clear, are all meshed, unrecognizable, together. For a moment, he ceases breathing, life coursing through him, undeniable and immense.

'That's it then,' a volunteer shouts from the other side of the bridge.

They all make their way across and wait for the driver to inch the truck's way over. Moments later, they once

218

again load the jugs of water onto the back of the truck and race down the highway.

When the temporary ceasefire was announced the day before and Ziad had asked him if he would be willing to join the volunteers on a trip to Sidon, Kamal had jumped at the chance. He had been wanting to come down south to see what was happening first hand for a while but thought Layla might object because of the dangers involved. Still, he was unable to resist the opportunity when it finally came up and had told Layla when he left early that morning that he would be visiting with an old friend for the day.

The last time he had come through Sidon was during the day trip he took with Layla and Margo. The setting is the same but the city seems utterly different. The streets are empty, shops are closed and boarded up and there is little sign of human life. Here, rather than soothing, the stillness is eerie. For the first time since the beginning of the war, Kamal feels his body tremble with something resembling fear.

They stop in front of a large, one-storey concrete building with a Red Cross van parked outside. The volunteers get out of the truck and begin to unload the water jugs. A woman comes out to meet them. She is small, dark-skinned and wears large-framed glasses that hide her fine features.

'Thank goodness you got here in time,' she says, smiling. 'We had almost run out of drinking water.'

Once all the containers are unloaded, the woman invites everyone into the refugee centre.

'Try not to be too shocked by what you see,' she says.

The quiet that Kamal had encountered outside only moments before is totally absent from the huge hall that they now find themselves in. There are hundreds of people milling about, sitting or lying on foam mattresses on the floor, walking around seemingly aimlessly or talking to one another. Children run through the melee, mostly shouting, and a strong smell of unwashed bodies permeates the air. It is very unlike the school in Beirut where Kamal and Layla have been helping the refugees.

The woman turns to Kamal.

'We've been unable to bathe, of course,' she says with a wry smile. 'All the spare water was used for drinking or sanitation purposes, so please excuse the stench. I know it's there but now I'm pretty much impervious to it. We've been here over two weeks.'

She motions for them to follow her to a corner of the auditorium.

'Come and sit down all of you,' she continues. 'You must be exhausted. I'm Mona, by the way, and I'm in charge of this refugee centre. Welcome to our foundation's headquarters.'

As they sit down, she explains that the charitable foundation she works for usually runs social and cultural events here but since the bombardment began they have been taking in displaced people from villages further south.

'We're ill-equipped for this kind of work and aid is very slow in coming through, especially since the bombardment has been so fierce,' Mona says shaking her head. 'We keep hoping the things will let up long enough to allow some of these people to make their way to Beirut where they have relatives to stay with. If we had fewer numbers staying here, we could work on improving conditions. As it is, more and more are coming in every day, including some who have been injured.'

'Haven't you been able to arrange something with the Red Cross or the UN to have them evacuated?' Kamal asks.

'We've been prepared to take that risk only with the really serious cases which have been taken to hospitals in

Beirut,' replies Mona. 'Otherwise it's just too dangerous, even for ambulances.'

A man arrives with a bottle of water and passes it around to the volunteers.

'Drink up, please,' Mona says. 'You'll need it before the drive back.'

She sighs and seems momentarily distracted by her thoughts. Kamal wonders what she is thinking.

'The ceasefire is due to end in less than an hour,' Mona says looking at her watch. 'You'd better go now, please.'

Kamal wonders how they could possibly leave this brave woman behind and head back to the relative safety of Beirut.

'I'll be alright,' she tells him as he shakes her hand goodbye. 'It'll have to end eventually, you know, and I plan on being right here to help put this city back together again.'

They pile into the truck, Kamal getting into the front seat with the driver. As they begin to move, he hears the sound of a reconnaissance drone flying above them.

'The planes will follow very soon,' Kamal says. 'Maybe we should stay here for the night.'

The driver shakes his head.

'We're better off getting back to Beirut as soon as possible,' he says. 'Don't worry, *ya akhi*. I'll get us there in one piece.'

Within thirty minutes they have driven through Sidon, made it across the makeshift bridge and arrived at a Lebanese army checkpoint where a young soldier approaches and bends down to look briefly into the cab of the truck before motioning the driver to go through. Later, when Kamal allows himself to think about what happened next, he remembers the soldier's face, lean and sharp-featured and a hint of something in his dark brown eyes. He likes to imagine also that in that last moment of

221

connection, he had somehow managed to connect to the young man on a human level.

As they advance past the checkpoint, Kamal hears the rumble of a plane overhead, a sudden silence, then a huge explosion, the impact forcing the truck forward, whooshing sounds imploding inside his head. The driver shouts out and grips the steering wheel with both hands in an attempt to steady the vehicle.

'That was right behind us,' he yells.

Kamal puts his head out the window. The checkpoint is on fire, black smoke rising from the debris. He watches in horror as a figure staggers through the flames before falling to the ground.

'Stop, stop,' he shouts at the driver. 'We have to help them.'

The driver ignores him, pushing down on the gas pedal so that the truck lurches suddenly forward.

'What are you doing?' Kamal continues. 'Some of the men in the back of the truck might be injured too. We have to stop.'

'There's no way any of the soldiers could have survived that explosion,' the driver says. 'And if any of our men are injured, we need to get them to hospital. Besides, I'm not going to allow us to become a sitting target for the next fighter plane that comes along.'

The driver puts his head outside the window and bangs with one hand against the truck's exterior.

'Is everyone alright back there? Hang on tight, now. We're almost there.'

As the truck races down the road to Beirut, Kamal knows he will never be able to talk about what just happened, not even to Layla. This is something that will stay with me forever, he repeats silently to himself, this is where, for once, words have no choice but to fail me.

*   *   *

Layla knows Margo and John would have had their golden moments too, when he was kind and attentive, whispering his love into her ear, helping her on the steps that led down to the riverbank and then holding her hand as they walked. And one night, as they ate dinner at a small bistro not far from their room, Margo cut into her steak, chose a choice morsel and offered it to him, and in that moment understood that this man meant more to her than her own self. This is love then, she thought as she watched him eat, this is where it all begins and where it will no doubt end, and there is nothing whatever that I can do about the direction in which it moves.

Was it merely chance that had brought them together or were they, as Layla likes to think, soul mates who had found each other in the most difficult circumstances? Their backgrounds were not dissimilar, after all, and they both believed fiercely in fighting the evil that had taken over Europe, but was there anything else that joined them besides desire and perhaps the realization that life was ephemeral?

Time would have meant something different for them. Uncertainty has the capacity to do that, to make hours stretch into forever one moment and shrink to separate instances of utter dread the next. It is conceivable that once Margo knew her fate would always be tied to the vacillations of this great love, she willingly did as John had asked and put an end to her pregnancy. It is also possible that this very act caused a breach between the two lovers that they would not be able to overcome.

And through all this would have been the spectre of crushing loss. Did they ever talk about it, Layla wonders? Did Margo turn to John one day and say through tears, I cannot bring myself to picture my parents in their suffering, John, cannot bear to imagine what might be happening to them now, while you and I lie here, happy in each other's arms. That is, perhaps, what had caused the guilt that would haunt Margo throughout her life.

She sees Margo standing somewhere in the dim dark, her legs weak so that she fears she might at any moment fall to the ground. The inside of Margo's head is spinning and as she opens her eyes wider, she can eventually see the outlines of objects past and present, here a narrow single bed in a tiny attic room, there the corner of her parents' garden where rose bushes grow and a jasmine tree, its blossoms fragrant as the air in heaven, leans gently in the wind, and just within reach, an image of her long lost love, his arm outstretched, his eyes reaching into her soul.

Her world now is a jumble of reality and dreams, of past sadness and happiness so intense that it is ever-present, no longer bound by time or place. Her body too has become malleable, ageless and somehow detached from everything that surrounds it, from time and place and the endless pull of longing.

These are the things, Layla now understands, that I saw in her without really knowing how or why. If she seemed to embrace me with her love, it was because there was a place and a moment when she could no longer be touched. If Margo was other-worldly, if that is how she drew upon her almost insurmountable strength, then what have I become for having known and loved her?

The children are precious friends now, running to Layla as soon as she arrives, thrusting their little hands into the plastic bag she is carrying, asking her what is inside it. Today, she has brought slippers in different colours and sizes in the bag because she has once or twice noticed many of them running around in bare feet. She sits down on the floor in the centre of the classroom and turns the bag upside down to empty it of its contents, red, blue, green, pink and yellow plastic slippers that the children reach for with giggles of delight.

'Let's all sit down in our circle now and I'll check the sizes for you,' Layla says, leaning over to push the little ones gently away. 'Come on, Mahmoud. In your place in the circle, please. You too, Aisha, put that down and sit in the circle.'

Once the children have quieted down and are sitting down looking at her with anticipation Layla puts her own slipper-clad feet out for the children to see.

'I've got the same thing on as well,' she says. 'You just put this bit here between your big toe and your other toes, see?'

Then she takes each pair of slippers out of its plastic bag and hands them out to the boys and girls one by one.

'Try these on, Ali, I think they'll fit you. And these pink ones are for you Fatima. Here you are, sweetheart.'

'She's too little to put them on by herself, miss,' Mahmoud tells Layla. 'You'll have to help her.'

Fatima has on thick socks and a pair of heavy navy blue booties which Layla helps her remove. Her feet, small and soft, are sweating in the heat. She wriggles her toes and seems delighted when Layla looks at her and laughs. Layla tickles the soles of the little girl's feet and watches as Fatima's eyes open wide and she begins to laugh. Then as soon as Layla stops tickling her, Fatima wriggles her toes once again and looks up at Layla who obliges the little girl by chuckling loudly.

Once everyone has their slippers on, Layla stands up and tells the children to do the same.

'Now, let's see you walk in them,' she says.

One by one, the children begin to walk around the classroom, the older ones allowing the slippers to make a slapping sound against their feet as they walk, those younger doing an awkward shuffle in an attempt to stop the flip-flops from slipping off their feet.

'OK everyone, stop now,' Layla claps her hands together. The children freeze.

'Mahmoud, I want you to show us how it's done.'

Mahmoud nods and proceeds to move around the room with ease.

'Well done, *habibi*. I can see you've worn slippers like these before. Now let's all try it together and see how much noise we can make.'

Soon, the sounds of stomping feet and happy children fill the room.

'Layla?'

Ziad sticks his head through the door.

'Oh, are we making too much noise?'

'It's OK,' he says with a smile. 'We were just listening to the news in the office and it looks like they've finally managed to negotiate a permanent ceasefire. I just thought you'd like to know.'

They go to bed that night feeling more than usually subdued. As they prepare for sleep, it seems to Layla as if they are already moving through dreams, disparate thoughts wandering wordlessly between them, their movements deliberate and stilted.

She slips in under the covers and turns to Kamal. In the dim light of the bedside lamp, she sees the shadows beneath his eyes.

'*Habibi*,' she says, beginning to weep.

He wraps her in his arms and holds her for a moment, the gentle sound of his breathing filling her ears.

'Hush, hush, my love,' Kamal whispers.

Moments later, Layla pulls away and reaches for a box of tissues.

'It's difficult to believe that it will all be over soon,' she finally says.

'I know.'

'The children were so wonderful today, Kamal,' she sniffs.

'When I'm with them, I manage to forget everything and everyone else.'

He sighs.

'Children live only in the moment,' he says. 'When exactly do we lose that ability?'

'Are you alright, *hayati*?'

He shakes his head but says nothing.

She reaches out to trace his lips with her fingers.

'Hey,' she says. 'Tell me what you're thinking.'

'I'm tired, Layla,' he says, turning away from her to look up at the ceiling. 'Tired of all the anger and the hatred, tired because we don't seem to learn that war is never a solution.'

There is so much she wants to say to him but doesn't know quite how, things like it is all bearable because of you or we will come through this somehow or, as Margo once told her, this too will pass. In these past weeks, she has felt frailty in her body, from the tips of her fingers to her toes, in her limbs and down into her bones, and seen in her lover, his dark skin taking on a greyish pallor, the same transformation from apparent strength to a state so unfamiliar that they have had to adjust themselves to it slowly, day by day and as time inexorably moves on.

When she looks again, Kamal has closed his eyes, his eyelids fluttering delicately, like the wings of a butterfly, his breathing even. Layla leans forward, plants a gentle kiss on his cheek and lies back to sink into sleep.

PART SIX

Hope

Just when the weather starts to cool in Beirut, when the early scents of autumn begin to permeate the air, the heat suddenly returns, bringing with it scorching sunlight and oppressive humidity. I dread these Indian summers, and often wish I could somehow step out of my skin, bruised and made brittle by months of a pitiless sun, to finally encounter coolness.

In the days that immediately follow the end of the war, after the swift return of the hundreds of thousands of refugees to their ravaged villages in the south, my beloved Beirut is a stifling ghost town. I think of the images in American Westerns of dirt streets empty of people, huge balls of tumbleweed drifting in the hot wind, and wonder how a city so vibrant, so enduring, could have been reduced to this.

The neighbourhood is slow to come to life in the mornings. Many of the shops remain closed, their owners not yet returned from the places they fled to at the start of the war, while business is slow for those that are open, perhaps because many who remained here find returning to a normal pace of life still too difficult.

I visit my office for the first time in weeks, opening the

window to let in the fresh air and running my fingers across the now dusty bookshelves. I am uncertain where to begin with work for the coming year, and feel, for the first time ever, little enthusiasm for it. When my colleague Roula comes by and asks me if I will join her for lunch at the university cafeteria, I jump at the chance. I am in no mood to be creative, I admit to her, and she only nods in agreement. Nor am I, she says in return.

Sitting down under the shade of a canopy on the cafeteria terrace, we talk about the war as best we can, concluding that despite everything, we are very lucky to have held on to our lives as well as our homes.

'My husband and I took the children up to my parents' house in the mountains as soon as we realized the fighting was likely to go on for a while,' Roula says. 'We tried to keep news of the war from the children as much as possible so they at least were happy up there.'

'That is something to be grateful for,' I nod.

'You stayed in Beirut?'

'Yes, I did. My parents wanted me to get on one of the ships evacuating foreign nationals to Cyprus. I just couldn't bring myself to do it.'

Roula gives me a wry smile.

'I would have given anything to have had the chance to get my children out of here,' she says shaking her head.

'I probably would have left if I had a family,' I say quietly. 'As it was I just didn't want to leave my apartment and my life here without knowing when I'd be able to get back.'

'I understand, Layla,' she says. 'I wasn't being critical when I said I would have fled with my family if I'd had the chance. I just feel so depressed about everything. What kind of future are the children likely to have here now?'

We remain silent for a moment.

'Anyway, tell me about your reading list for this year,'

she says with a bright smile. 'Anything interesting on it that I could use for my own students?'

I tell her about a novel I have just read by an Anglo-Indian author which is beautiful and devastating and puts the whole issue of loss as a result of conflict in such profound perspective that one cannot help but be changed by it.

'I'm hoping the students will be able to gain some understanding from it that will help them deal with their own situation,' I say. 'But somehow I'm not too hopeful, after what happened when I had them read Orhan Pamuk's *Snow* last year.'

'They didn't like it?'

'That book left me dazed for days after I finished it,' I continue. 'The stories he weaves, the flawed characters who stumble through one political and social upheaval after another, their vulnerability and the errors of judgement they make. I was so moved by the quiet sadness of it all.'

'I loved it too.'

'We read parts of it in class and I tried to show my students how resonant it is of our own story, how close this wonderful writer comes to describing this country's anguish. Do you know what one of them said to me?'

Roula shakes her head.

'It's only literature, Miss. Real life is something completely different.'

We both laugh.

'Perhaps we're just out of touch when it comes to the views of young people,' says my colleague. 'During the civil war, it was literature that we turned to for the truth about our lives and not the distortions of reality that people in power try to fabricate. Sometimes I think that contemporary authors from this part of the world are writing books only to have their work translated for a western audience.'

On my way home, I decide to take a detour to visit my old neighbourhood, taking the steps that lead from the top of the campus where my office is down the hill towards the sea. I turn into the far end of the street where I lived as a child and notice a newsagent's and stationery shop that I used to visit often. I loved to browse through the racks of Arabic, English and French magazines, fingering the stationery, lined notebooks, reams of white paper and pens and pencils of all colours, while contemplating the rows of chocolate bars on the counter by the till. I am amazed and pleased that it is still here.

On Saturdays, as soon as I was given my weekly allowance, I would walk down to this newsagent-cum-corner-shop and decide what to spend the money on, usually a comic book and a chocolate bar made up of six bulbous squares with fruity fillings. Once I had paid for my purchases, I would walk down to the end of the street and sit down on the wide stoop of an old house with my back leaning against the black iron gate. I would place the comic book on my lap, open the wrapping around the chocolate bar and put it on the stoop beside me. As I read, I bit into the soft, already half-melted pieces of chocolate, slurping in the thick, fruity filling and chewing slowly to make the bar last as long as possible. I read with equal deliberation because the comic books, American and filled with illustrations of girls and boys with fair skin and blond hair who lived in houses with fireplaces and front lawns, weren't as long as I would have liked them to be. I often wondered what it would be like to be one of those children instead of who I really was, a skinny young girl from a crowded city by the Mediterranean that was as close and as blue as the sky above it.

I walk around the neighbourhood and note how much it has changed since I was a child. Still, there are corners that are familiar, this shop, for instance, the YWCA down the street where my mother took flower arranging lessons every Tuesday and the petrol station my father once owned, although the new owners have introduced some changes to it, adding a small kiosk for sweets and soft drinks as well as an extra pump for unleaded petrol. The building the family had lived in has also survived but the old house with the stoop where I used to sit is gone and in its place is a parking lot where dark, sleek German cars and four-wheel drives are lined up next to one another.

I get to the end of the street and pause by the statue of Gamal Abdel Nasser around which cars turning off or onto the Corniche manoeuvre with skill. The acrid smell of car fumes and a damp, pungent breeze blowing off the sea fill my nostrils. It all seems so familiar that for a moment I am transported in time, not to one particular period in my life but to a kind of amorphous past that continues to enfold rapidly passing moments, Layla here and now and all the Laylas who have ever been.

'I've been asked to speak at a conference in Berlin in a couple of weeks,' Kamal announces one evening.

'Oh?'

'They called this morning, from the university where I used to teach. They want me to let them know within the next few days whether or not I'll be able to attend.'

'Well, of course you must go,' I say. 'What will the talk be about?'

We are in the kitchen preparing dinner. I am cooking and Kamal is setting the table.

'The conference is on the Middle East and they want a special paper on the aftermath of the July war. It's a last minute decision to have me participate but they thought it was important that the war be discussed, especially in terms of the costs on a human level.'

He pauses.

'I'm not sure I want to go, though,' he continues quietly.

'Why not?' I ask as I stir the vegetable stew.

'I don't like the idea of leaving you here now, with things still so unstable. And I have to admit the idea of returning now after all these years is a bit daunting.'

'Why is that?'

He shrugs.

'I don't know. Maybe I just don't want to be reminded of my life as a young man.'

'You were happy there, weren't you?'

I feel momentarily puzzled.

'Yes, I was,' he says, his voice strangely quiet.

I understand what he is trying to say.

'Maybe it's time you went back, Kamal. It might help you understand what you're feeling about being here right now.'

'Layla, I . . . I feel so unsure about everything at the moment.'

I nod, my heart beating more quickly now.

'Yes, I know. But the war is over, thank goodness, and I think it would do you good to get away from here for a while. You'll come back with a better perspective on things.'

I spoon the food into two plates and sit down. Kamal fetches a loaf of Arabic bread from the refrigerator, tears off a piece and hands the rest to me before sitting down.

'But things are still very unsettled here,' he says.

'That doesn't mean I won't be able to manage without you. Besides, I've got a lot of work to do before the semester begins so I'm going to be very busy anyway over the next few weeks.'

He nods and continues eating.

'What do you think you'll say in your talk? Do they want you to focus on the politics?'

'I want to look at how the war affected people on a human

236

level, how it has changed their lives and how they're coping now, what the consequences will be for them in the near future. It's not entirely clear in my head yet but I'll have to provide some political background to the whole thing, yes.'

I put my fork down and take a drink of water. Disparate thoughts of the summer begin to enter my mind but I quickly push them away.

'You know, it's all still so immediate that I don't think I could to talk about it and make sense,' I say.

Kamal closes his eyes and sighs.

'To tell you the truth, there's a part of me that feels the same way.'

I put my fork and knife down and reach out to touch his hand.

'For the first time, I suspect that being able to write about this experience won't do anything to help me understand it,' he continues. 'How can war and hatred and so much violence ever make sense?'

He shakes his head and turns away to put his plate in the sink.

'I think I'll go down to my apartment to start work on this paper,' he says. 'You don't mind doing the dishes on your own tonight, do you?'

'No, of course not. Just let me know if you need anything. I'll be right here.'

He nods, kisses me lightly on the cheek and moments later is gone.

I stand at the kitchen sink and look out of the small window in front of me. Through the shuffling darkness of night I imagine my lover at his table, pen in hand, a small vein in his neck beating a steady, visible rhythm as he bends his head down to write.

I see a place of refuge where my life at last gathers itself together, memories and longings, expectation and discontent, people, beloved and unknown, and an all-consuming solitude that glows quietly inside me until I feel myself dissolving into countless, unequal pieces.

My eyes closed in half-sleep, I picture a room with a high ceiling and light coloured walls that are fluid in appearance. It is sparsely furnished, with rows of shelves lined with books and windows so high that I cannot reach them although they let in rays of light that drop rainbows on the bare floors. In one corner is the front door. I reach out to open it, feeling a frisson of excitement at seeing the bustling street beyond, this is some Western city, I am certain as I look out, where peace and anonymity can be taken for granted. Then, standing in the doorway, half-in, half-out, in that moment before I can decide which way to go, I wake up gasping, unsure where I have finally ended up, and alone.

I turn on the bedside lamp and pull myself up in bed. Since Kamal left for Germany earlier in the week, I have swayed between feeling free and constrained. At moments like this, with only myself to contend with, I am reminded of a less defined self and alternate between frustration at my frailty and exhilaration at the prospect of what I might be capable of on my own.

Once out of bed, I put on slippers and go into the living room. I can do whatever I like, I say out loud in my brave self's voice. I can do simply anything I like. To prove it, I turn on the overhead light, lift up my arms and begin to twirl around the room. Stumbling, I place a hand on Margo's old Morris chair and stop, feeling a little dizzy. This is the one piece of furniture belonging to her that I had wanted to keep. I lower myself into it, feeling the rough texture of the thick cloth with my fingers, and sit down, my eyes closed, my breathing a little heavy. Don't sweetheart, I hear Margo's voice hovering around me. Don't what? I want to ask, but the voice disappears and I am left, once again, with no one to turn to but myself.

The line is clear but I still hear myself shout as though I am afraid of not being heard.

'I'm fine, *mama*,' I bellow into the telephone receiver. 'How are you and dad doing?'

'You mean besides worrying about you, dear?'

'Please, mum.'

'We're doing very well, thank goodness. But we want you to come home.'

'I know you do, *mama*,' I say in a resigned voice.

I wonder how my parents, of all people, could think that leaving this place would be easy? It was difficult the first time round, I want to say to my mother, and it would be even worse now, I know. I am beginning to think that the enthusiasm my mother and father had hoped I would acquire for our adopted home had settled instead in their own hearts where it would remain forever.

'Talk to your father and please promise me you'll take care of yourself, dear?'

I hear my father clear his throat as he takes the receiver.

'*Habibti*, how are you?'

There is a faint trace of an Australian twang in his voice that makes me smile.

'I'm very well, *baba*. I'm preparing for the semester to begin now so I have lots of work to do.'

'I thought you were going to think about coming back here, Layla, until things sort themselves out a bit.'

'*Baba*, please. Let's not get into that discussion again.'

'But things seem to be falling apart over there. There's even talk of another civil war starting.'

'It's just a few politicians flexing their muscles. Things will eventually calm down.'

'How can you be sure?'

'I can't be certain of anything but that's hardly the point, is it?'

'You tell me what the point is, Layla,' he is beginning to sound impatient.

'*Baba*, you know I thought a great deal before making the decision to return home and I'm not going to run away just because things happen to be difficult right now.'

'What makes you think you would be running away?'

'Oh, for heaven's sake,' I retort impatiently. 'What else would you call it then?'

There is a pause.

'I'm sorry,' I eventually say, ashamed of myself. 'I didn't mean it to sound that way.'

I close my eyes and take a deep, calming breath.

'Layla, this is not about false loyalties. You have a right, after all, to keep yourself safe from harm and you're lucky that you have that opportunity. Many Lebanese would love the chance to leave and begin new lives away from all the turmoil.'

'What guarantees that once I leave I won't be longing to come back again? That's what happened the last time, isn't it? In any case, isn't it an illusion, *ya baba*, this idea we all have that our lives can always continue smoothly without being interrupted by events around us?'

As I ask the question, I realize how anxious I am to receive an answer to it that would help me understand the chaos around me.

'What am I to do with you?' my father asks softly. 'How can I make you see?'

'But that's just it, *baba*. You have to let me see for myself.'

On my own, I begin to follow a routine, waking up early in the morning and eventually making my way down to Hamra Street where I sit down in a pavement café for a cup of coffee and something to eat. It's a relatively quiet time of day, the shops opening one after the other and people walking past unhurried, some carrying briefcases, others just meandering by, the atmosphere relatively relaxed before the real morning rush begins.

From a passing vendor, I buy a newspaper which I usually read right through, although there are days when my eyes only skim over the headlines because I feel too disheartened to delve beyond them.

In the café, all talk is of the impasse between the government and the opposition, a conflict that tends largely to fall along sectarian lines and which is creating tensions between different communities and has come about largely as a result of the war we have just had to endure. Because I sit on my own, I can listen in on conversations around me without interruption. It is clear that most people have only one thing on their minds: when will we be able to resume our normal lives again? But it is the sense that we are helpless in the face of regional political interests that makes them particularly angry. How is it that we have put ourselves in a position where everyone and anyone except ourselves seems to have a hand in our fate?

I walk down to the university and into my office where I spend a few hours every day preparing for the coming academic year. I have chosen a number of new novels to include on my reading lists and am also planning to approach Kamal again about the possibility of his giving a lecture to my students on the war and the difficulty of writing about it. Perhaps if the students had some kind of intellectual framework to help them get around the shock of the past few months, they would be better equipped to deal with it. Confusion, I now know, is what is most likely to stop them from moving forward.

The university is still virtually empty and I can wander through the campus freely, enjoying the vista of sea and greenery, losing myself in the beauty for moments at a time, then coming to again at an unexpected sound or some drifting thought.

I spend evenings alone too, eating at the table in the kitchen and perhaps watching television or reading before going to bed. In Kamal's absence, the apartment feels larger, not so much because his presence fills it so completely but because, I suddenly realize, being a couple is like growing into a new and larger self. Life is bigger when I am with Kamal, bigger and wider in scope and in being so becomes more precarious somehow, less predictable.

The night Kamal telephones to tell me he has decided to delay his return, I feel an unexpected fear at the distance in his voice.

'How long will you be, *habibi*?' I ask slowly. 'I miss you.'

'I'm not sure yet, Layla. Listen, I . . . I've been offered a full-time job at the university here and I'm thinking of taking it.'

I am too stunned to speak.

'Are you there, Layla?'

'You mean you're thinking of not coming back?'

'Even if I do take the job, I'll have to return for a short while to organize things before I leave again. We can talk then.'

His voice sounds cold and indifferent. I push a fist into the centre of my chest to ease the pain I am feeling there.

'What are you saying, Kamal? Are you telling me that it's over between us?'

' I'm just tired of it all," he sighs. " I just need to get away from Beirut for a while. I'm not sure it's where I want to be anymore.'

'But I'm here.'

'Yes, I know,' he says, sounding tired now.

'Do you honestly think you're the only one feeling like

this, that I don't have the urge to run away from all this too?'

'Layla, you have told me again and again that you don't want to leave Lebanon, regardless of what happens, that you'll stick it out no matter how difficult it gets. I'm not sure I want that kind of uncertainty in my life anymore.'

He pauses.

'Things are so much easier here,' Kamal continues. 'I'm finally beginning to feel like myself again and I know I could do some good writing once I settle down. What's wrong with wanting a life without constant conflict?'

'When did all this start, Kamal?' I ask him. 'I'm supposed to be the unsure one, not you. How did everything change so suddenly?'

'I don't know. Maybe coming here has made me see things differently.'

He laughs nervously.

'You know how Lebanon has a way of sucking you into it, of making you feel there's nowhere else that matters,' he goes on. 'I just need time, that's all.'

'Time? I don't understand.'

'To decide what I want to do.'

'Time to tell me whether or not you'll be leaving me. Is that it?'

'I . . . I don't know anymore, Layla,' he says after a pause.

I feel my whole body begin to shake and sit down on the floor. I want to tell him that he is the only man I have ever truly loved, that after being alone all these years I finally feel that I have begun to find my way home, but I don't.

'Layla?'

'Goodbye, Kamal.'

'Layla, please, listen to me. This is not how I meant this conversation to go.'

'This is too difficult for me, Kamal.'

I hang up, put my head in my hands and sob with all my heart.

I am sitting in a café reading a newspaper when I see him walking past.

'Bilal?'

The young doctor stops and turns towards me.

'Oh, hello Layla,' he says. 'How are you?'

I stand up and we shake hands.

'I'm very well, thank you,' I reply. 'It's good to see you too. Please, won't you join me?'

'Yes, I'd like to thank you,' Bilal says, sitting down at my table. 'I have a few minutes before I have to be somewhere.'

'How do you take your coffee?'

I notice that he looks less tired than he did when I last saw him.

'Just black, thank you.'

I return to the table with our coffee and sit down.

'You're looking well, Bilal. What have you been up to since I last saw you?'

He smiles.

'Trying to recover mostly,' he says quietly. 'But yes, I do feel a lot better now. How is Kamal doing?'

'He's away at a conference in Germany at the moment. I haven't seen him for some weeks now.'

He looks puzzled and I decide to change the subject.

'I suppose all the refugees have left your village by now?' I ask.

'They left within the first few days following the cease-fire, so our local school will be opening on schedule and things are slowly going back to normal.'

'And are you practicing at your clinic in the village again?'

He shakes his head.

'Actually, I'm planning on leaving soon.'

I look at him in astonishment.

'You're leaving the country?'

He reaches for his coffee cup and shifts in his seat.

'I've had an offer from a hospital in the USA and I've decided to take it.'

'I'm sorry to hear that.'

A man selling national lottery tickets comes by our table and holds out his hand, the coloured tickets arranged like a fan in his fingers. He moves away when I shake my head at him.

'When will you go?' I ask.

'It'll be a couple of months yet, I think. I'll have to close up my clinic here and attend to a few things. I'm due to start the new job sometime in December.'

'But what about your parents, your family? How do they feel about it?'

'They're not happy, I guess, but mostly they understand.'

I cannot help probing further.

'But why? You were doing so much good here . . .'

He takes a deep breath before replying.

'What kind of future is this country likely to have now, Layla? Do you really believe people like us will have a say in what happens next?'

He speaks with a forcefulness that surprises me.

'Surely, it's up to us to make our voices heard?' I protest. 'We can't abandon this country just because things happen to be difficult.'

'Look, Layla, I went down to the south a few days ago to check on some of the families who came to us during the fighting. You can't imagine the extent of the destruction there. Thousands of people are living in tents and conditions aren't much better than the places of refuge they just left. The party has promised to give them funds to rebuild their homes, so has the government and the aid agencies that are helping, but it's going to take a long time.'

He frowns.

'The UN troops there are supposed to protect the borders but what guarantee is there that fighting won't erupt again sometime soon?' he continues. 'What will happen to the people then? After all, nothing has been resolved.'

He gestures: nothing.

'I'm just tired of it all,' he sighs. 'I need to think of my own future now.'

'I can understand why you might feel that way, Bilal. I've sometimes felt like giving up too since this wretched war started. But I can't help but be sad to hear you're leaving just when we need people like you most.'

He stands up.

'I'm sorry, Bilal,' I say, getting up to shake his hand once again. 'I wasn't trying to make you feel guilty or anything.'

'Don't worry about it. I felt plenty guilty on my own before I was able to make my decision. I know it won't be easy but I'm certain I'm doing the right thing. Thanks for the coffee. It was great to run into you like this. Please say hello to Kamal for me and let's get together when he gets back. I'd like to see you both before I leave.'

The front gate of the school is open. I step inside and make my way to Ziad's office. I find him busy at his desk and knock on the door.

'I hope I'm not disturbing you, Ziad.'

'Ah, Layla. Not at all, please come in.'

'Thank you. I just thought I'd come by and see how you were doing. We haven't seen you in a while.'

'We're busy preparing for the coming academic year.

All the work I would have done over the summer had to be postponed, of course, so here I am.'

He smiles.

'And how are you?' he asks. 'Ready for next semester?'

'Not quite yet, I'm afraid. I've been procrastinating but I will have to get my act together soon, I suppose.'

'And how is Kamal?'

'He's fine. He's in Germany at the moment presenting a paper on Lebanon at a conference.'

'Lucky him,' he says. 'I wouldn't mind a chance to leave and get a fresh perspective on things.'

'Hmm. By the way, I saw Bilal on Hamra Street the other day. Did you know he was leaving?'

Ziad sits back in his chair and reaches up to run a hand over his shaven head.

'Yes, he phoned me last week and told me he was going to America to work. Can't blame him really. It's not likely he'll get an opportunity like that over here.'

'Doesn't it upset you though, that he might never come back again?'

He shrugs.

'He has to think about getting ahead in his profession and this place doesn't have much to offer right now.'

'So why are you staying?' I feel impatient with him now.

'I'm not the type to make it overseas, too attached to this country I guess. What about you? Why do you stay on?'

I lean forward and look closely at him. I won't tell him that I don't have an answer to that question.

'I worry about those children so much, Ziad. Whatever's become of them, do you know?'

'You mean the families we had staying here? I heard from one of the men recently. You know Mahmoud's father?'

I nod.

'He said they're all fine, that things are a bit tough back in the village but they're managing fine. They seem confident their homes will be rebuilt and that life will eventually return to normal. They're much better off at home.'

'But Bilal said he'd been down to south since the ceasefire and the situation is dire.'

Ziad looks disapproving.

'I've known Bilal since we were both children. His problem is that he's always been a bit of an idealist. That kind of attitude doesn't work in this country. No one can afford to be so sensitive when trouble is always around the corner.'

'Being compassionate is a problem?'

'Come on, Layla. We both know that when you come from this part of the world you have to accept everything that comes with it. This region has always been unsettled and things are not likely to change for the better very soon.'

'You're so cynical, Ziad. How could you possibly think like that? How can there be hope for change when young people like you and Bilal are unwilling to fight for it?'

'Is that why you stay here, because you have hopes that things can eventually be different?'

I pause to consider his question. Is living in Lebanon, despite all the unrest and the constant uncertainty, only worthwhile for me because I feel duty bound to try to improve it in some way?

'No,' I reply, my voice hesitant. 'I have my doubts just like everyone else but I can't imagine myself being elsewhere anymore. I just don't want to take on the role of newcomer again, of starting over and trying to put together a life of sorts in an unfamiliar city. It would be like being in between lives all the time. Nothing feels certain or even real when I'm away from here.'

His eyebrows lift up as if in surprise then he smiles at me.

'Maybe you're like me, Layla,' he finally says. 'Maybe you're meant to put up with this country through thick and thin.'

It is Saturday afternoon and I hear a knock at my front door.

'Fouad, how lovely to see you. Please come in.'

'I meant to telephone,' Fouad begins. 'Then I thought since I was planning to come down to Beirut anyway, I would pass by on the off-chance of finding you and Kamal at home. I wanted to see how you're doing.'

'I'm fine, thank you. *Ahlan, Ahlan.*'

He bends down, picks up a large plastic crate off the floor and steps inside.

'I brought you some things from the garden,' he continues.

'Thank you, Fouad. Here, let me help you with that. It looks heavy.'

He follows me into the kitchen and we set the box down on the table.

'Oh, my goodness, there's so much here,' I say. 'You really shouldn't have.'

There are tomatoes, apples, a huge cabbage, runner beans, two heads of lettuce, as well as several bunches of parsley and mint.

'This looks wonderful. Thank you so much. You must have been working very hard on the garden.'

'The apples are still a bit green but they're delicious.'

'I'm sure they are. Come on, let's go sit down.'

We move into the sitting room and settle down.

'I'm still waiting for you and Kamal to come and stay, you know,' Fouad says. 'I think it'll do you both good to get away from Beirut for a few days.'

'Actually, Kamal's away at the moment. He was invited to a conference in Germany and won't be back for a while.'

Fouad raises his eyebrows.

'You didn't go with him?'

'It was a very good opportunity for him so I insisted that he go,' I continue, my voice trembling a little. 'They asked him to present a paper on the war. The talk went very well and he received a lot of positive attention.'

I hear shouts coming from the children playing in the alleyway.

'Look, I was just about to make myself some tea,' I say, not wanting Fouad to ask me more about Kamal. 'Or would you prefer coffee?'

'Tea would be fine, thank you.'

'I'll only be a moment. Please make yourself at home.'

In the kitchen, I make tea and arrange slices of a cake I baked a few days ago onto a plate. I am touched by Fouad's thoughtfulness and generosity. When the tea is ready, I take the laden tray into the sitting room.

'This was in Margo's flat wasn't it?' Fouad asks, indicating the Morris chair he is sitting in. 'She used to lean against it while she sat on the floor.'

'Yes, I wanted to keep it because it reminds me so much of her. Sometimes I imagine her sitting there looking at me.'

I pour out the tea, place a piece of cake on a plate and hand it to him.

'I know what you mean,' he says. 'I think about her often too.'

'It's impossible to forget someone like Margo,' I laugh. 'I realize that now.'

He takes a sip from his cup and nods.

'And she will always be with you, you know,' he says. 'She loved you very much.'

'I still think about her dying all alone like that,' I shake my head. 'I wish I could have been with her.'

'*Habibti*, there is a point in one's life when the inevitability of death is a constant and even comforting presence. But perhaps you are too young to understand that. Margo was ready to go, I'm sure of that.'

I smile.

'How was Prague?' Fouad asks. 'I telephoned after you left and Kamal told me about your trip.'

'Kamal told you why I went there?' I ask.

'I do understand why, Layla.'

'It's not that I felt betrayed because she hadn't told me all the truth about herself . . .'

He looks at me with a slight frown.

'Alright, maybe I was a bit upset,' I admit. 'But it was more than just curiosity that made me want to go to Prague. I felt I might understand Margo better if I knew more about her past.'

'And do you?'

'The strange thing is that after all that's happened in the past couple of months, it doesn't really matter any more, you know? It certainly doesn't change the way I will always feel about her.'

'Exactly,' Fouad says.

I wonder how I can ask him the next question without sounding as though I were accusing him of something.

'But I suppose you could have told me all I wanted to know about Margo?' I ask quietly.

'Layla, my dear,' Fouad says, leaning over to put a hand on my arm. 'Whatever Margo told me about herself was in complete confidence. I could not have said anything even if you had asked me.'

I nod and smile.

'I know. I . . . I shouldn't have mentioned it, really. I'm sorry.'

'No, you don't need to be sorry. I do understand.'

He picks up his plate and takes a bite of the cake.

251

'This is delicious, thank you,' he says. 'I suppose that you and Kamal will be ready to get married now.'

I look away.

'I'm sorry, have I said something wrong?' Fouad continues.

I stand up and move towards the half-open window. I stick out my hand, feel a gentle breeze and again imagine that if I were to turn around again I might find Margo sitting in her usual place with her back against the old armchair. A shiver goes up my spine.

'Layla, are you alright?'

I turn around and look at him.

'But my dear, you're crying. What has happened?'

'Kamal and I are no longer together and I am heart-broken, I think.'

I fetch a tissue and sit down again.

'But you seemed so happy together,' Fouad says softly.

'I don't think we want the same things. He's likely to stay on in Germany permanently now.'

'I am so sorry about this. Look, why don't you come up to the mountains and stay for a few days? It'll be a good break for you.'

'I might very well take you up on that offer,' I say, sniffing loudly. 'There's a long weekend coming up soon.'

'Promise me you'll come.'

'I promise.'

After Fouad leaves, I go up to the third-floor landing and stand outside Margo's door. The young couple who moved in recently are clearly not interested in plants because there are none anywhere to be seen. I notice that they haven't even bothered to put a welcome mat on their doorstep. I sigh, turn to lean against the concrete balcony and stare at the city below.

*   *   *

When I arrive at the National Museum, a number of women are already gathered on the front steps leading up to the main building. It is late afternoon and the vigil is set to begin at sunset. Several large banners have been placed on the columns of the museum entrance, slogans such as No To Civil War, and Lebanese Women For Peace emblazoned across them in bold, black letters.

At the bottom of the steps is a small table where demonstrators are lining up to sign a petition that will be sent to politicians on both sides of the divide demanding that they work towards a peaceful solution to the political conflict. I put my name down before moving away to stand by the other demonstrators. I don't know many people here but I feel at ease nonetheless.

'Would you like a candle?'

I turn to the woman standing beside me. She is small and thin and her skin is clear and white.

'Yes, please, Antoinette,' I smile. 'It's good to see you again.'

The nun smiles and hands me a candle.

'We'll be lighting them as soon as everyone is here. It looks like there'll be a decent turnout.'

'Sister Antoinette, how are you?'

A woman dressed in a floor-length dress and a head-scarf walks up to stand on the step below us. I watch as the two women embrace one another. Antoinette is the chief organizer of the vigil.

'I'm very well, thank you.' The nun pulls away from her friend and smiles. 'Oum Hassan, it's so good to see you. Thank you for coming.'

'I've brought my neighbor with me,' Oum Hassan says to introduce her friend. 'This is Sister Antoinette and this is my neighbor Oum Mohammed.'

Then she turns to me with a smile.

'It's good to see so many women here, isn't it? Maybe there's hope for this country yet.'

I laugh.

'I certainly hope you're right. I'm Layla.'

In the moments that follow Oum Hassan manages to get all the women around her to talk to one another.

'I'll be damned if I'm going to allow those stupid politicians to steer us into another civil war,' she says and everyone nods in agreement. 'I have two sons and I'm not prepared to sacrifice them for the sake of leaders who care about nothing but their own interests.'

She grabs her friend and continues.

'Oum Mohammed and I have been neighbours for the past twenty years and we love one another like sisters. Just because she is Sunni and I am Shia, our leaders think they can turn us against each other. We're not going to allow them to do that to us.'

Moments later, a school bus drives up to the museum and we watch as dozens of children dressed in white descend to join the demonstrators. More candles are passed around and the banners are handed out to those who want to carry them.

'Everyone, we're ready to begin now,' Antoinette calls out in a loud voice. 'Please help each other light the candles and we'll stand to attention for the national anthem.'

I notice one or two television cameras and a number of photographers taking pictures. Cars going past on the main road that runs just at the bottom of the steps to the museum slow down to watch what is going on. This location is significant because it is where the infamous Green Line between the east and west of the city was marked during the fifteen-year civil war of the 1970s and 1980s and where many battles between warring sectarian factions were fought.

Dusk begins to fall. When the first notes of the national

anthem play on a loudspeaker behind us, I look back. A huge Lebanese flag is hanging between the two main columns at the top of the museum steps. Below it are rows of women and children standing still, hands shielding the candles they are carrying, tiny flames fluttering in the breeze. I mouth the words to the anthem silently, unable to raise my voice, and feel tears fall slowly down my face. In that moment, I wonder how long we will all be able to hold out like this. How long before we give up on Lebanon and decide to leave it forever?

It is not the last time we speak but a few days before that, though I cannot remember exactly when. I know I was surprised to see Margo at my door at that late hour but I let her in, of course, hold her arm as she walks into the kitchen and falls into one of the chairs with a little thump. She seems unaware that it is close to midnight, that I am in my nightgown and everything around us is eerily quiet. She says she will not have any coffee today but a glass of juice would be fine, something to smooth the persistent dryness in her throat. I grab a couple of oranges from the fridge and squeeze them, my back turned to her as I try hard to hide my astonishment. I have never seen Margo look so disoriented and vulnerable. It is unsettling and a little frightening too.

How lovely to see you, Margo, I say quietly. How are you?

She looks at me and smiles.

I'm fine, I'm fine, she says. I'm doing lots of thinking these days, of course, but I suppose that's a good thing.

What are you thinking about, I ask, sitting down beside her at the table. I reach out to touch her hand and she goes quiet for a moment.

It's nice to have someone to talk to, she finally says. It's good to have you with me, sweetheart.

I am taken aback. Her hand trembles beneath mine and I am not certain what to do.

Did I ever tell you about my mother, Margo suddenly asks. She was a beautiful woman, nothing like me.

She chuckles.

Beautiful and gentle and everything a mother should be.

I nod and wait for her to continue.

And she loved me, despite all the trouble I caused her.

Her head shakes as she speaks, and for a moment there is a vacant look in her eyes that makes me anxious.

Margo, Margo, I am whispering now. Listen to me.

She turns towards me again.

Perhaps that's what she loved most about you, I say, insistent now.

What do you mean, she pulls her hand away.

Perhaps that's precisely why you were so precious to her, Margo, the fact that you were so daring and different, everything she had never been. Have you ever thought of that?

The house is made of limestone and has a beautiful garden that overlooks a valley where rows of dark green umbrella pines make a small forest. I park the hired car in the driveway just beyond the front gate and get out carrying Margo's urn. Fouad comes out to greet me before taking me through to the living room balcony to have lunch.

The weather is perfect, sunny and dry, softened by the intermittent presence of a cool mountain breeze; and the view to Beirut, with the airport at one end and the Damascus highway at the other, is stunning.

'I'm so pleased you were able to come,' Fouad tells me. 'So many friends who spend their summers here left when the war started and haven't yet returned. To tell you the truth, I've felt a bit lonely here in the past couple of months.'

I suddenly realize that in being so caught up with my own concerns, Margo's death and Kamal's absence, I have been oblivious to the feelings of people around me.

'Losing Margo cannot have been easy for you,' I say.

He shakes his head.

'I'll always miss her,' he says quietly.

'Me too.'

In the early afternoon, once the table has been cleared and Fouad has gone back inside, I decide to linger on the balcony for a moment. A soft mist begins to rise from the valley. The weather here is always cooler than Beirut. I watch the slow swirl of cloud and shiver at the sudden dampness in the air. The house is eventually surrounded by fog and for a moment it seems almost as if everything were suspended in mid-air. I close my eyes and sigh, then step inside to join my host.

'Ah, there you are, Layla,' Fouad says coming through the French doors. 'Would you like to go out in the garden?'

I move closer to him and put a hand on his arm.

'I'd like to do it now, if I can, Fouad,' I say, feeling suddenly nervous.

When I phoned a few days ago to tell Fouad I was coming here, I also told him that I wanted to find somewhere to scatter Margo's ashes, somewhere where there were lots of trees.

Fouad nods.

'Yes,' he says quietly. 'There's a baby cedar in the front garden that I planted only three years ago. I was thinking that might be a good place for her.'

I fetch the urn and follow Fouad back through the front door and out into the garden. We walk past a trellis draped in jasmine and large terracotta pots filled with African violets, flowering gardenia and lavender. At the far end of the garden, well away from the house and with plenty of room to spread itself, is the cedar tree. It is

257

about four feet tall, with a mottled brown trunk and branches that are a rich emerald green, the colour of seaweed when it is still damp from the sea. I bend down to touch it. How can something seem both so fragile and so solid at the same time? I manage, for a moment, to forget my anxiety and begin to see the possibility of finding spaces of quietness where one can breathe freely, intervals during which life is momentarily unfilled by the disorder of circumstance.

'It's like the real thing only in miniature,' I say softly. 'It's beautiful.'

When I open the urn, Margo's ashes are just that, grey dust that is powdery to the touch. I tip the urn over and deposit its contents in a near even line around the base of the young cedar. I straighten up and look down at the ashes. This is not you, Margo, I whisper to myself. This is just me saying goodbye.

I tiptoe downstairs to the living room. It is close to sunrise and after waking up suddenly I am unable to go back to sleep.

'Are you feeling restless too?'

Fouad turns on a side lamp and looks down at me with a smile. He is dressed in flannel pyjamas and tufts of his snow white hair stick up on his head.

I blink.

'I'm sorry, I must have woken you,' I tell him.

'Not at all, my dear. I always have trouble staying asleep. It's one of the curses of old age.'

He motions for me to get up.

'Come on, let's go get ourselves some coffee. We're not likely to go back to sleep now.'

The kitchen, like the rest of the house, is high-ceilinged and spacious. A whiff of cold air comes in through an open window. Fouad rushes to shut it and invites me to sit down at the small breakfast table set against the wall. He opens a door and walks into a large pantry whose shelves are stacked with bags, tins and packets of food.

He takes a packet of ground coffee beans off one of the shelves and lights a burner on the stove.

'With or without sugar?'

'Without, please.'

He fetches two small cups and saucers from a cabinet above the stove and places them on the table.

'Would you like something to eat?'

'No, thanks. The coffee will be just fine.'

He brings the pot to the table and pours the dark liquid into the cups. I breathe in the aroma of coffee and cardamom.

Fouad sits down beside me.

'I remember sleepless nights long ago when Margo and I used to sit together like this,' he says after a pause.

'You were lovers?' I ask, suddenly feeling brave.

He smiles.

'It was always the friendship in our relationship that was most important to us, you know,' he says.

I lift the cup to my lips and sip slowly at the hot coffee.

'Margo was a very complex person,' Fouad continues. 'When I first met her in London just after the war she was desperately unhappy and there seemed very little I could do to give her comfort. It was a while before she told me about what had happened to her family, and even then she was very reluctant to do so.'

Fouad sighed.

'There were so many people around at that time whose lives had been irrevocably changed by the war, so many people who lost loved ones. It wasn't that she wanted to keep her past secret, I don't think.'

'What was it then?'

'I think Margo was trying very hard to go beyond what

had happened, to find meaning to her life in spite of it. She didn't want anyone to feel sorry for her because she didn't feel sorry for herself. And she did manage to pick herself up afterwards and get on with her life.'

I nod in agreement.

'She was never one for self-pity, that's for sure,' I say. 'But I would have thought she would seek solace from her friends.'

'My dear, you must know that there are situations in life that can never be resolved no matter how much one talks about them,' he says gently. 'Margo always knew when acceptance of circumstance was the best answer.'

It occurs to me that had Margo lived, her reaction to this war might have been very different from my own. Would she have seen it as just another misfortune that had to be borne and which would eventually pass?

'People were very different when I was young,' Fouad interrupts my thoughts. 'Sometimes I think we were better able to cope because we had fewer expectations. You can't be disappointed or surprised by what happens to you when you understand that life does not necessarily owe you a better existence.'

We sip at our coffee and sit quietly for a moment or two. The silence is comforting.

'This house is very beautiful,' I finally say.

'Well, Layla. You know you're welcome to come and visit any time at all.'

'Thank you, Fouad. You know, I've always had a dream about living in the mountains. Maybe I should try to find a place for myself up here.'

'Why don't we take a drive in the area later this morning?' Fouad asks. 'Who knows, maybe you'll find your dream home.'

*　　*　　*

260

Margo and John would have been sleeping all afternoon, partly because they wanted to get some rest and also because it was the best way to dispel the apprehension that always preceded important missions. Plans to help a group of refugees flee to England had been in the making for several weeks and John was to lead the escape that night.

Margo got out of bed and prepared coffee. She knelt by the bed and put a hand on her lover's shoulder, shaking it gently.

'Sweetheart, it's time to get up now,' she said with a soft voice.

He stirred and opened his eyes.

'Sit up and drink your coffee,' she continued, and when he obeyed her placing a tray in his lap. 'You'd better have some of this bread as well. It'll be a while before you'll have the opportunity to eat again.'

Minutes later, as he prepared to walk out the door, John turned to look at her.

'Make sure you have a good night's sleep,' he said with a smile. 'If things go well tonight, we'll have to go out and celebrate tomorrow, maybe go for a picnic somewhere.'

'We can take that bottle of wine I've been saving, and I'll get some food in the morning,' she was excited at the prospect of them having a day alone together.

She went to him and they kissed.

'Wish me luck,' were his final words to her.

Later she would struggle to remember exactly what they had said to each other in those last few hours, strain to hear the tone of his voice again. Had it been light and hopeful or was there an underlying note of apprehension in it that she had somehow missed at the time?

It would be a while before a true image of his face would begin to fade from her memory although, at times, she would recall individual features precisely, his sharp

261

nose and thin lips that disappeared whenever he smiled, and could put them together to make up a kind of composite that fell just short of capturing his spirit.

When morning came and John had not reappeared, Margo would have known that something had gone terribly wrong and that she would have to make an escape to a safe house before she too was discovered. She did not give herself time to weep, but dressed quickly, put a few things into a small canvas bag and walked out of the room without looking back.

I sit up and blink. I have been dreaming again. What would Margo have seen in her dreams in the nights that followed John's disappearance?

Trying to imagine the suffering of someone you love is unbearable because you are unable to bring the strength of their endurance to mind. Perhaps Margo eventually found a way to elude the pictures that constantly made their way into her mind. Is that why she always told me that in expecting nothing, neither good nor bad, one's eyes opened to a vast emptiness, an endless expanse of stillness where suffering simply did not exist?

We drive up into the hills, several kilometres further than the town where Fouad's house is situated and above a small village of stone houses with red rooftops.

'I want to show you the view from up here, Layla,' Fouad says. 'It's very different from what you see from my place.'

The road narrows and twists as the car moves further up into the forest. I open my window all the way and put my head out to smell the air. I notice a small stone structure ahead and point to it.

'What is that?' I ask Fouad.

'It's just an old house. It's been empty for years. Would you like us to stop to have a look?'

262

'Yes, please.'

Fouad parks the car by the side of the road and we get out. There are stone steps built into the hillside which lead down to the house.

'Careful, Layla,' Fouad says, following me. 'Those look steep.'

The cottage has a small front yard with a low wall defining its edges. I look through the empty front door frame into two small rooms with dirt for a floor.

'The windows and flooring have been stripped. Don't go inside, Layla. We don't know if it's safe or not.'

I move away from the house and into the front yard to look down into the valley, through a forest of umbrella pines and down to the village below. I am struck by the gentleness of the view. There is nothing to overwhelm here, no wide expanses, nothing majestic, just an intimate, quiet beauty of trees and red earth and a bright, open sky.

'It's lovely, isn't it?' Fouad says, sitting down on the low wall.

I take a deep breath and smile.

'I can see myself in a place just like this,' I tell him. 'In a small house overlooking a quiet valley, warming myself by the fireplace in winter and sitting in the shade of a grape vine in summer, sipping lemonade and nodding at the sun.'

Fouad chuckles and motions for me to sit next to him.

'You know, even during the fighting there were moments last summer of such peace up here that I would forget what was really going on,' he says.

'Almost as if the war was merely an illusion because life continued regardless of it?'

'Yes, exactly that.'

'I felt that too, in Beirut.'

'This country is really something,' I continue. 'One minute I love it with all my heart and the next I hate

263

it so much that I want to leave and never return. I wasted years longing to come back and never really allowed myself to settle anywhere else, to have a real relationship or even to think about what I really wanted out of life.'

I look at Fouad.

'It was so insistent, you see, this feeling that I had to come back. I just couldn't shake it off. And now look where it's got me. Everything is falling apart, Fouad, people around me are leaving, people are giving up on Lebanon . . .'

'Have you imagined what your life would have been like if you hadn't returned, Layla?'

I shake my head.

'Think about it for a moment. You were clearly following your instincts when you longed for Lebanon even if you weren't consciously aware of it. There must have been a reason why you felt you had to come back. You just have to ask yourself what it might be.

'I've seen this country go through its best and worst times, my dear, and I've always felt exactly as you do about it. But sometimes I think that my generation took advantage of the glory years of Lebanon and gave very little in return.'

'What do you mean?'

'Well, we settled for a political set up based on sectarian loyalties, and we were mostly interested in making money and being successful and didn't really think about building a spirit of community that might have helped cope with the challenges we later faced. The civil war broke out and everything began to fall to pieces and there was nothing that could be done about it.'

He puts a hand on my shoulder.

'We all need to look deeper into ourselves, Layla, to make sense of things. How else would we manage to follow our hearts? The turmoil this country is going through now only makes this task seem more urgent, that's all.'

It's how things smell and look here, how happiness feels and the silence that fills me once I let it in, something akin to peace. In this once-house, walls caving in and sky drifting through without obstacle, I am at last untroubled. Here too is where I find you, Margo, and the boundless love to which you lead me. I am mindful of purpose, everywhere and at every moment.

Beirut seems overbuilt and crowded on my return, a world away from Fouad's idyll in the mountains. I feel strangely detached from my surroundings as a result and it is a few days before I can readjust to being in the city again. Then one morning, I am surprised by Kamal at my front door.

'You're back!' I cry, not certain how I want to react to his return.

He is looking good, much rejuvenated since he went away two months ago.

'Don't look so shocked,' he says with a nervous laugh. 'I arrived last night and would have come up to see you then if it hadn't been so late.'

'You didn't let me know you were coming.'

I cannot leave the rebuke out of my voice.

'Can I come in?' he finally asks.

'I was just on my way out, actually. I'm teaching a class in half an hour.'

He frowns.

'I need to talk to you. Can I come by later then?'

'I don't know, Kamal.'

He clears his throat.

'I know you're feeling hurt. I know that you're angry with me right now, but I have to see you.'

'I don't expect any explanations from you, Kamal. What's the point of talking?'

265

He steps back, looking pained.

'I really have to go now,' I tell him and he turns and walks away.

I am unable to focus on work for the rest of the day and end up sending my students off to the university library to do research for their course projects. Back in the office, I sit at my desk and leaf through the papers on it but don't succeed in getting any work done. I finally get my things together, lock the office door and make my way home.

Much later that night, I walk up to the landing on the third floor and find Kamal waiting for me there.

'I think I knew you would be here,' I say with a sigh.

'I couldn't keep away.'

He laughs.

'Shhh,' I tell him, pointing to Margo's front door. 'The new tenants will hear you.'

'OK,' he whispers. 'I promise to be very quiet.'

We look out at the city for a few moments and then at each other again.

His face is dear to me still.

'I had to come back, you know,' Kamal finally says. 'Because of you.'

'Don't,' I interrupt.

I squeeze my eyes shut because I don't want to cry.

'I'm sorry,' he says. 'Please let me explain.'

I open my eyes again and look at him.

'No, Kamal. Before you say anything else, I have something to tell you.'

'Tell me, Layla.'

I struggle to begin.

'I'd been thinking too about what I wanted to do even before you called me that day to tell me you were thinking of staying on in Germany,' I say quietly. 'Then I went up to the mountains to see Fouad and during one of our conversations he asked me if I knew why I had come back to Lebanon in the first place.'

'You went to Fouad's?'

I nod.

'It's just as beautiful there as we imagined. I scattered Margo's ashes in the garden, under a young cedar tree.'

He looks troubled.

'I know you loved her too, Kamal, but I had no idea when and even if you would ever be back. I couldn't wait.'

'It's OK. I'm glad you were finally able to say goodbye, that's all. I'm happy for you.'

He reaches out and touches my cheek. I move away.

'I need to say this, Kamal. Fouad was right. There was a reason why I returned and it wasn't simply about having grown up here and about being attached to this country, or even because I never felt I belonged anywhere else. I . . . It's difficult to explain it now that I'm trying to.'

'You can tell me,' Kamal says softly.

'Yes, I know. You're probably the only person I can tell.'

'And Margo too, if she were here.'

He smiles and I cannot help but smile back.

'And Margo, of course. I know now that not coming back was never really an option for me, that if I hadn't returned I would have continued to drift along without purpose as I had been doing for years.'

I take a deep breath.

'I met Margo here and loved her. Our friendship helped me make sense of so much that was confusing me. She told me it was no use to want things to be different, that in accepting them as they were I would finally see the beauty that is always there. Keeping so much of her history to herself wasn't a betrayal of our friendship. Margo was just being human, trying to cope as best she could like the rest of us.'

267

I begin to cry.

'Beirut is also where I met you, Kamal. You are my only love. And you know what? Even if you are leaving me, I will still know that with you I finally gave myself a chance, that I didn't turn away from this one true thing that has brought so much meaning into my life. Now that I see all this, I wouldn't change any of it, not a single moment of it.'

He takes me in his arms and lays his cheek on the top of my head.

'Forgive me, Layla,' Kamal whispers. 'Forgive me, *hayati*.'

We decide to take advantage of the last days of the heat and go to the beach, leaving early in the morning laden with towels and books and sun creams. Although the day is warm and the sun is already out in full force, there is a refreshing breeze that blows in off the water and onto the terrace where we sit in deck chairs facing the distant horizon.

Kamal is lying on his back with his eyes closed, his head lifted up towards the sun. His body seems fragile like this, slender and sagging slightly in places, his olive skin pallid where it has not been exposed to the sun, his feet hanging loosely over the edge of the deck chair and appearing overly large. I love you, I begin to say, but reach out to place a hand on his knee instead.

'Everything OK?' he opens his eyes.

'I'm going to take a dip in the pool,' I say. 'Would you like to come with me?'

We cannot swim in the sea because of the oil spilled on the shoreline by a barge that received a direct hit during the bombing.

'Perhaps a bit later. I'm enjoying the sun too much now.'

I put a toe in the water. It is cool enough to send a

shiver up my spine. I bend forward at the waist, lift up my arms and dive in. As I come up for air, I breathe out through my nose and watch the bubbles break through the surface of the water. I am reminded of my childhood, when touch, smell, hearing, taste and sight defined existence, when the feel of the elements on my skin, water like this or even the air itself, made light of the more disparate aspects of my life, emotions that I did not always understand and the fears that arose in their wake. I move to the edge of the pool and smooth my hair back off my forehead, then I launch myself into the crawl and cover the length of the pool once, twice and back again until I am slightly out of breath.

Once out of the water, I rush to fetch a towel from my bag and wrap it tightly around myself.

'You're dripping all over me.' Kamal jumps up from his seat laughing. 'Was it cold?'

I laugh.

'This is bliss, isn't it?' I say, sniffing loudly.

We look out at the sea, a deep dark blue. Buoys bob up and down in the waves close to the shore. In the pool behind us, children screech with delight as they enter the water, and in the distance, through a haze of feathery cloud, is where sea and sky meet.

'Why are we drawn back to this place again and again despite all the problems, all the anxieties associated with living here?' I ask.

Kamal stands up and comes to sit beside me. He places the palm of his hand on the centre of my back. It is warm and comforting. I straighten my spine and pull my shoulders back. He laughs, lays his arm over my shoulders and leans forward to kiss me lightly on the lips. As we move apart again and Kamal removes his arm, I feel a current of cool air on the back of my neck. I shiver and look down at the goose bumps that now cover my skin.

Beirut is our refuge, the place where we all feel we belong, I suddenly realize, just as love is for all of us, wherever we are and whoever we may be.

The plane is only half-full. We sit to the left of the aisle. I am by the window and there is a vacant seat between us. The flight to Cyprus will be short and we will only stay there overnight, long enough to go through the civil marriage ceremony that is not available in Lebanon for couples from different religious backgrounds.

I look at Kamal. He has his glasses on and is reading a newspaper. With his head bent down like this, his features appear fluid and less defined, but his skin, as always, is smooth and dark.

'Hey,' I call to him.

He looks up and smiles. It is more like a beam, really, than a mere smile.

'Ready?' Kamal asks.

I nod.

'Do you want to come and sit here to watch the plane take off?' I ask, patting the seat beside me.

'Alright.'

He folds up the newspaper, puts his glasses in the pocket of his jacket and moves over to sit next to me. Instantly, I begin to feel better. We do up our seat belts and sit back as the plane begins to slowly move forward on the runway.

'I wish,' I begin but immediately stop myself. There is nothing, after all, that can add to the joyfulness of this moment.

Kamal takes my hand and leans forward to look out of the window with me. The plane roars ahead and takes off into the air. Beirut and the sea lie below us. Slowly, the sharp edges of concrete and sand begin to recede and what emerges instead is a nebulous picture of grey, blue and yellow, a mix of all the world's colours, the songs of my heart. I squeeze Kamal's hand and feel my soul take a leap.

Author Note

I began writing this novel in early 2006. It was going to be the story of an extraordinary friendship between two very different women. In July of that same year, Israel launched a month-long bombing campaign against Lebanon following the kidnapping by Hizbullah of two of its soldiers in the south.

It was a conflict that would result in the death of over a thousand people as well as the displacement of hundreds of thousands of others, and would have a profound effect on the future of a country that had only just begun to recover from a long and bloody civil war. It was also an experience that would completely alter the way I viewed the world.

My husband, young daughter and I spent the duration of the war in the relative safety of my parents' summer home in the mountains forty kilometres to the east of Beirut. It is a beautiful haven of quiet, surrounded by umbrella pines and high enough for the air to be scented with sweetness.

There, the constant din of fighter planes overhead and the violent bombardment of Beirut on one side of us and the Bekaa valley on the other filled our days and nights.

275

There also, two weeks into the conflict, my elderly father closed his eyes one morning and died.

I stood by his bedside afterwards, a view of the beloved mountains of his childhood through the window before us, and wondered how all the things of which I had once been so sure could so suddenly fall apart. I wanted to ask him why he had always encouraged me to love a country that now seemed too fragile to embrace. For the first time since the war began, I felt enclosed in silence.

Some time after the war had ended, we returned to Beirut and I finally sat down to write again. The story I had originally conceived would have to change, I knew, though I did not immediately understand how. I would eventually discover the answer in the writing.

I decided to look into Lebanon's history since independence in 1943, not just to go over the facts that I had been taught at school but also to talk to people who had experienced the birth of this country first hand. While the 15-year civil war that broke out in 1975 had been the defining reality for my generation, I wanted to try to understand what it was about Lebanon before that conflict that had inspired my father and so many others like him.

In the period that I spent researching and rewriting, I began to see how the "sense" of a place could be just as important as its physical reality, to understand that Lebanon is just as much an idea of what it had the potential to be as it is a nation with borders and a population of some four million people from eighteen different religious communities.

In a region that has for so long struggled to define itself, where authoritarian governments continue to rule, Lebanon has always represented the opportunity for a different kind of Arab society, one that is open and tolerant, where the freedom to be oneself, regardless of religious or political affiliation, was a right rather than a privilege.

But Lebanon has not always managed to live up to its promise. We seem to experience a major upheaval every decade or so that makes us question the authenticity of the intervening years of peace and prosperity. But do we really understand the part we have played, as individuals and as communities, in creating this confusion?

Throughout that terrible summer of 2006, I found myself wondering whether Lebanon was a viable nation any longer, whether choosing to stay here despite all the turmoil was enough to make this country real. Perhaps the one thing I learned while writing this novel is that the answer to that question keeps fluctuating. There are times when our feelings for Lebanon, our belief in it as a place unlike any other in the region, as a haven for democracy and freedom, make it so. While at others, it seems like the last place in the world anyone in their right mind would want to be.

Walking along the Beirut Corniche, waves rising and falling to one side of me and my city of dreams stirring just as close on the other, I begin to understand that, rather than my mind, it is my heart that will always speak for Lebanon.